Enchanted

While You Can

by

Emilie Ocean

Copyright

© 2024 Ocean Publishing

All rights reserved. No part of this book may be reproduced or used in any manner without the prior written permission of the copyright owner, except for the use of brief quotations in a book review.

All characters and events depicted in this book are entirely fictitious. Any similarity to actual events or persons, living or dead, is purely coincidental.

The following story contains mature themes, strong language and explicit scenes, and is intended for mature readers.

Editing and proofreading by Nikita Catherine (Instagram: @author_nikita_catherine), Eóin O'Donnell, and Patricia O'Donnell

Irish translations by Rosemary Lahiffe (rosemarylahiffe@gmail.com)

Cover by Rahma Ayman (Instagram: @thebookcoverwitch)

First Published 2024

ISBN: 978-1-7385528-0-1

Also by Emilie Ocean

Chronicles of Protectors Series

A Warrior's Requiem: Protectors

To Eóin,
with whom I have shared my first, only, and last Irish fairytale, and will continue to do so.

Acknowledgements

To my partner, Eóin. Thank you for your unconditional love and support. I appreciate the time you spent reading the rough drafts, editing and proofreading; I know it was a lot but you still did it!

To Gedi, who answered every question I had about Lithuania and listened to all of my nonsense without ever complaining (out loud). You are a true friend x

To Nikki; my emotional support throughout this entire writing process; the amazing woman who reviewed, edited, and proofread my manuscript. Thank you so much for your compassion and the non-judgmental space you kept open for me. I am eternally grateful.

To Patricia. Thank you so much for your edits and suggestions. Your feedback was invaluable. I appreciate your help and devotion.

To Rahma, my talented book cover designer. You have surpassed yourself!

To Rosemary, my Irish translator. I appreciate all your hard work and quick turnaround. Go raibh maith agat!

To Vic, who shared many tips with me on formatting and more. I really appreciate it!

To Darren who offered me his continuous support and unwavering encouragement.

And to you, my beautiful readers. Thank you from the bottom of my heart for taking the time to read this novel, following me on this journey, and helping me make my dream come true.

My heart is filled with gratitude for all that I have.

XOXO

Trigger Warnings

Explicit sexual content

Child abuse (brief)

Strong language

This novel is intended for **mature** readers.

Glossary

A
Aoife: *ee-fah*
Amrah: *am-rah*
An Garda Síochána: *awn gar-dah she-oh-cawn-ah* Irish police/Guardians of the Peace
Ayan: *ah-yahn*

C
Claddagh: *klah-dah* A ring that represents love (heart), friendship (hands), and loyalty (crown)

D
Daniyal: *dah-nee-yaal*
Delfi: Lithuanian online media
Doliprane: *doh-lee-prahn*
Duwamish: *doo-wah-mish*

E
Eejit: *ee-jit* Idiot
Éire: *eh-rah*
Elmas: *el-mahs*

F
Féidhlim: *fey-lum*
Fleur Fané: *flur fah-neh*

G
Gardaí: *gahr-dee*
Gâteau patate: Reunionese dessert

H
Hakimi: *hah-kee-mee*

K
Karam: *kah-rahm*

L
Léo: *leh-o*
Lrytas: Lithuanian online media

M
Máire: *maw-rah*
Mamie: Grandma
Marché forain: Reunionese farmers market

O
Oisín: *o-sheen*

R
Rivière: *ree-vi-ehr*

S
Salomé: *sah-low-meh*
Sézi: *seh-zee*
Sgian-dubh: single-edged knife

T
Tatie: Auntie
Tonton: Uncle

V

Vilius: *vil-ee-us*

Z
Zain: zayn

Other
15mn: Lithuanian online media

Spotify Playlist

Table of Contents

Prologue..1
Chapter 1..4
Chapter 2..13
Chapter 3..26
Chapter 4..34
Chapter 5..43
Chapter 6..50
Chapter 7..59
Chapter 8..67
Chapter 9..77
Chapter 10..88
Chapter 11..98
Chapter 12..108
Chapter 13..119
Chapter 14..134
Chapter 15..144
Chapter 16..154
Chapter 17..166
Chapter 18..174
Chapter 19..189
Chapter 20..200
Chapter 21..211
Chapter 22..220
Chapter 23..226
Chapter 24..235
Chapter 25..248
Chapter 26..256
Chapter 27..268
Chapter 28..279

Chapter 29..289
Chapter 30..301
Epilogue..313

Éire

Bainbridge Island

Reunion Island

Prologue
Juliette

I take a deep breath, anticipation coursing through my veins and making my insides churn. My fingers fist the fabric of my royal gown, the white satin crumpling under my touch. Soon, I will be face-to-face with my future marital partner, a male I have never met before.

The magical gates shine bright like the sun, the loud jingle of the pickets echoing through the royal gardens as the doors shimmer away to let the carriage in. Four majestic white stallions flap their wings once more before allowing the pumpkin-like coach to land on the ground. The security system goes back up over the gates the second the guests are in, a wave of magical dust enveloping the material like a shield. No one is allowed in without the royal council's authorisation, and I am certainly not allowed out either.

"They're here," Léo announces, his thin fingers wrapping around the edge of the white stone balustrade of the parlour's balcony, the warm honey of his skin contrasting with the cold material.

His golden-brown eagle eye takes in the three males stepping out of the carriage, the heels of their shoes clacking their way to the palace onto the large stony path, pebble stones grinding under their weight. They glance at the walkway, the long-lasting passage my parents built when I was only a young witch and Léo in my mother's belly, extending over a hundred yards.

Léo's dark-brown eyebrow arches, unimpressed as one of the males—the one whose jet-black hair is so dark it almost shines raven-blue—looks up at the warm May sun, his face screwing up. His pale hand gets a hold of the pocket square from his suit jacket before gently tapping his forehead with it.

Léo rolls his eyes to the cloudy sky. "Vampires… always so dramatic!" he exclaims, which only makes the corners of my lips curl upward into a mocking smirk. "Whatever you do, do not choose this one, Jules…"

I sigh, my chestnut eyes squinting at the gardens down below. My throat tightens, a suffocating knot expanding at my predicament, but I shove it down.

"Would you rather I go for the werewolf?" I grimace, watching as the second male—the one with a ponytail—swings the wooden handle of a large axe over his right shoulder, showing off just how beefy his frame is under his egg-white tunic.

"What about the fae?" Léo shrugs, the motion of his shoulders light and relaxed, though I know he can sense the anxiety radiating out of my pores. "He looks like mate-material, no?"

I follow his gaze, my head cocking and my black curls bouncing sideways against the small of my back.

The fae strolls ahead of the group, his head high, his fair hair reflecting the golden rays of the sun, while his piercing cerulean eyes remain on the white marble staircase leading them to the floor-to-ceiling entrance doors of the palace.

"He looks… confident," I say, "but I don't know yet that he'll be a good king and mate."

"Jules, you need to lower your standards." Léo pats me on the head, playing big brother despite the fact that I am five years his senior, the soft pads of his fingers petting my hair as if I were a cat. "They're the only bachelor princes available!"

Chapter 1

Féidhlim

I stand by the floor-to-ceiling window in the parlour, my gaze glued onto the gardens, where the four white stallions patiently wait by the carriage that brought us here only a mere half an hour ago. A silent sigh escapes my lips and I force my muscles to relax, hoping no one notices my lack of composure and fidgety hands.

I have come to Reunion Island for one reason, and one reason only: To convince Princess Juliette, the eldest daughter of the Rivière royal family—one of the most venerable families of witches in the world—to accept my marriage proposal. While love is a matter of the heart, power is purely political. And if what I heard is correct, the Rivières are in dire need of a strong international alliance to secure their position amongst larger magical nations who have been threatening an invasion. In all honesty, it is a miracle the island has managed to remain independent for so long considering its size; a mere dot in the Indian Ocean.

I lean against the windowsill behind me, my arms crossing over my chest as I glance around the white-sage-incensed room. My two rivals, Prince Elmas and Prince Kai, are here, too. I only met them a couple of times in the past at galas and charity events, but I think I have them figured out already.

Prince Elmas stays away from the window, preferring the artificial light from the chandelier to the soft rays of the natural sun, despite the enchanted family heirloom wrapped around his little finger that allows him to walk in broad daylight. I suppose I wouldn't want to risk it either if I were a vampire.

Prince Elmas is a direct descendant of King Vilius of Lithuania himself, which makes him a legacy vampire. His vampiric bloodline extends through at least seven generations if my source is correct. Their paranormal skills sharpen with age and their political alliances expand beyond the vampiric community. But if the rumours I have heard are true, Prince Elmas has been living a life of debauchery ever since he became old enough to understand the meaning of the word.

I hide a smirk behind the pad of my thumb as Prince Elmas nervously runs the flat of his hand along his black suit jacket, brushing away invisible creases. I doubt he is here of his own volition… *Did King Vilius have enough of his protégé's objectionable behaviour?* I wonder if he forced Prince Elmas to contribute to the welfare of their kingdom by securing a magical union, too.

"Dude, those little rings are so good!" Prince Kai cries, interrupting my train of thought, his pink tongue generously licking his sticky fingers where the snacks left a thin veil of honey behind. He turns to the guards by the door. "What are they called?" he queries, pointing at the golden tray on the sideboard along the back wall, his index finger only an inch away from the ring pastry filled with liquid honey.

My gaze jumps from the guards, who don't react, to Prince Elmas, who rolls his eyes at the plastered ceiling that reminds me of a wedding cake with Spanish influence.

"I don't suppose you know their name?" Prince Kai asks me next, not in the least vexed by the guards ghosting him, a childish smile painting his suntanned face.

"No, sorry…" I shrug.

"Want one?" Prince Kai gets a hold of the tray to wave it in my direction.

"No, thank you," I decline politely, although, truth be told, I have been eyeing these little honey rings for a while, too.

"What about you?" He turns around and gestures toward Prince Elmas before pausing abruptly. "Oh… can vampires eat normal food?"

Prince Elmas' brows arch, a stark expression hardening the features of his face.

"Normal food?" he repeats in a slow voice, his tone sharper than Kai's axe.

Prince Kai swallows, awkwardness making his movements falter as he places the tray back down on the sideboard.

"Nah, buddy, I didn't mean it like that—"

"Then, what did you mean exactly?" Prince Elmas asks, the grey of his eyes darkening as he squints.

But to Prince Kai's relief, a throat clear echoes through the room, and the herald—most aware of his courtroom-formality duties—marches in. He taps the bottom of his wooden staff against the shiny white tiles, ready to speak up.

"Their Majesties, King Daniyal and Queen Blanche," the herald announces, his loud voice bouncing off the walls.

I swiftly turn around, watching as a short male in a white cotton tunic and matching bottoms walks in, the soles of his leather ankle sandals quiet as a mouse against the floor. King Daniyal's head bows slowly and he turns around, his arm extended to welcome his marital partner—his mate—Queen Blanche. The female joins him, eager, a wide smile stretched across her face. Her jade-green eyes skim across the room and I feel them invade my soul the second they land on me; my insides twist at the intrusion.

Thump.

Thump.

The herald's staff hits the tiles once again.

"Princess Juliette and her brother, Prince Léopold," he announces as the king and queen settle down on one of the divans facing us.

I hold my breath, apprehensive to meet the person who will determine the fate of my kingdom at last.

Princess Juliette steps in, her white satin gown flowing around her golden figure, her hips swaying from side to side as she makes her way to the second divan, her brother following her closely. She sits down without saying a word, her hands wrapping over her knees. A soft smile spreads across her face, lighting up her innocent features, as she and Prince Léo share a silent thought.

When Princess Juliette looks away and her almond eyes rest on me, piercing and mysterious while they take me in, my heart somersaults in its cavity. A delightful spark pinches the bottom of my spine, goosebumps rippling over my alabaster skin in an unexpected, yet delicious, wave of electricity.

So this is the female I have been sent to seduce, huh?

"Welcome!" King Daniyal starts, getting back to his feet, his arms opening wide.

He twirls slowly, like a peacock proud of his feathers, making sure to lock eyes with each one of us.

"This is my daughter, Princess Juliette," he says next, the guttural sound of his Rs gritting my ears.

While English is universally spoken, being the political language of choice, King Daniyal seems to be reluctant to use it. But I am glad he makes the effort to do so anyway because my Reunionese isn't as sharp as I wish it were.

The flat of King Daniyal's hand points at his daughter across the room. She smiles shyly but stays put.

"Please, come forward and introduce yourselves," King Daniyal encourages, nodding at us before regaining his seat.

Prince Kai's hand rises like a schoolboy seeking permission to speak as he clears his throat.

"Uhm, should we introduce ourselves to you, Your Maj, or you, pretty lady?" he asks, his puzzled gaze flickering from the king to the princess. "I mean, I think you have my CV, no?"

King Daniyal winces at the question but his daughter's lips roll into a thin line to hold in a giggle. My stomach twiddles with disgust; if she likes jokesters, then it seems Prince Kai will have no problem scoring points.

"Introduce yourself to my daughter," King Daniyal blurts out, arms crossing over his chest, unimpressed with the prince's display.

"Alright!" Prince Kai chirps, not in the least fazed.

He takes a step forward, his muscular fingers running through his ponytail to tame the wild strands of black hair.

"Wasup." He arches an eyebrow at Princess Juliette, a charming smirk lifting the right corner of his lips, his head bobbing slightly. "I'm Prince Kai but my friends call me K, like the letter, you know?"

I suppress a wince at the lack of need to shorten a name that is already monosyllabic.

"Nice meeting you… K," Princess Juliette greets in a composed fashion, extending a hand out to him.

K cocks his head, his eyes resting on her delicate fingers for a second. His large hand wraps around hers but, against all odds, he urges her fingers to close so that they can fist-bump each other. She bursts out laughing, taken aback by the informality of the gesture, while King Daniyal snorts with sheer disgust, eyes rolling to the ceiling.

"Next!" the king exclaims, head shaking at the childishness of the prince before his daughter.

"If I may," Prince Elmas voices from his corner of the room, his eyes locking with mine.

I nod politely so he quietly makes his way to Princess Juliette, the soles of his Derby shoes moving slowly like he was gliding along the polished flooring.

"Your Royal Highness, it is an absolute pleasure to finally make your acquaintance." He gently brings the back of her hand to his lips. "I am Prince Elmas of Lithuania."

She smiles, their eyes meeting, and I frown, remembering how the tabloids like to depict Prince Elmas as Lithuania's modern-day *Don Juan*.

"You are even more beautiful in person." He kisses her hand again, her cheeks flushing magenta under his gaze.

My jaw clenches, anger simmering in my insides at my direct competition. *Why the hell did I let him go first?* I curse under my breath.

"Enough touching!" King Daniyal groans at his daughter, aversion rendering his stare icy. "Next!"

My heart thuds in my chest as Prince Elmas takes a step back and retreats to the bright shadows of the room. It is now my turn to finally meet Princess Juliette. I have one chance, and one chance only, at making a great first impression on her.

The pressure is on.

My feet begin to move, my spine straight and my head high, my body exuding confidence but my ears buzzing with anxiety. Anxiety that I don't allow to transpire, however, because I would rather fake it until I make it.

"Princess Juliette," I rasp, kneeling in front of her, my head bowing low in respect. "Please allow me to introduce myself. I am Prince Féidhlim of Éire. It is an absolute honour to make your acquaintance."

I dare to look up, my gaze snapping straight to hers… and she is breathtaking. Big brown almond eyes and warm honey skin framed by bouncy dark curls. And Gods, I don't know how long I stare at her but she cracks me the sweetest of smiles, her naturally rosy lips stretching wide across her round face.

"The honour is mine, Prince Féidhlim," she tells me, never breaking eye contact. "I have read a great deal about Éire. Is it true what they say about the rain?"

"I'm afraid so…" I confess, my muscles relaxing. "You're very lucky to have grown up in such a hot nation."

"Am I?" She cocks her head, staring out the window behind me.

I watch as her smile drops but before I have time to respond, the herald's staff strikes the floor once again and we are prompted to the dining room.

Chapter 2
Juliette

I exhale deeply, lying down on my super-king-size bed, my eyes glued to the painted ceiling, retracing the outlines of the drawn stars and moons over the dark-blue mural. Though he has now returned to his own quarters, Léo and I came straight back to my room after dinner to assess the princes and put our thoughts together.

Today wasn't so bad after all.

Prince Kai—*K*—is goofy but funny. His joyful nature is endearing, and I am glad he broke the tension in the parlour earlier. I was so nervous, my heart drummed in my ears. I could barely hear him at first but then I relaxed, the easiness radiating out of K contagious. I chuckle, remembering the exasperation on my father's face every time he opened his mouth to share his thoughts with the room. It was priceless!

If my research is correct, K is the youngest of six siblings, who have all already mated with other royal werewolves like them. I am surprised the queen and king of Spain allowed their youngest to seek a marital union with a witch.

Next, there is Prince Elmas, who is, as I suspected, a player. I read enough tabloids depicting him as such to know what to expect from him. Plus, I am well familiar with his night-owl lifestyle. I already know he is going to get bored out of his mind here between the four magical walls of the royal grounds.

And last but not least, Prince Féidhlim…

Oh…

Prince Féidhlim is…

My cheeks flush as I remember his sharp cerulean eyes locking on me, his head bowing as his handsomely tall frame knelt before me. But my face screws up almost instantly because I can't believe I talked about the weather with him. *The freakin' weather!* I cringe, burying my face in my hands. That is what I get for having no social interaction outside the palace walls.

I had been dreading my twenty-first birthday my whole life, knowing damn well my parents would force an arranged marriage on me. And sure enough, the day I turned twenty-one, they summoned my brother and me to their private business chamber to confirm the inevitable.

Three years went by with no luck—an abnormal drought in the pool of international suitors that is usually so generous. While my parents were deeply disappointed, I was relieved I didn't have to engage in courtship so soon after my twenty-first birthday. But the queen and king were relentless in their search. They eventually got their hands on three princes—Kai, Elmas, and Féidhlim—who apparently were way too eager to start the courting process.

It took my parents two months of negotiation with the rulers of Éire, Lithuania, and Spain to come to an agreement with my choosing a marital partner. So here we are, a week after ironing out the terms of the election, opening our doors to three complete strangers because my parents are hoping to sell me off to the most advantageous nation to secure their political power amongst the rest of the world.

Although Léo sees this as an opportunity to get some dick and possibly leave the island—the only home I have ever known—all I feel is anger simmering in my insides at the betrayal. How could my parents live with themselves, knowing their daughter is about to marry a male she barely knows? Sure, all three of my suitors are princes, but royals have issues, too. My parents don't care, though. They never did. Bile rises in my oesophagus, prickling my eyes. To them, I am only a vulgar piece of property they can toss around to secure their future and that of the island.

While I do want to contribute to the welfare of my nation, I do not wish to trade myself for it. I want to govern like a real queen does; with smart decisions and faithful alliances. Alas, all I can do is smile and act pretty until I say yes to one of the princes.

What am I saying? I won't even get to choose; my parents will.

Clink.

Clink.

Clink.

I prop myself up on the bed, my eyebrows drawing in at the sound of hail hitting the glass doors of my Juliet balcony—or *"Juliette's balcony,"* as I call it.

Clink.

Clink.

Clink.

I swiftly approach the window, my fingers wrapping over the white fabric of the curtains, which I pull to the side with a brisk motion of the wrist. And right there, on the mango tree rooted deep in front of my room, a male stands on the strong branches, his shadow lurking in the dark, hidden away from the guards below. I quietly open the French doors to step onto the cold tiles of the balcony.

"'Evening, Princess Juliette," the familiar voice whispers, its echo travelling through the empty space between us until it reaches my ears. "Don't be afraid—"

"I'm not," I blurt out, eyes rolling, unimpressed.

The shadow frowns, taking a step closer, allowing the rays of the crescent moon to light his features.

"It's me, Elmas," he mutters, a charming smile twisting across his face, revealing perfect white teeth and pointy canines.

"I know," I tell him, amused.

He cocks at me, taken aback by my obvious poise.

"I'm clairvoyant," I explain, leaning against the railing.

"Oh," is all he says with a shrug, not in the least intrigued.

I am sure Prince Elmas is well accustomed to witches and their gifts by now. That is what the tabloids seem to believe anyway; they love him! And Prince Elmas *loves* females.

He looks down at the guards before locking eyes with me, his smile turning into a smirk.

"Are you coming?" he asks, his right hand extending to the balcony.

"Where?"

My brow arches, my gaze jumping from the tree to the witches patrolling around the gardens.

"Anywhere! Come on, Princess, don't tell me you never sneak out." His hand waves encouragingly but I don't move. "Or would you rather I come to you?"

My eyes widen, anxiety running through my veins.

"No!" I snap a little too loud.

I stare down at the guards—all magic wielders—but none of them seem to have heard me. I take a deep breath.

"I'll come with you," I tell him.

If my parents find Prince Elmas in my room, I don't know what they will do to me, or him for that matter.

I swing my legs around the balcony railing, my suitor's grey eyes sparkling under the stars the second they rest on my bare thighs.

"Well, what are you waiting for? Give me a hand!" I urge, placing a foot over the mango tree.

Prince Elmas hurries to me, wrapping an arm around my legs, the other behind my back, to effortlessly scoop me up. I can't help but stare at him, amazed by his strength, and frankly a little aroused by his dominant frame against mine as his soft fingers press into the bare skin of my legs. No male has ever carried me off the ground—or a tree—like this before, making me feel like a feather they need to keep safe.

My eyes flicker to where my hand rests against his chest. I can feel the chill of his pale skin through his black polo shirt, which surprises me considering it is twenty degrees Celsius.

"Everything okay, princess?" he asks in a low voice, his gaze meeting mine.

His grip tightens around my thighs, and he turns around to near the tree trunk.

"Yes, sorry… I didn't mean to stare."

"No apologies needed. I don't mind beautiful females staring at me," he rasps, a charming smirk spreading across his face.

A shy smile adorns my features as I can't help but wonder how many females he has flirted with this way already. Possibly more than I can imagine.

"Ready?" he whispers.

I make a face, confused, but he doesn't give me the chance to reply. He jumps down a solid eighteen metres, and my heart pinches as I try my best not to scream. His feet quietly touch the ground below us before he lets me down. I stagger, my legs shaking from the adrenaline, but Prince Elmas' hands wrap around my waist to steady me and help me stand.

His index finger flies to his lips next, hovering over them vertically. A guard gestures in our direction, and Prince Elmas' body presses against mine, my back sinking into the hard outer bark of the mango tree. A warm breeze swooshes between us, his spicy vanilla cologne filling my nostrils with delicious hints of cardamom and cashmere wood. My eyes flutter close as I inhale his manly scent, my chest heaving against his torso. His long fingers wrap around my hips, and I look up at him, our gaze meeting in the shadows of the tree, the leaves cocooning us from the rest of the palace grounds. Prince Elmas smirks again, his lips skimming over the shell of my ear, which only sends a luscious spike of electricity down my spine, butterflies dancing in my insides.

"Come with me," he tells me under his breath.

Prince Elmas' slender frame pulls away, his hand wrapping around mine to guide me through the darkness of the gardens. We pass by the star-shaped pond, where families of moustache catfish swim idly in the clean water. At first, I am taken aback by the assertiveness in his steps, watching as he avoids every hidden rock and above-ground root, until I remember he is a vampire. Vampires are known to have excellent night vision.

"How do we get over the wall?" he asks me eventually once we reach the far end of the garden, where stone benches lay between generous bushes of roses and frangipanis, their floral scent sweetening the air around us.

My face screws up as my eyes sadden, resting over the three-hundred-and-fifty metres high magical barrier in front of us; higher than the Eiffel Tower, or the Shard.

"We don't," I sigh.

"What do you mean?" His eyebrows shoot to his hairline. "How do you usually sneak out?"

A low chuckle leaves my chest, my head shaking profusely.

"Do I look like someone who sneaks out at night?" I giggle, truly amused. "I mean, look at me…"

And he does. His eyes shine in the moonlight when he takes me in; my loose curls brushing against my bare shoulders, my white flowing gown contrasting with the blush of my chest, its skirt stroking my thighs.

"I like what I'm seeing, Julie," he rumbles, his gaze snapping back to mine.

Heat settles in my middle at the compliment like a swarm of butterflies taking off in my stomach. I feel my cheeks redden, fervour surging through my pores.

"Can I call you *Julie*?" he wonders, his tone as casual as the serene stream of a river.

I nod.

"Huh-huh," I mutter with a nod, holding his stare until his tongue swipes across his upper lip and I can't help but follow the motion with my eyes, mesmerised. "Prince Elmas—"

"El. Call me *El*," he demands, tucking a wild curl behind my ear, delightful goosebumps growing over the otherwise smooth skin of my arms.

"*El*," I say softly, the pet name rolling over my tongue with grace, making the corners of his mouth stretch into a satisfied smile. "The magical walls are powered by witches at 08:00 in the morning, and then again at 08:00 in the evening. It's unbreakable…"

His eyebrows draw in.

"That's a bit excessive, don't you think? Who's gonna break into the royal family's grounds? I mean, you guys have guards at every corner of the palace," he chuckles. "Who are your parents trying to keep out?"

"Not keep *out*, but keep *in*," I correct, my fingers nervously twisting in front of me.

El lifts a brow, waiting for an explanation.

"My brother and me," is all I say next.

He blinks.

"I don't follow." He nonchalantly scratches his chin. "You two have curfews... like non-magical people?"

"No, curfews are a luxury you get when you're allowed outside," I clear my throat, "and Léo and I haven't had permission to exit the royal grounds in..." I count on my fingers, "eleven years."

El's eyes widen with incredulity.

"I don't even remember what our cities look like anymore," I admit.

"Are you serious?"

"I'm afraid so..." My lips close in a thin line as I shrug. "An extrovert like yourself will find my company very boring—"

"You are anything but boring, my sweet Julie," he murmurs, his voice low and hoarse, the tips of his shoes now against mine. "And I can't wait to get to know you better, whether it is here, or out there."

He points at the darkness on the other side of the barrier with a furtive motion of his eyes, then hooks his index finger under my chin. The pad of his thumb gently strokes my lips, while El watches me through a hooded gaze. I hold my breath, my mouth parting to meet his when sudden words of warning flash through my brain.

Hide! it hisses. *Guards! Mind the guards.*

"Three guards are coming," I breathe, snapping out of the trance to focus on El again.

"I can't hear, or see, a thing," he murmurs, turning back around to check our surroundings.

The gardens are empty, not a soul in sight, only night herons perched on the branches of the mango trees framing our path.

"And you won't. Some of our witches are magically cloaked," I tell him in a whisper, swiftly pulling onto his arm to urge him to hide behind a pink rosebush.

And surely, a trio of night guards marches by on their habitual patrol, the echo from their heavy steps swallowed into the ground beneath their feet.

"Thank Gods for your clairvoyance…" El sighs once we are alone. "I don't wanna know what your dad would do if he found out I went out for a stroll with his daughter in the gardens after dusk."

"Don't mind my father. He's a brute but he's all bark on his own." I shake my head, coming out of our hiding spot. "It's my mother you should fear."

He frowns but I don't bother explaining that Queen Blanche is the true mastermind controlling everything around here. My father simply follows her like a puppy, ready to do her bidding so that she keeps her hands clean and her reputation intact.

While the population disapproved of it and solely blamed my father, it was my mother's idea to put up a wall around the royal grounds to limit mine and Léo's contact with the outside world and cut all ties with the rest of our paternal family. My father, of course, is at fault for not stopping her but, ultimately, it was my mother's initiatives that impacted us the most.

My mother is the king of France's baby sister, and her relatives are the only ones we get to see here at the palace once a year on their annual visit. Every February my uncle, his mate, and their younglings come to Reunion Island to see us to check up on us and ensure the political relationship between our two nations remains intact. I never bonded much with them, though; we have very little in common.

The chill of the evening suddenly wraps its arms around me, a shiver carving its way up my spine, forging gooseflesh on my skin.

"I better go back inside," I say, now feeling awkward. "I don't wanna catch a cold."

El and I walk in silence, our fingers occasionally brushing as we follow the path leading to the mango tree directly facing my balcony. He takes me into his arms, and I let him, before he jumps up onto one of the stronger branches, agile as a cat. He grips my fingers tight, following me to the edge of the balcony to help me over.

"Goodnight, Julie," he purrs, his eyes never leaving mine.

He brings the back of my hand to his lips.

"Goodnight." I smile, cheeks undoubtedly flushing bright crimson.

"And don't worry, I'll find a way to get past the magical barrier," he says when my hand closes around the gold handles of the French doors.

"What?" I ask in a whisper, surprised by his statement.

I turn back around but he is gone already.

Chapter 3

Féidhlim

It has been three days since I arrived at the Rivières' palace, and I am gutted I haven't got the chance to have a tête-à-tête with Princess Juliette yet. I have, however, joined King Daniyal in his business chamber for an impromptu chat, where he offered me one of his *Romeo y Julieta* Cuban cigars. Now, I am not too sure if this is common practice around here, but my understanding is that Prince Elmas and K didn't get the same honour. Hopefully, this ranks me first on the princess' list.

I sat on the oakside upholstered armchair opposite King Daniyal, who couldn't wait to tell me all about his escapades with his two brothers on the Emerald Isle in his early days as a young male; how they climbed the Cliffs of Moher with the help of local winged fae, hiked across the Connemara region through rain and sunshine, and took shelter at Kylemore Abbey that same night thanks to a magical portal—a transporter of sorts—to then end their trip two days later with a fresh pint of Guinness and a hot bowl of stew at the well-recommended Brazen Head gastrobar, the oldest pub in Dublin.

I was amazed to hear of Éire's reputation so far away across the globe when other powerful nations have made more of a mark in history. And since Reunion maintains a close relationship with the other islands within the Mascarenhas Archipelago (for location purposes) and France (Queen Blanche being the French king's sister) I assumed the Rivières had very little business going to Éire.

My interest piqued, remembering the way Juliette's eyes shone bright, her brown irises shimmering golden, as she asked me about my country. She had read about it. Something warm fizzled in my insides then; most people think of England when rain is mentioned, not Éire.

"The Éirean fae folk have had their fair share of ill-treatment throughout the years... just like us," King Daniyal observed, interrupting my thoughts. He stared at the thick rings of smoke escaping his dark lips. "We're more alike than we think, despite our physical, cultural, and magical differences."

His statement prompted me to settle in the palace's library, where I am now comfortably sitting at one of the bulky oak tables, my laptop shining light over my tired eyes as I scroll through the history of Reunion Island—research I would have done before leaving home, if I had the chance.

The island was coveted by the Europeans and Asians as early as the 1500s for its natural magical ley lines, which explains the rich multi-ethnicity of its natives. The Rivières—Well, their family name was Hakimi at the time—were already in power back then, and have been ever since. The royal family has relentlessly fought against the pressure of the more imposing magical nations, who have tried to swallow the island whole and subdue them, wishing to acquire more power. Always more power. To no avail.

Reunion Island is small in size—only covering a mere 970 square miles—but their witches, which are their predominant supernatural population, are strong, their ancestors' magic and wisdom flowing through their veins thanks to the ley lines.

"Well, that explains how they managed to keep their independence for all these years!" I exclaim out loud, my fingers interlocking behind my head as I stretch against the back of the office chair.

"So you can understand why it would be a shame to surrender now and give in to those same bully-nations…" the familiar voice that has haunted my dreams for the past two nights sighs, the melodic accent music to my ears.

My spine straightens, my heart surprisingly thudding against my ribs as I jolt around in my seat to see Princess Juliette lounging on the brown leather couch to the left of me, a couple of feet away, an open book on her lap.

She smirks, amused, a brow arching at me.

"Sorry, I didn't mean to scare you," she says.

I clear my throat, composing myself, my fingers consciously dragging the edge of my short-sleeve polo shirt down to cover the skin that was showing. Her eyes follow the movement, her gaze burning my flesh with a delicious flame I didn't know I needed in such a hot country.

I take a second to revel in her natural beauty, admiring the way she looks just as enticing in civilian clothes. Princess Juliette's long black hair curls around her face to drape over her oversized t-shirt, the crotch of her shorts barely visible under the fabric.

"Have you been here long?" I ask, forcing my eyes to snap away from her bare legs, relief seething through me at the trained aplomb in my voice.

"A while." She shrugs casually, her shoulders causing her breasts to raise under her loose top, her pebbled nipples grazing the black material. "I'm on page fifty." She waves the book at me. "I can go read elsewhere if you prefer," she adds swiftly, uncrossing her legs, the white soles of her runners tapping the tiled floor as she readies herself to get up.

"No, stay," I blurt out, dread clouding my brain at the thought of Princess Juliette feeling unwelcome in her own home at my expense. "Please." I smile warmly, and she smiles back the sweetest of smiles, her face lighting up her innocent features. "Maybe when you're done, you can help me learn more about your island. I have a lot of ground to cover, so any help from the expert that you are would be most appreciated."

Princess Juliette's lips stretch into a grin and she eagerly closes the book in her hands.

"I can finish it later!" she rejoices, tossing her novel onto my desk before enthusiastically grabbing the heavy chair beside mine to join me at the table.

"Okay, then," I mumble, contentment blooming in my chest at the keenness of her movements. I slide my laptop in her direction, the blue light reflecting over her warm skin. "Can you see?" I ask her, pointing at the screen with a subtle bob of the head.

"Uhm…"

She wriggles in her seat, dragging her chair closer to mine, our arms now touching. My eyes meet hers, the warmth of her small frame urging a singeing spark to twist the organs in my middle as I secretly long for more physical contact. The sensation reaches my balls, their throbbing a light fizzle; short and sweet.

I have been thinking a lot about Princess Juliette; every time I am alone in the confines of my guest bedroom or away from prying eyes in my en-suite. The moment I saw her, I knew she would be occupying an important place in my mind. While I am not looking to engage in a traditional romantic courtship, Princess Juliette's physical attributes do sweeten this political deal I need to secure for my nation.

Her skin is soft, its golden complexion inviting. Wondering if she minds the proximity of our bodies, I lean closer to see what she does next; she doesn't move. She simply stares at the screen and starts reading. She occasionally bites the inside of her cheek, her almond eyes squinting at the text. Her head cocks, the tropical scent of coconut escaping her curls, and I picture what it would be like to sink my fingers through her mane and grip it tight as I bend her over the table.

"How about you ask me a question and I try my best to point you in the right direction?" she suggests, her stare making my insides flutter.

I allow myself to dive into the rich chestnut of her eyes for a second before nodding, the composed features of my face never betraying my thoughts.

"Okay."

It takes us two hours—which is a lot more time than I expected—to go through the map of the entire island and the predictable seasonal forecasts for the upcoming months, to skim through heatwaves and monsoons, and then end on natural disasters, such as volcanic eruptions and tornadoes.

"What about tsunamis?" I query, amazed at the array of eventful opportunities such a small island withholds.

"No, we don't have those, thank Gods!" she giggles, my cock twitching at the sound. "That'd be detrimental to our sharks."

"Sharks?"

"Oh, yeah! Loads and loads of them," she confirms, nodding profusely, a mischievous smile curling upward. "But don't worry, I'll ask them to be nice to you."

She winks and I can't help but smile back, her cheekiness beguiling.

I watch the way her smirk turns into a beaming grin and her curls bounce up and down as her soft facial features come to life, while she proudly tells me all about the island's sharks guarding the shore and protecting its people. I relax beside her, allowing my back to slouch slightly, my left hand to rest over the back of her seat, and my bare knee to press lightly against hers. Satisfaction courses through me when she doesn't flinch but instead leans into the touch. And it takes every fragment of my willpower to stop the muscles of my fingers from running along the flesh of her thighs to find the invisible hem of her shorts.

"Oh, and have you ever swum with dolphins?" she asks next, her fingers excitingly tapping the beige material of my chinos.

I shake my head, revelling in the happiness radiating from her and wishing her touch would linger a little while longer.

"Me neither, but I would *love* to someday, Féidhlim—Sorry… I mean, *Prince* Féidhlim."

She winces, her cheeks blushing, her demeanour instantly shifting as she sits back on her chair.

"Féidhlim… is more than fine," I reassure her swiftly, silently cursing at the formality that only holds barriers between us.

I have made tremendous progress with Princess Juliette in the span of a mere two hours; I would hate to backslide now. For *political* reasons, of course.

"Princess—"

"Juliette is enough," she cuts in, her cheeks now crimson-red and her lips rolling into a thin line. I smile, delighted, until she adds, "My brother calls me Jules, but El gave me a new pet name; *Julie*. I think I like both."

And just like that, my features darken, a sucker punch hitting me in the gut out of nowhere at the mention of Prince Elmas' term of endearment for the princess. *El and Julie.*

"Is that so?" I mutter, my voice more hoarse than I intended, patches of green staining my heart.

Chapter 4
Juliette

Léo winces beside me, his arms crossing over his grey stringer vest, his hazel eyes squinting at the arrow that left my bow to miss the dummy he previously wrapped around the banana tree by the neck.

"I missed again…" I mutter, unimpressed with my performance.

"Maybe it's the target," he says, hands over hips. "What if I add something of Papa's to it?"

I chuckle, amused, because I know Léo is serious. Our current dummy is a stuffed doll of mine with pink hair that our mother gave me as a toddler.

"No, it's not the target." My face screws up and I walk up to the tree, the soles of my bare feet enjoying the cool of the earth beneath them.

My fingers close around the aluminium shaft of the arrow, its long spine sliding out of the hole the bullet-point dug in the hard bark, its head soon exiting the warmth of the banana tree as I pull.

"It's me… I can't focus," I go on.

"Why? Because you thought you were gonna get some fae dick, but instead all he gave you is a cold shoulder?" Léo cackles, his bow pointed at the pink doll.

My eyes roll. He somehow summarised my thoughts better than I ever could in one sentence.

"Where to?" he asks, his features regaining their composure, patiently holding back until I tell him where to shoot.

"The heart," I reply.

Léo waits for me to join him again before swiftly pulling back the string on his bow, his elbow up as he releases the arrow. As always, the bullet-point lands in its target, impaling the shabby doll's ribcage, the metal shaft sinking deep inside the imaginary organ.

"Wow, dude, slay!" K's voice suddenly echoes behind us.

Léo and I swing around to see the prince stroll his way down to us, his bare feet as comfortable against the green lawn as ours, the richness of his brown skin almost shining under the bright rays of the scorching sun. An impressed whistle blows out of his lips as K takes in the tortured toy tied to the banana tree. His six-foot-two frame pauses between my brother and me, the warmth radiating out of K's bare chest a comforting bubble despite the midday heat.

Though I have plenty of books about werewolves and their magical qualities, I had yet to meet one in the flesh. K's body heat is as balmy as I thought it would be.

Werewolves are known for storing warmth within themselves to survive the coldest of temperatures.

"Can I try?" K asks, his chin bobbing at Léo's bow.

"Okay…" my brother agrees in a voice lacking conviction.

"Sweet!" K chirps.

He turns back around to plant the axe in his right hand inside the only tree stump behind us. He swiftly jogs back, his fingers reaching for Léo's bow.

"I've never done archery before," K confesses. "How do I position myself?"

"Like this," Léo tells him, lining his body up to the target in a perpendicular fashion. "Are you right-eye dominant?"

"I don't know." K shrugs.

While Léo shows him the ropes, I glance around the glade; the secret place my brother and I like to disappear to to escape our parents. *How did K find us?* The glade is situated deep inside the royal gardens, past the rocky ground where nothing has grown in years. The soil there has been damaged for so long, I can't even remember what the place looked like when nature framed it.

It used to be my paternal grandmother's personal garden, where she would grow leafy vegetables such as pak choi and chow chow leaves, back when she lived with us at the palace. That was eleven years ago before my parents got into a heated argument with my father's side of the family, who were never allowed on royal grounds again. No one has been beyond what used to be my grandmother's garden ever since, not even the gardeners themselves.

"'Princess Juliette' has way too many syllables," I hear K's bubbly voice babble. "Can I call you PJ instead?"

PJ?

I don't know that I like this new nickname but it doesn't really matter; I doubt my parents will choose K as my marital partner. For all I know, I will never see him again once this courtship comes to completion.

"Yeah, PJ's fine," I agree casually over my shoulder.

"Score!" K exclaims before releasing the arrow.

I don't watch as it reaches its target but the proud humming escaping Léo's lips tells me K is a natural at archery.

"Jules, your turn!" my brother calls, readjusting the dummy over the tree.

"You guys keep shooting without me." I shrug, slipping my toes between the straps of my rose-gold flip-flops. "I need a break."

"Is that what we call *it* now?" Léo cackles again, joining K, who stares at us, puzzled.

By '*it*', he means '*dick,*' of course. That is all my brother has been talking about ever since puberty hit him.

My head shakes. I ignore them both, sauntering out of the glade, the narrow leaves of the tall grass brushing against the bare skin of my calves. I sigh, unable to chase away the intrusive thoughts that have been haunting me for an entire week.

First, I told Féidhlim about the pet name El gave me. *Stupid*... I am pretty sure Féidhlim made a point of ignoring me after that because I only saw him at the mandatory dinner meals we are required to attend in the company of my parents. Needless to say, not much happens at those; only polite chitchat about the princes' stay and how they have been adapting to the heat.

But then, as I silently sat at the table yesterday evening, lost in my thoughts, wondering where Féidhlim had been disappearing to during the day—never to be found within the enceinte of the palace at regular hours—the answer was given to me on a silver platter. Disgust burgeoned in my pit as my father, reading my mind, openly disclosed the fact Féidhlim had been visiting his business chamber to bond with him over *Romeo y Julieta* cigars. Féidhlim locked eyes with me over the table, a proud smile stretching across his face. And my disgust was soon replaced with anger.

Anger because Féidhlim would rather spend time with my father than with me.

Anger because my parents are meddling in my marriage business.

Anger because Féidhlim is their favourite, too.

Anger because the look he gave me told me he knew exactly what he was doing; that bonding with my father was more beneficial to him and his country than getting to know me. Of course, he isn't wrong. I simply despise the way he supports my parents' arbitrary rules. I somehow expected more from Féidhlim. If El was able to make time for me, why couldn't he do the same?

I had to excuse myself then, faking a headache, refusing to sit and watch as my parents took *my* choice away. I always knew I had very little ground to hold but confirmation stings like a motherfucker.

I now march down the halls of the palace, determination coursing through my veins, making my heart thump in my ears like circus drums. I need to get out of here, and El will help me do it. But first, I impatiently head to my room, nodding occasionally at the housekeepers as I meet them in the arched corridor, the rubber soles of my flip-flops flapping loudly against the cold white tiles. My fingers wrap around the gold knob and I close the door behind me, eager to do what I haven't done in a long time.

I swing my sandals around, letting them bash against the wooden chest of drawers by the entrance, the bare soles of my feet tingling at the sudden temperature change. I take a deep breath, gathering my favourite candles—pink, purple, and black—and lighting them, the melted coloured waxes diffusing the sweet scents of roses, verveine, and cedarwood in the air. I pull the curtains next, while magically scanning the perimeters to ensure no one is watching me before sitting comfortably on the bed.

Here goes nothing...

I hope this is like riding a bike, and I still have the hang of it!

My eyes flutter shut and I inhale deeply, praying I won't have to wait long. I relax the muscles in my jaw and the tendons in my shoulders, my hands resting idly over my thighs, my palms facing up.

Are you here? I ask silently, focused on establishing a connection.

I don't get a verbal answer but a sudden gust of icy wind swooshes between the four walls of my room, sending a shiver along my spine. I smile and keep my eyes closed.

Thank you for coming, I tell the dead ghosting around me with my mind. *I'm sorry it took me so long to get back to you...*

A puff of cold air rushes through my hair in response, making my curls tickle my neck.

I'm sorry. I promise I'll be more social!

Nothing happens.

I'll burn incense and white candles for you every day for an entire month if you help me. Please.

Still nothing.

And I'll keep the connection open so you can come with me on my new adventure, I add swiftly, hopeful.

The air warms up, the goosebumps on my arms vanishing.

Okay, we have a deal then, I rejoice, the corners of my lips stretching into a satisfied grin. *Please, tell me how to get past the magical barrier surrounding the royal grounds without being detected.*

I stroll down the arched corridors once more, this time heading straight to El's bedroom, barely able to contain my excitement.

"El!" I cry, impatiently swinging the door open. "I know how to—" I pause, my heart uncomfortably pinching in my ribcage as my eyes flicker from El to... Féidhlim.

El, casually sitting at his desk, looks up at me, a sexy smile on his face.

"Hello, my sweet Julie," he purrs.

His eyes linger a little too long over my body, drinking in the shape of my breasts under my white tank top and the nakedness of my legs under my denim shorts. I feel my cheeks flush under his hungry stare, the butterflies in my middle fluttering with a life of their own.

"Princess Juliette," Féidhlim mutters my name *and* title, which only chases the delicious swarm away to replace it with an uneasy knot.

So I guess we are back to formalities, then...

Féidhlim clears his throat, his spine straightening as he shifts his weight away from El's windowsill to stand fully instead. Though I am upset with the fae prince's doing, I can't help but take a moment to observe his frame, all dominant and virile, as his strong biceps flex when his arms unfold. The butterflies in my stomach come back to quiver one more time but I remain unmoving.

"What can I do for you, love?" El asks, slouching in his seat, allowing his back to sink against the ergonomic padding of the chair, his knees spreading generously to draw my attention to the space between his legs.

My lips part, my eyes meeting El's again, but I hold my horses, swiftly glancing at Féidhlim with apprehension as I wonder whether it is safe to share the details of my plan with him, too.

Chapter 5

Féidhlim

I sigh heavily, massaging my eyelids with the pads of my index finger and thumb as I allow my hamstrings to press against the windowsill in El's room.

"Don't beat yourself up," El tells me, his long fingers wrapping in front of him while he swings his office chair around. "How could you have known?"

I shake my head, annoyed at myself for not noticing it before, although it was obvious as hell. Of course, Juliette doesn't see eye to eye with her parents. Not once did I see her entertain a conversation with them; she never does anything in their presence without her brother there. I was so focused on winning this competition—on winning her hand—that I didn't take the time to step back and observe the true object of my political desire.

"You don't care what Julie thinks of you anyway, do you?" El asks, resting his cheek against his fist, his elbow propped over the armrest of his chair. "I mean, you've already won her father over."

"I don't know that I have yet," I argue, arching an eyebrow.

"Well, I, for one, was never invited in his business chamber to smoke cigars, and neither was K." El shrugs, the tips of his left fingers tapping the wooden surface of the desk. "I suppose congratulations are in order."

"Congratulations?" I repeat, my voice half-hearted. "I don't think so. Princess Juliette despises me."

"So? She doesn't have a say in the union."

"What?" I frown, taken aback, a line drawing across my forehead.

"Yeah, she told me so herself," El goes on, sitting up.

His piercing grey eyes squint at me, an amused smirk brightening his pale face.

"You didn't know?" he asks after a moment, observing the gobsmacked expression keeping my mouth agape.

My head shakes and a genuine chuckle escapes his throat.

"And there I was, admiring how smart you were for going after her father first!" he exclaims. "It turns out you had no idea what you were doing!" I pull a face at his comment, somewhat feeling insulted. "Ah, Fé… this is a disguised arranged marriage," he explains. "King Daniyal and Queen Blanche will be choosing one of us on behalf of poor little Julie. How did you miss that?" He snorts. "And it seems, you're their favourite. So, again, *congratulations*."

A lump grows in my oesophagus, embarrassment unexpectedly flushing my cheeks magenta at the revelation.

No wonder Juliette has been avoiding me these past couple of days. She probably thinks I have been conniving with her parents to trap her in a union she does not want.

"Why are you still here if you know Juliette won't get to choose her mate herself?" I ask El, curiosity suddenly piquing my interest.

He smiles, revealing two perfect pointy canines.

"I like her," he says, not an ounce of hesitation or uneasiness in his tone.

I swallow, the words slicing through me like a sharp knife. My heart begins to race against my ribs, my stare darkening as anger simmers in my veins, making my blood boil. For *political* reasons, I do not want another male—especially my direct competition—to think for one second he can have Princess Juliette's heart.

I know El and Juliette have been sneaking out of the palace at night when the lights turn off and the château goes to sleep. I have seen them myself more than once, strolling through the gardens, staring at one another through googly eyes under the moonlight, giggling like two teenagers as they hide away from the guards. It sears my heart every time, the scorching burn in my ribcage darkening the organ that pumps my blood green.

My mouth parts, my arms crossing over my chest when the door to El's room slams open. We both turn around, startled by the intrusion, and my heart somersaults in its cavity; Juliette barges in, her cheeks rosy with excitement, a beaming grin brightening her features.

"El!" she cries. "I know how to—"

She pauses, her golden eyes jumping from El to me, uncertainty taking over. My chest pulls at her reaction, envying the way she looks at El and despising the uneasiness radiating out of her pores in my presence.

El, casually sitting at his desk, looks up at her, a smile worthy of a predator curling upward from the corners of his lips.

"Hello, my sweet Julie," he purrs, the echo of his voice spreading goosebumps of disgust along my skin.

His eyes linger a little too long over her body, and it takes every last bit of self-control I have for me not to punch him in the face. My stare snaps to Juliette, who doesn't seem to mind El's attention in the slightest, which only makes me want to roll my eyes and pull my hair.

"Princess Juliette," I say instead.

She locks eyes with me, her glare dark and icy. I clear my throat, uncomfortable with her animosity, my spine mechanically straightening as if gaining a couple of inches will help my confidence regain its authority. So I shift my weight away from the windowsill, standing tall, faking it until I make it.

"What can I do for you, love?" El asks in a suave voice, his back sinking against the ergonomic padding of his chair, his legs spreading wider.

I watch as Juliette's gaze instantly softens when she takes him in; his tall and slender frame slouching in his seat, his jet-black hair perfectly gelled back with a single strand falling over his forehead, the muscles of his arms showing under his black short-sleeve shirt. And when her gaze lowers to his crotch, I squeeze my eyes shut, my head instantly turning to the side, unable to keep my composure.

Juliette's lips part eventually before closing again. She glances at me, apprehension smearing her face, which only makes my heart break.

"Princess Juliette, it's nice seeing you," I say softly, a shy smile curling upward from the corners of my mouth.

She nods slowly, lips in a thin line, arms crossing over her white tank top. I wait a few seconds, dying for her to open up and share her news with me, too, but she doesn't. She remains quiet, her body as stiff as a stick.

From the corner of my eye, I see El's gaze bouncing from Juliette to me, his index finger hiding a satisfied smirk. Anger surges in my insides again at the cocky bollocks enjoying Juliette's aversion toward me.

"I'll catch you later, pal, okay?" El tells me, jumping to his feet, before condescendingly patting me on the back.

He leans against the door frame next, a dismissing nod urging me to leave. My jaw clenches, and I can't help but glare at him, losing composure at last. A low chuckle rumbles in El's chest, mocking and taunting, before he winks at Juliette beside me. So I march out, my vision turning red, every fibre of my being screaming at me to unleash my rage and show Juliette just how much of a male I am—after all, I am Prince Féidhlim of Éire and I had to undergo extensive fae magic and skills training for many years. I could win a fight against a vampire. I could take down Elmas in the blink of an eye. But I choose not to.

Later that night, I lie in bed, my heart racing with anticipation when I hear the swift sliding of the French doors from El's bedroom onto his Juliet balcony next door. Without wasting another second, I zip up my black bomber jacket, put my phone on silent, and slip it into the front pocket of my black chino trousers. I wait for El to jump down first and take a few steps ahead before I follow him.

While, contrary to popular belief, we—magical beings—don't fight like animals every chance we get, I have been thoroughly prepared for raids in case of an invasion. I don't have vampire strength or speed, but I am well able to stealthily monitor my target's whereabouts when needs be. Surveillance is of the utmost importance when training in the art of espionage.

I could fly down but I have a feeling El would notice the fae dust gathering around my body as I do so even miles away. So I climb down my balcony instead, my feet and hands using the capital of the white marble column for support before I agilely slide down its shaft to reach its base. I dash after El in the darkness of the night, the air warm around me, the fresh scent of frangipanis and roses perfuming the gardens. I hide behind a rosebush, watching as El jumps up, disappearing amongst the high branches of the full-grown mango tree in front of Juliette's room.

Her balcony doors open and I see her small frame slipping between them. She swiftly passes her legs over the railing, her black-and-white runners finding their balance over the closest tree branch next. El is beside her in no time and I hate what I see. Juliette's lips brush the shell of his ear before she jumps up into his arms, her legs easily wrapping around his waist. El smirks, the paleness of his skin reflecting under the moonlight, one hand against the small of her back, the other gripping the black material of her leggings over her thighs. And then, they jump down.

I wait for them to hit the ground but they never do. I frown, squinting my eyes at the poorly lit tree, searching for the pair, to no avail.

Where did they go?

Chapter 6
Juliette

We watch the conniving spy, weighing up our options, my head shaking. I spotted Féidhlim the second I stepped out onto my Juliette's balcony, my clairvoyance warning me like an alarm bell. So I whispered into El's ear and jumped up into his arms, knowing he would easily be able to get us out of Féidhlim's sight.

"I bet you he's spying on us on *Tonton* Daniyal's behalf," the ghost whispers in my ear as we hide behind the rosebush facing the mango tree—the one opposite Féighlim's—a mocking cackle swooshing past her thin lips.

I roll my eyes at Amrah, my paternal first cousin, who tragically passed away five years ago.

No one truly knows what happened to her. Amrah was a writer in her living days; a demanding profession that often prevented her from leaving her bedroom at my aunt's residence by the sea. She was, however, in love with life so none of us saw it coming when one day she was found in her bed, unconscious. One moment she was well and healthy; the next, she lay unalive under the covers, her blood thick and icy under her flesh, her eyes bulbous and red-rimmed in her skull.

"Do you think your father sent him?" El asks, as if able to hear Amrah.

"I don't know," I mutter, watching as Féidhlim innocently scratches the back of his head a couple of feet away from us, his muscular fingers diving through the short blond curls of his hair.

I check the time on my phone, anxiety coursing through me; only one hour until the palace wakes up.

"Only one way to find out!" El exclaims, sensing the urgency in my demeanour, leaving my side to sneak behind the fae prince.

His steps are quiet as he nears Féidhlim and leans closer to him.

"*Boo!*" El whispers, a wide grin spreading across his face, his canines shining like the sharpest of knives under the soft rays of the moon.

Féidhlim swiftly turns around in a jump, his features stark, his hands closed into fists, ready to fight.

"Oh, he's cute!" Amrah chirps, clapping excitedly, her dark-brown gaze devouring his tall frame with undoubtedly the dirtiest of thoughts.

"What the fuck!" Féidhlim snaps, his fists lowering, his muscles relaxing, recognising the male before him at last. "What's wrong with you?"

Emilie Ocean 51

"With me? You're the one spying on us," El chuckles, not an ounce of remorse in his voice. "Be grateful I didn't bite you. You're lucky I excel at self-control!"

I wince at the empty threat because I know for a fact vampires have a distaste for fae blood with a passion, finding it too acidic for their refined palates. The same goes for witch blood, for that matter.

Though he wouldn't have bitten Féidhlim, I was expecting El to at least kick him in the stomach or punch him in the face—not that I condone violence; far from it, in fact. I guess the rumours about nightwalkers and their inability to stay away from fights are flawed, which shouldn't surprise me in the slightest. Non-magical beings are known to expect the worst from us.

My eyes narrow on Féidhlim in the darkness of the gardens, my hands over my hips. I force my expression to go bleak, pretending not to notice how handsome and smart he looks dressed in black.

"Well done, Prince Féidhlim." I fake a smile. "You caught us. Go ahead and report to my father—"

"Your father?" Féidhlim's brow shoots to his hairline, his expression genuinely stretching into thick wrinkles of confusion. "No, Juliette, I'm not here because of your father. I… simply wanted to make sure you were safe."

My stare can't help but soften at his words, my heart flinching against my ribs. Whether he is telling the truth or not, my cheeks blush crimson-red at the attention, my stomach quivering.

52 Enchanted

"As you can see, she's perfectly safe. Goodbye," El tells him, entwining our fingers to pull me away.

I look back, locking eyes with Féidhlim, who follows us closely, clearly annoyed at El's response.

"He's so handsome when he's mad!" Amrah giggles, her bare legs hovering over the dewy grass beside me. "Can you introduce us?"

I sigh heavily, regretting the deal I made with her already.

"What are you guys up to?" Féidhlim asks, stepping ahead to face us.

"Nothing," El grumbles, guiding me through the gardens toward the magical wall.

"Oh, this is so fun. Our first adventure together!" Amrah cries beside me. "Can you tell them I used to be a model? Oh, and that I'm wearing some kind of sexy lingerie right now? Thanks!"

I grimace at my cousin, looking her up and down. Her black curly hair is all over the place, and patches of yellow stain her nightgown; the very one she died in.

"I'm coming," Féidhlim exclaims, no ifs, ands, or buts.

"Dude…" El's head shakes, his face screwing up at the intrusion.

But Féidhlim doesn't back away.

"I don't know what you are doing at four in the morning in the gardens," he starts, "but—"

"We're clearly gonna fuck, Fé," El blurts out, his stare holding Féidhlim's, his most serious expression on.

My eyes widen with embarrassment and shock at El's statement, my face turning magenta as I lock eyes with Féidhlim.

"El!" I snap, appalled and, frankly, irritated because the clock is ticking.

"Oh…" Féidhlim mutters, his brows drawing in, his cerulean gaze shying away from me.

"Wait a second… did you drag me all the way out here so I can watch you fuck the vamp?" Amrah exclaims, cross, her feet heavily landing on the ground. "That's fucked up, cuz! I mean, yeah, I get it, he's hot, but you do realise he drinks people's blood, don't you? Oh wait, have you kissed him yet? What does his breath smell like?"

"Enough! We don't have time for this, Amrah," I hiss, my patience reaching its limits, my glare murderous.

Féidhlim grimaces, staring at me like I am some kind of magical narwhal lost in the Indian Ocean. His eyes rest on Amrah to the left of me, except to him it is just an empty space with no one there.

"Who is she talking to?" Féidhlim asks El in a whisper as if I wouldn't hear him.

El's index finger draws small circles beside his temple, a low whistle escaping his lips.

"She's coo coo, Fé. You should leave while you can," El warns him.

"Come on, we have half an hour left to pass through the wall and get away with it," I point out, ignoring El's mischievous smirk and Féidhlim's frown. "We need to be quick so I can come back for Léo before the château wakes."

"Who's Amrah?" I hear Féidhlim ask El again, ignoring what I just said, his voice quieter this time.

"The ghost who's been haunting the palace," he announces, his stare darkening, but his lips grinning. Féidhlim rolls his eyes. "I'm serious, pal," El carries on. "She's Julie's cousin, who died five years ago. Amrah, sweetheart, meet Fé, fae prince of Éire."

Amrah squeals with delight, tightly grabbing Féidhlim's hands in hers.

"What a pleasure to meet such a hunky young prince!" she rejoices. "I'm single, by the way."

Féidhlim—unable to hear, feel, or see her—shivers uncomfortably, his eyes swiftly checking our surroundings, anxiety forming thin lines at the corners of his eyes. Amrah blows him a kiss next and he winces, feeling the air around him cooling down.

"I really don't like this…" he confesses, his gaze darting to mine.

"She's harmless, don't worry." I shrug before turning around to face the magical barrier.

I take a deep breath, readying myself.

"Amrah, are you ready?" I ask with determination.

"Yep!"

"Ready for what?" Féidhlim wonders, looking up at the dusty veil shielding us from the outside world.

"We're sneaking out, Fé!" El rolls his eyes, hands over hips and feet rooted in a warrior stance.

Footsteps echo behind us and my heart sinks, my blood growing icy at the thought of my parents finding out about our plan before we have time to put it into action.

"And you were gonna leave me behind?" Léo's voice exclaims, shock making his brow arch as he steps closer, K after him. "*Merci...*" (Thanks...)

His thank-you is sarcastic, of course.

"Léo? What are you doing here?" I query, shocked to see him in the gardens this early in the morning.

"Finding out my sister's abandoning me, apparently," he says, unimpressed.

"I was gonna come back for you if it worked!" I deadpan.

"Uh-huh," Léo hums, his lips now in a thin line.

"If *what* worked?" Féidhlim asks in a cry, clearly exasperated from not being kept in the loop.

"Amrah?" Léo cuts in, head cocking at our cousin. He too can see the dead, although he doesn't use his magic much.

Amrah's fingers gesture into a peace sign, a beaming grin lighting her smooth and dark skin.

"What is she doing here?" Léo goes on, casually nodding at her as if having her around was the most natural thing in the world.

"Turns out the security system only keeps the *living* on either side of the barrier," I explain proudly. "So Amrah is gonna briefly possess each one of us, just long enough for her to step through the wall while in our bodies."

"No way!" Léo blurts out, wide-eyed. "Are you telling me we have no defence against zombies?"

"*Argh...*" Féidhlim sighs in a grimace, ignoring my brother's comment. "I don't like this... Is there another way?"

"Yes, if you die you can ghost yourself out, too," I tell him bluntly.

"I volunteer to be your executioner," El offers generously, taking a step closer, his canines out.

"I should've brought popcorn," Léo rejoices, a mischievous giggle escaping his throat.

"No one's killing anyone," I rasp. "Féidhlim, you don't have to come with us..."

He swallows, his head shaking.

"No, I want to come," he confirms, though his voice lacks conviction.

"Guys, guards are coming," K—who I forgot was here—warns, his fingers tightening around the handle of his axe.

"Okay, let's go, Amrah!" I urge, my heart pumping blood faster than ever through my arteries.

I close my eyes, inhaling deeply as I surrender my body to my cousin, hoping she is right about the magical shield.

According to Amrah, the security system loses some of its power throughout the day—and night—its magical battery depleting. At this hour, it should be weak enough to let the dead walk through while inhabiting a living body.

Fingers crossed this works!

Chapter 7

Féidhlim

I can barely feel my body as it passes through the magical gate, Amrah commanding my limbs like they are hers. I have never been possessed before, and it isn't something I wish to do again. What a strange sensation to be in one's own body without the control that is supposed to come with it. I hear my thoughts but also Amrah's, the one making my muscles and organs function.

Relax, Fé. I won't hurt you, I promise, the ghost tells me sweetly in my head. *Stop fighting my presence or you'll be stuck here alone.*

She urges me to look up at the rest of the group on the other side of the magical veil, my heart hurting as Amrah forces me to watch El lean over Juliette, the pair locking eyes before fondly smiling at one another.

Okay, let's go! I say through gritted teeth.

No need to shout! she retorts, exhaling heavily.

Emilie Ocean 59

I will my mind to go quiet, granting Amrah complete access to my body. She uses my lips to giggle, excited, and we effortlessly jump through the wall.

We step out of the taxi, the scorching midday sun forcing my eyes to squint as I take in our surroundings. We decided to head to Saint-Gilles, an area by the sea on the west coast of the island that is for the most part a resort village. Juliette couldn't wait to go to the beach—one that isn't on the royal grounds, that is—and swim with dolphins.

"Fuck… It's way too bright…" El hisses, using his pale hands to protect his forehead and eyes from the beaming light. "I need to get inside…"

"I'll carry you, buddy!" K offers generously, his fingers wrapping around the vampire's waist.

"Stop that!" El snaps, irritated, nostrils flaring. "I can still walk!"

"Chill, El. I was only trying to help," K retorts, eyes rolling.

But the vampire prince swiftly leaves his side to cross the road, where *Fleur Fané* Resort awaits, its doors welcoming behind the white classical columns.

"Maybe we should've gone somewhere more discreet?" Juliette mutters, chewing her cheek nervously.

"Julie, sweetheart, I need a five-star hotel to soothe my nerves," El argues, hurrying inside the building.

She sighs, her head cocking back at the clear blue sky, and I can see just how nervous she is, far away from the palace for the first time in eleven years. Small little wrinkles form between her hazel eyes, her fingers fidgeting in front of her, and I wish I could do something—*anything*—to comfort her.

"I don't think anyone will pay much attention to us here," I voice instead, daring a shy smile at Juliette.

"No?" Her tone is soft but uncertain, her voice a gentle whisper that makes me want to hold her hands tight in mine to reassure her.

But I don't.

I swallow, my Adam's apple bobbing in my throat, focusing on keeping my composure.

"Why would your parents look for us here? As you said, we should've gone somewhere more discreet," I tell her.

Her lips close in a thin line and she nods.

"I don't care where we are, as long as I have my own room," Léo announces, eagerly joining El at reception.

Juliette shakes her head before staring at the empty space to the left of her.

"No, you're not getting a room…" she breathes, tossing her curly hair behind her shoulders.

"Sorry?" I frown, puzzled.

"Are you talking to me?" K asks her, his index finger innocently pressing against the swollen pec of his bulky chest.

"No, guys, I mean *Amrah*."

She tilts her head in the invisible ghost's direction and K grimaces.

"Oh… she's still here?" I ask, hoping for her cousin to go her separate way soon. "How long will she stay with us for, do you know?"

"Until we get back to the palace," Juliette says to my utter disappointment.

"We *are* going back to the palace?" K wonders carefully, weighing every word he breathes out.

"Eventually… yes." Juliette shrugs. "Amrah's staying with us until then. We made a deal."

I have nothing against Amrah—apart from the fact she is a ghost and ghosts make me nervous. I don't know where they are, what they do, or what they say. I find the complete lack of control disturbing.

Léo and El soon join us, key cards in hand. We get one each and head to our respective rooms on the top floor.

"Should we meet downstairs in ten and go to the beach?" Juliette suggests once in the lift, the corners of her lips finally stretching upward.

"Gods, no!" Léo cries, lazily leaning against the glass behind him. "I'm not leaving my room until dinner."

"Léo, you haven't been outside the royal grounds in over a decade! Aren't you curious to see what we've been missing out on?" his sister replies, eyebrows arching in disbelief.

But he shrugs, clearly uninterested.

She winces, turns to El, and asks, "Are you tired?"

He sighs heavily, an apologetic smile smearing his face.

"Sorry, sweet Julie," is all he says.

"That's okay, I get it," she replies softly.

"I'll be at the bar if anyone needs me," K announces casually, slipping his hands into the pockets of his denim shorts.

Juliette nods, focusing her gaze on the digital numbers indicating the second last floor.

"I'll go with you," I offer, spinning to face her fully, breaking the silence.

I hold my breath as her eyes meet mine, hoping she won't reject me.

"I want to go to the beach… and swim, though," she explains, hesitant.

"Yeah, me too."

I give my head a slow bob, although my heart is pounding frantically, adrenaline at the prospect of spending alone-time with the princess pumping in my veins.

"Aren't you afraid of sharks?" she asks me as the doors open and we step out onto our floor.

"Of course not." I shake my head, faking my confidence. "You said you'd put in a good word for me, didn't you?"

I smirk and she giggles, her curls bouncing up and down around her face, the tight knot in my stomach loosening instantly.

"I'll see you downstairs in ten, then," I tell her.

She nods, her laugh turning into a charming smile before she disappears inside her bedroom. And I can't help but grin, delighted she is giving me a chance to show her I am not her parents' puppet.

I watch as her door closes, my chest filling with warmth and excitement. When I turn around, however, my features regain their trained composure as El holds my stare, a dull expression painting his face. We don't say a word to one another and I slip inside my own room, my eyes never leaving his.

Eight minutes later, I am refreshed and determined to make the most of this unusual situation, knowing only too well it mightn't present itself again. Juliette is too excited about being away from her parents right now to

64 Enchanted

hold a grudge against me, it seems, which only works to my advantage.

I reach the reception hall and look around for her when I spot her shiny curls in the hotel souvenir shop.

"Hey, you ready?" I ask, swiftly joining her by the sunglasses display.

"Yeah, I got everything!"

She taps the braided tote bag hanging over her shoulder. She suddenly looks me up and down, my stomach clenching, something fuzzy coming alive in my insides.

"You're not wearing swim shorts?" She cocks her head innocently.

"Hm…"

My brows knit, my gaze snapping to my beige chinos.

"I got my bikini over there," she says, looking past me.

Her index finger mechanically hooks around the red lace of her bikini top. I follow the motion with my eyes, mesmerised by the bright scarlet of the fabric against her soft honey skin under her white sundress.

"They have swimwear for men, too," she lets me know.

"Right," I breathe, locking eyes with her.

"I'll show you."

She walks past me, the sweet scent of coconut enveloping us, and I wish I could wrap her black curls around my hand and whisper dirty words in her ears as I bend her over the closest wooden shelving unit.

"What about these?" She waves a pair of black-red-and-white swim shorts at me.

"Yeah, I'll take them," I tell her swiftly, grabbing the piece of clothing to cover my cock, now hard against the zipper of my chinos.

I pay for the shorts and head to the changing area to put them on, willing myself to get my act together, wishing my dick stopped acting up already.

Chapter 8
Juliette

I squeal as Féidhlim's strong arms clasp around my stomach, preventing me from swimming any further. He holds me flush against his tall frame, my back sinking against his sturdy chest, his abs contracting below me.

"Stop fighting me, Jules!" he says, his grasp tightening. "I won!"

"That's not fair!" I cry, wriggling my way out of his embrace. "You're taller and stronger."

"*And* faster," he adds cheekily, the sound of his voice causing my insides to flutter, a kaleidoscope of butterflies taking off with a mind of their own.

"You haven't won yet," I blurt out, gathering the strength to mask my arousal. "I'm still in the water—"

But I pause, Féidhlim's hands brushing my skin to wrap under my knees and back, a delicious shiver travelling my spine under his touch. He stands up, the defined muscles in his arms lifting me above the silky surface of the seawater, my feet now dangling into thin air.

"I won," he declares confidently, his cerulean eyes gazing into mine with such intensity that I feel my cheeks flush instantly. "Now I get to collect my prize," he says, his expression softening as he continues to hold my stare.

I nod slowly, dazed at how handsome he looks in the water; his blond hair glowing under the beaming sun, his blue eyes piercing, his bare chest strong and bulky with bright speckles of fae dust floating around us.

"Okay. What do you want?" I rasp, struggling to keep my breathing under control, a delicious burn coming alive between my legs.

"A kiss… from *you*," he whispers, gently placing me back down, his fingers wrapping around my hips.

I swallow, short for words.

"Okay," I manage, my bottom lip curving around my teeth.

I let Féidhlim twirl me around, his grip tightening to draw me closer to him, my pebbled nipples now pressing against his bare skin. I wonder if he can feel my heartbeat racing in its cavity, or see how turned on the proximity of his body makes me.

The palm of his right hand grazes my flesh, moving upward until it cups my cheek, Féidhlim's long fingers diving through my curls for support. He takes his time, the pad of his thumb stroking my bottom lip, his gaze plunging deep into mine. My lips part, impatience getting the better of me, and when my face nears his, Féidhlim mimics the motion until our mouths join. His tongue claims mine, my heart stuttering. I close my eyes, revelling in the warmth of his breath, a delicious wave of electricity pulsating in my sex.

His grip tightens over my hair, his hand levelling the back of my head, and our kiss deepens. My fingers fly to his strong back, my palms stroking his smooth skin and defined muscles. Féidhlim's mouth applies just the right amount of pressure and suction to mine, making me ravenous. But our lips eventually part and I am left with a racing heart and rosy cheeks, unsure what to do next.

"You're stunning, Juliette," Féidhlim whispers, pulling me closer, his arms closing around me into a loving embrace.

I blink, warmth filling every fibre of my being as my head rests against his torso. And I can't help but notice just how fast his own heart beats beneath his sculpted musculature. Whether it is for me, or not, I know I am the cause of it, and that is enough to make me happy. My eyes flutter shut and my arms wrap around his slender waist as I allow myself to enjoy every second of bliss I can hold onto.

"We should rent a motorboat," he suggests a moment later, his lips pressing against my hair.

I look up at him, puzzled, so he points at the rental shop a couple of feet behind us.

"To swim with dolphins," he adds.

My mouth stretches into a wide grin, excitement taking over.

He remembered!

His large hand wraps around mine to guide me out of the water. Our toes sink into the damp white sand on the shore, our wet bodies glistening under the sun as we approach the store.

"Wait, wait…" I beg, a lump forming in my throat.

"What is it?" he asks, his voice soft and patient, his fingers cupping my face.

He leans down to be at eye-level with me and squints, his brow drawing in.

"What if someone recognises us?" I whisper, anxiety preventing my legs from going any further.

"Uhm…" he hums, a genuine look of concern painting his face.

I look around.

"I mean… We've been lucky so far but… do you think the retailers would know who we are?" I offer, guarded.

I have no idea whether the Reunionese population knows what I am supposed to look like (maybe my parents have been sharing photos of Léo and me with the public without us knowing about it), or if they are versed enough in Éireann politics to recognise Féidhlim.

He pulls me closer to wrap a reassuring arm around my shoulders.

"I don't think anyone will recognise *me* this far from home, Jules. Wait here. I'll get the rental boat sorted."

My mouth parts to argue but his thumb presses against my lips, a sexy smirk curling upward on his suntanned face.

"Please," he presses.

I nod shyly.

I don't like having other people do my bidding for me, but I would rather have Féidhlim take the lead on this one. The last thing I want is for someone to recognise me and alert my parents. Plus, letting Féidhlim dictate what we are to do next is a huge turn on for me.

I march back to get my tote bag from the sandy beach, while he fetches us a motorboat, a million thoughts racing through my mind. I replay our kiss in my head, analysing every single detail of it, wondering if it was as good for him as it was for me.

Thank Gods, Amrah stayed behind at the hotel with Léo; she would not approve of me sharing an intimate moment with her crush. My cheeks flush crimson, butterflies taking off in my stomach once again.

I kissed *Féidhlim*.

"Ready?" I hear him ask in the distance, snapping me back to reality.

I look up, happiness radiating from me before my smile drops.

"What is that?" I point at the white forty-foot vessel with my index finger, my eyes widening.

"A yacht," Féidhlim announces, grinning like a youngling. "A 39 Open Flybridge to be exact!"

"Féidhlim, I don't know how to pilot that thing. Do you?"

"Don't worry, I have one just like it at home."

"You do?"

My eyebrows crook at the luxury of having one's own yacht.

"Yeah… Éire's an island, too, you know."

He shrugs casually.

I smile because that isn't why I am surprised. Sometimes I forget other royals have regular regal lives. They can come and go as they please, never to be confined between the four magical walls of their estates.

"Don't be nervous, Jules," Féidhlim tells me, his fingers wrapping around the handle of my bag to carry it for me. "Just think about the dolphins."

He winks, and every ounce of stress poisoning my every thought evaporates from my body, something warm and fuzzy in its stead.

Féidhlim extends his other hand to me, so I eagerly grab it, the air crackling between us as our skins touch.

Ten minutes later, I sit on the sunlounger on the foredeck, my back sinking against the black pillow behind me. My head cocks at the sky, my eyes fluttering shut as the sea breeze caresses my face, the late afternoon sun rays brushing against my skin like a veil of warm velvet. And I can't believe I have lived twenty-four years without ever experiencing bliss from the sea.

Féidhlim soon joins me with two glasses of bubbly, which he places in the drink holders by the sunlounger to keep cool. My heart cartwheels against my ribs when he lies down beside me like it is the most natural thing in the world. And maybe it is because I have never felt safer in my entire life. This is what peace feels like; right here, right now, with *him*.

"Are you good at chess?" he asks me, the pad of his fingers stroking my forearms as we lock eyes.

"Yes, why?" I reply confidently, propping myself up onto an elbow to face him.

"That won't do, then…"

He winces, his gaze reverting to the serene blue of the water. I cock, puzzled, and he smiles, his left brow hiking at me.

"You see, I need to find a way to win again so I can kiss you," he lets me in on his plan.

His blue eyes hold mine, prompting my cheeks to go scarlet of their own accord. My stomach flinches at the thought of Féidhlim's lips on mine again, the delicious kaleidoscope of butterflies now back in my stomach.

"You don't need to win to kiss me, Fé," I mutter to my own surprise.

I don't know if it is the fact I am away from the palace, or on this yacht, or this beautiful sunset, but I feel alive as never before. And I want to enjoy every second of it, while it lasts.

So I lean closer, watching through hooded eyes as he does the same, our mouths opening slightly before meeting. My eyes flutter closed eventually, allowing me to revel in the taste of sea salt sprinkled over his lips; his tongue is sultry, his breath minty. The palm of his right hand moulds over the back of my head, our kiss intensifying. A sudden rush of electricity dashes to my middle and I can't help but let out a quiet moan.

Féidhlim's hands roam my back before wrapping around my hips, urging me closer; so close that I am now practically on him, a leg over his thigh. I inhale deeply through my nose, never breaking our kiss, as I feel the rock in his swim shorts, his erection protruding against my red bikini bottom.

"Féidhlim, wait…" I manage, out of breath.

"Are you okay?" he asks, my breasts uncomfortably cold as he instantly backs away from me.

I nod, gathering my thoughts.

"Yes, I just…" I exhale, kicking myself for ruining our moment.

"What is it, Jules?" His eyes search mine, genuine concern forming little wrinkles between his brows.

"Uhm... I don't wanna be presumptuous, but I think you should know that I've never... uhm... I'm not very experienced at... well, you know..." I attempt to formulate my thoughts as best I can. "I wasn't allowed out of the palace for over a decade so... I'm still... you know..."

I look away, embarrassment making me forget how to talk. And judging by the heat surging to my cheeks, I can safely assume I am as red as a ripe tomato.

"Was I too touchy?" A grave expression twists across his face as he takes me in. "I'm sorry, Juliette—"

"No, you were... *perfect.*"

I smile shyly, hoping I haven't ridiculed myself beyond repair and the beautiful male in front of me won't run away the second we get back to the shore.

But he cracks me the sexiest of smiles before tucking a curl behind my ear, giving my lungs permission to relax and breathe.

"Perfect," he repeats, his gaze locking on mine, the pad of his thumb gently stroking my cheekbone. "Perfect isn't accurate enough to describe you, Juliette," he purrs music to my ear.

My lips stretch into a wide smile at the compliment. I hold his stare for long seconds, grateful to have agreed to come to the beach with him. When I finally break eye contact to look past him, I spot a pod of dolphins playing in the sea. Féidhlim turns around, following my eyes.

"Jules!" he cries, excitement in his voice. "Come on, let's go!" he encourages, his hands gripping mine to pull me up.

Chapter 9

Féidhlim

We have been at *Fleur Fané* Resort for four days. Four whole days of swimming in the sea and playing with dolphins with Juliette.

I still cannot believe my luck, if I am being completely honest.

El can never come out of the hotel in daylight, the sun rays too harsh for his vampire flesh despite the enchanted ring he wears around his little finger. Léo and K pass their time at the hotel arcade, playing video games all day long. And I don't know what Amrah has been up to because I never ask.

With everyone out of the way, I have had Juliette to myself, and the more I get to know her, the more I want our union to occur. Every evening, however, as we meet the others downstairs for dinner at the hotel restaurant, I am reminded I am not her only suitor.

"Love, will you pass me the salt, please?" El asks Juliette, his pale hand wrapping around her delicate fingers over the table.

My blood boils in my veins despite the gentle breeze keeping our bodies cool in the open area, anger raging in my middle at the way El touches her like she is his. If only he could see us at the beach. The way *my* tongue dives deep in Juliette's mouth, claiming it as our taste buds blend and our salivas meld. The way *my* pelvis playfully grinds against hers until her body shudders under mine and she battles for composure. The way *my* name escapes her delicious lips when I touch her and she begs me to keep going.

"Sure," Juliette exclaims, reaching for the glass container.

El sprinkles the pink crystalline substance over his rabbit-blood soup, stirs, brings a spoonful of the red mixture to his lips, and slurps. I wince, looking away, my stomach turning. Léo suppresses a peal of laughter at the expression on my face, and I curse under my breath for losing composure.

What is it with these people and my lack of self-control?

"Will you please stop?" Juliette snaps crossly, the unexpected melody of her voice making the muscles of my stomach quiver.

My eyebrows shoot high, uneasiness stiffening my every muscle at being reprimanded, until I realise it isn't me Juliette is talking to.

"Amrah, you can't even *eat* food!" Léo adds, coming to his big sister's rescue.

Their gazes meet and they both roll their eyes.

At this stage, El, K, and I have stopped asking questions, preferring to ignore Amrah's shenanigans altogether. I have grown to accept her ghostly presence, but I still refuse to take part in her invisible deeds. She has been driving my Juliette insane ever since we got here, so I will not allow myself to bond with Amrah. The last thing I want is for Juliette to think I am teaming up against her again; this time with her dead cousin.

"Are you all going to movie night after dinner?" K wonders, the tips of his fingers sinking into the soft bun as he bites into his juicy hamburger. Ketchup smears the corners of his mouth, and his pink tongue swiftly swipes across. "They're playing *Casper*." A loud chuckle rumbles through his chest. "I bet you that's Amrah's favourite movie—"

Smack!

Without any warning—and to our utmost surprise—the back of Léo's hand smacks against K's arm, the impact resonating through the entire area, ricocheting off the ivory walls and rippling over the swimming pool behind us. If we were indoors, the vibrations would have been much louder, judging by the red mark on K's raw flesh.

"Léo!" Juliette cries, appalled.

"Hey, what's your problem?" K roars at him, gently rubbing the pain away with the flat of his hand.

Léo blinks once, twice, his face livid. His brows knit closer in slow motion, and I have no problem picturing the gears rotating inside his head as Léo processes what he just did.

"That wasn't me," he manages at last, his voice trembling, a genuine expression of dread dimming his features. He turns to the left of him, toward Juliette. "You did this?"

I frown because I was watching his sister the entire time, and I can certify she did not lift a finger.

"What?" she voices, her expression mimicking her brother's. "You can do that?"

I lock eyes with El and K, suddenly realising they are talking to *Amrah*.

"K, I'm sorry. It wasn't me," Léo apologises, his hand patting our friend gently where the flesh is bruised.

K swallows, wincing.

"It's okay… but please don't tell me Amrah did it…" he manages, uneasiness twisting the innocent lines of his face.

Léo nods, his lips thinning.

"She… took possession of my hand," he slowly confirms in disbelief. "I didn't even know she was strong enough to control the living."

Juliette sighs heavily, head shaking.

"Only briefly and to those with no mental-shield training, Amrah says," Juliette repeats her invisible cousin's words, her stare focusing on the vacant spot between herself and her brother.

"No mental-shield training?" Léo repeats, his eyes squinting at the ghost. "I have trained plenty, I'll have you know!"

"Hm-hm—" Juliette winces, unconvinced.

"Don't you dare say I'm weak!" her brother spits, vexed.

"All I'm saying is that those whose minds aren't tightly concealed from Amrah can be possessed any time," Juliette explains, shrugging innocently.

"Great... So, all of us, then!" El hisses, defeated by the situation. He locks eyes with me across the table. "You better change your attitude toward our wonderful Amrah or you'll be next, Prince of Éire!"

I grimace, knowing feckin' well he is right.

"So, Amrah could've possessed any one of us at the palace, too?" I ask, curious as to why she decided to keep her ghostly abilities a secret until now.

Léo and Juliette stare at the space between them for a couple of seconds until Juliette's cheeks flush magenta, and Léo bursts out laughing.

"No way!" he cries out, his palm flying to his lips in an attempt to stop himself from grinning. "Jules!"

His mischievous chestnut eyes jump from his sister to me, his teeth biting his bottom lip as he tries to keep his cackle under control.

"How could you do this to poor Amrah?" Léo asks Juliette, choking on his words with amusement.

Juliette's face turns red—the same way it does when she is embarrassed—and I couldn't find her more adorable.

"What is it?" El jumps in, a hand behind Juliette's backrest as he leans over her to get the goss.

Léo grins and turns to Amrah before exclaiming, "With your crush, huh? Where?" Another quiet chuckle and his gaze darts toward the beach. "I knew it!" he turns to us next. "So, apparently—"

"Léo!" Juliette cuts him off, her big-sister hat on as she shakes her head slowly in a threatening fashion. "The unsolicited possession only works if Amrah is… experiencing strong feelings."

"What does that mean?" K cocks.

"She's mad pissed, bro!" Léo blurts out, no longer able to suppress his laughter.

He starts giggling like a madmale, his eyes mockingly grinning at his sister, who glowers at him.

"But why?" K presses, at a loss.

"She's annoyed with me," Juliette says in a calm voice, getting back to her dinner. "That's all you need to know," she adds when we all stare at her in silence, waiting for more.

We decided it would be wise *not* to attend the *Casper* screening in the end. We don't want to piss Amrah off, especially now that we know she can possess the living at the snap of a finger. So, instead, here we are at the outdoor hotel bar. The place has a nice vibe to it, I admit. The infrastructure, built on the white sandy beach, is made entirely of bamboo with lampshades of the same woody grass hanging down from the ceiling.

We were lucky to get a table; the bar is packed with hotel guests and visitors, making it hard to have a conversation without having to shout. It seems Juliette's concerns about being recognised by her people were unnecessary; not a single person has given us attention, or the royal treatment I usually get around Éire for that matter.

I sit back in my bamboo seat, watching as we naturally divided ourselves into three distinct groups; Léo and K, El and Juliette, and, well… me. I may be a prince but social anxiety gets to me as much as it does anybody. I usually put on a brave face and pretend I am a fish in the water, but not tonight. Tonight it is okay to sit back and remain quiet, for a change.

I smile, silently listening to K tell Léo how he fought an alligator in the Bayou of New Orleans a couple of years back when he was only twenty.

"What!" Léo exclaims, eyebrows shooting high in wow. "I'm twenty, and there's no way on Earth you'll see me fight an animal in the Bayou, no matter how strong my magic is," Léo announces, nonchalantly, metaphorically giving himself a pat on the back. "What am I saying? There's no way I'll *go* to the Bayou!"

K's genuine laughter bubbles out of his chest in an echo of sheer happiness, Léo soon following his lead. My smile broadens and I soak in their glee before finishing my whiskey sour.

"I'll get the next round," I offer the table, getting up. I look at each one of their glasses. "JD and coke for Léo, Heineken for K, Red Martini for El." They nod. "And…" But I pause, frowning at Juliette's glass. "Are you still on the water?" I chuckle.

She smiles shyly.

"I got nervous and didn't know what to order…" she confesses in a small voice.

"Come with me, so. I'll help you pick a drink at the bar," I tell her, extending a hand, which she grabs eagerly, a wide grin twisting across her face.

I chance a glance at El, who is fuming I stole the princess away from him, before guiding her through the crowd. Her body presses heavily against mine as we carve our way to the counter. I take my time, enjoying the pressure of her hand against my bicep, delighted to finally have some time alone with her. I grab the drink menu next and lean in to scan it, our cheeks only mere inches apart.

"Sex on the beach?" she asks me, screaming from the top of her lungs to overcome the cacophony of voices, glass clinking, and music suffocating us. "What do you think?"

"Now?" I stare at her wide-eyed, my cock pulsating with want in my beige chino shorts.

If she wants her first time to be on the beach with *me*, who am I to disagree? She is, after all, the princess of this beautiful island. And as of two days ago, her wishes are my command. My heart picks up its pace, excitement pumping adrenaline through my veins at the prospect of taking our relationship—which, despite its casualness, has been nothing but hot and all-consuming—to the next level.

"Are you sure?" I double-check with her, nonetheless, because I will not make my move unless I am a thousand percent certain she is ready for this.

"What?"

Her brows pinch and she leans closer, a hand cupping her ear.

"Are you sure you want to go to the beach *now*?" I elaborate, my voice louder.

"No! *Sex on the beach*. The drink!" she rectifies, pointing at the cocktail on the menu with her index finger.

Cringe!

What a cliché...

I am not the first male to make a mistake and I won't be the last.

"Oh…" I sing, forcing my facial composure to remain.

Well, that makes more sense...

"You like it?" she wonders, her voice loud to overpower the music playing in the background.

"Yeah."

Though I wish we weren't talking about the alcoholic beverage.

Looking at Juliette in her floral-print dress, the collar of the fragile garment exposing the swell of her breasts, I am reminded of the effect of her body on me. How easy would it be to feel her tits when the space around us is so packed no one pays us any attention? Or slip my hand under her skirt to check if she too is horny, her folds wet and swollen? Every time the breeze swooshes around Juliette, the hem of her dress lifts to show me a teasing amount of flesh; just enough for me to picture the juiciness of her ass in her red bikini bottoms. The female has been giving me blue balls ever since we began to frequent the beach.

"I'll take it, then!" she chirps, closing the drink menu.

My reverie ceases and I nod casually before turning around to order our next round of drinks, embarrassment at my earlier presumption still making my stomach churn. I silently curse myself, watching Juliette from the corner of my eye, for (almost?) making a fool of myself in her presence. Hopefully, I played it cool and she didn't notice the disappointment in my voice at the realisation we weren't on the same page.

The bartender slides her cocktail across the bamboo countertop, and I hand it to her. Her lips wrap around the white straw to suck the beverage into her mouth.

Her eyes light up, a grin shaping on her face. "I love it!"

Chapter 10
Juliette

I can't help but groan when I wake up to the excruciating thumping in my head. My brain feels hazy, slow from the fog preventing my thoughts from enunciating clearly. My eyes flutter open and the second broad daylight flows through my irises, an imaginary hammer batters my skull, forcing me to squeeze my lids shut again.

What the hell is going on?

I wince, pulling the covers over my head, before I realise I am lying down on my stomach; a position I never fall asleep in because it hurts my neck.

Oh, my neck…

Another groan escapes my throat as I move slowly, contorting my body with care so as not to cause any further damage. I open my eyes one more time and take a deep breath, staring at the ceiling to squint at the two dainty black wire light shades.

"Huh?" I exclaim, frowning.

The ceiling lights in my bedroom are golden, not black!

I prop myself up onto my elbow to have a better view of the space around me when the white flat sheet falls, revealing my bare breasts, my nipples pebbled. I am *naked*.

What the fuck?

I freeze, my face turning to the left of me to see Féidhlim fast asleep on his back, a hand behind his head, the other across his clothes-free stomach. His chest peacefully rises and falls with each breath he takes, the motion measured but rhythmic. I take a second to watch him, forgetting all about the migraine pounding inside my head, the ache in my neck, and my comatose naked body. I quietly lie back down, my eyes never leaving him as I soak in his beauty.

I smile at how bright his blond hair looks after only a couple of days in the sun, his short curls beautiful golden locks. My gaze lands on his ears next, causing my brow to arch. I never realised how pointy the tips of his ears were because, of course, he is a fae.

Féidhlim is the first fae I have ever crosses paths with. I know that some of them have wings, others don't, despite the fact that they can all fly. I read that some fae from Greece and England even have horns! But Féidhlim has neither. If it weren't for his ears and the golden-and-silver fae dust sparkling around him when he flies, I wouldn't know he was a fae.

Féidhlim hums in his sleep, his head tilting left before his breathing resumes its steady course.

My smile broadens at the innocence radiating out of the handsome male by my side, my gaze softening. I skim his body with my eyes, my cheeks flushing at the bulge protruding below his pelvis from under the covers.

Holy shit!

He's hard!

I swallow, my eyes widening at the hidden stick as thick as a plantain, bobbing below his waistline. I squeeze my legs tight, heat surging between them at the thought of Féidhlim lying down in bed beside me, devoid of any kind of clothing.

My fingers shyly wrap around the seam of the sheet, greed and want dictating my next move, my heart pounding louder than the hammer in my head. I carefully lift the light fabric just high enough to have a quick look at his—

"Morning, Jules," Féidhlim mutters, his voice hoarse.

"H-Hi!" I say a little too loud, prompting the vibrations of the words to hit off the walls of my skull like rubber-bouncy balls. "*Argh.*"

I grimace, massaging my temples as I lie back down. Féidhlim chuckles, turning to face me.

"You're hungover," he states casually, an amused smile shaping his lips.

He scooches closer to deposit a light kiss against my forehead, his erection brushing my stomach as he leans down. So I act on my self-control, battling my natural instincts against the need to grab his dick to feel it in my hand. I want to feel his stiffness, his heat, his length. I want to hold his cock tight in my fist and pump him until he comes. The thought of it makes me wet beyond belief.

"Do you remember last night?" he asks softly, his piercing cerulean eyes diving deep into mine.

"Uhm…" My face screws up as I try to access my memories, but nothing comes up. "No," I confess, my irises flickering and my brain straining. "Did we…"

I lock eyes with him, brow arching.

"What? Have sex?" he elaborates for me, his tall frame backing away. "No. You were *drunk*."

Oh…

Am I disappointed nothing happened, or am I relieved? I don't know. Though, I suppose I would want to remember my first time with Féidhlim.

"It's just… I don't have any clothes on, so I thought—" I start, looking away as an embarrassing flush of red hue smears my cheeks.

"You threw up on yourself, then on me," he blurts out, the soft features of his face pulling into a grimace.

"Oh…"

Oh, my fucking Gods!

Kill me now…

"And then you lost your key card on the beach, and dropped mine on the road." He shows me the blackened electronic piece of plastic from his bedside locker. "A truck drove over it, and it won't work anymore."

"Oh…" I swallow, uneasiness forming a lump in my throat. "So, this isn't your room?"

I look around for his belongings but can't find any.

"No, the hotel manager wasn't there last night to replace our key cards, so I had to get us a new bedroom. This is all they had left," he explains, waving at the space before us with the flat of his hand.

I nod, bracing myself for what I am about to say next, unable to look him in the eye.

"And… what about our clothes?"

Féidhlim sighs.

"I didn't know how you'd feel about the others knowing we were sharing a bed, so I couldn't ask them for help. And the shop was closed."

I wince.

"Thanks," I mumble, readying myself to walk out of this room with dried puke all over.

I made my bed, time to lie in it.

I exhale heavily.

"I'm sorry, Fé—"

92 *Enchanted*

"I washed our clothes and hung them outside on the balcony."

"You what?"

"It's less awkward this way."

He shrugs casually as if washing spew off a silly princess' clothes is something he does every day. My skin crawls at the uneasiness settling in my insides as I picture my crush fiddling with my thrown-up dinner. I now wish I could hide under a rock for the rest of my life and never leave. My heart shatters at the realisation I will never be able to sway the way Féidhlim looks at me from now on: *Vomit princess.*

"Thanks," is all I can bring myself to say, my eyes growing glassy.

The knot grows thicker in my oesophagus but I swallow it down.

"Did you, hm, strip me naked, too?" I ask shyly after a moment.

My stomach twists, the blush of my cheeks scorching fire, hoping that somehow in my repulsiveness, he still found me attractive buck naked despite my making a total fool of myself.

"No… you did that on your own," he replies, a blank expression on his face, "before you asked me to sleep beside you because you were afraid of the dark."

My lips close in a thin line and I nod, unable to find my words, mortification and the after-effect of alcohol blocking my ability to think.

I am never drinking again!

"Here." Féidhlim casually hands me a small yellow cardboard box with navy and red writings. "The receptionist gave me this for you last night. It'll soothe the migraine."

My fingers wrap around the small container on which I read *Doliprane*. Paracetamol might ease my physical discomfort, but I doubt it will help with my self-esteem.

Later that day, after Féidhlim got us replacement key cards so we could shower and get changed in our respective rooms, I decided it was time I went to the farmers market, or "*marché forain*" as we locals call it. I am in dire need of escaping Féidhlim and getting a natural remedy for my hangover, so here I am under the midday sun, browsing stall after stall as I battle my way through the crowd.

Despite the stiffness of my body, my heart aches with nostalgia at the smell of freshly ground spices—cumin, cinnamon, cardamom, and whatnot— and my eyes swell at the vibrant green of the ripe guavas on display.

"*Mamzel, samoussas?*" (Miss, samosas?) one of the vendors catches my attention, wondering if I would like to purchase a couple of his homemade delicacies.

I smile, approaching the metal trays on the table, my mouth watering at my favourite filo pastry snack; my most cherished comfort food. So I gladly pick a couple, knowing only too well Léo will never forgive me if I don't bring him some, too.

"They look nice!" the familiar voice echoes behind me.

My heart stutters and my muscles go rigid under my t-shirt. I silently curse, not ready to face *him* so soon.

"You should try them," I manage nonetheless, turning around to face Féidhlim, a shy smile growing across my embarrassed face.

He nods, leaning closer to the trays.

"What's '*jambon-fromage?*'" he asks, a boyish grin brightening his features and putting me at ease instantly.

"Ham-and-cheese," I translate, my voice more timid than I intended it to be.

"Excellent," he cries, casually wrapping an arm around my shoulders to pull me closer. "I've tried samosas before but they were bigger and seemed spicier."

"You mean, you tried the Indian version?" I query, making conversation.

"Probably." He shrugs.

My stomach quivers the second his cologne whiffs its way to my nostrils, and I deeply inhale the fresh scent of his eau de toilette; top notes of grapefruit, lemon, and pepper.

"Ten of those, please," Féidhlim tells the vendor, pointing at the small ham-and-cheese triangle-shaped appetisers. "And I'll pay for whatever this beautiful lady is having, too."

"Oh, no, Fé, you don't have to do that," I interject, the muscle in my neck straining so I can lock eyes with him.

His grip tightens over my frame, pulling me flush against him.

"I know I don't have to, Jules. I *want* to," he explains before depositing a light kiss against my hair.

He nods at the vendor next and hovers his phone over the card machine to tap.

My thoughts race inside my hazy brain, another migraine surging as I wonder whether Féidhlim forgot about last night, or if he genuinely doesn't care I embarrassed myself the way I did.

"What else do you need to get?" he asks me, following my lead through the crowd.

My lips part, searching for a medicinal herbs stall when I unexpectedly freeze into place, causing Féidhlim to heavily bump into me.

"You okay, Jules?" He frowns, his hands gripping my hips from behind.

I don't reply so he follows my gaze, our eyes resting on the middle-aged female before us, her dark skin glowing under the sun like the healthiest of dates.

"Who's that?" he asks in a whisper.

I swallow, blinking once, twice, the palms of my hands growing clammy.

"Amrah's mother," I tell him.

Chapter 11

Féidhlim

I roll my eyes at El across the kitchen as I watch him talk to Juliette's grandmother. The bastard has been in my way for seven days straight, spending every single second of his existence charming the Hakimis to impress Juliette.

We ran into Amrah's mother, Juliette's aunt, at the farmers market last week. The female, Salomé is her name, scared me at first: Her dark-brown stare was inquisitive and cold, her features stark. She relaxed the second she realised her brother, Juliette's father, wasn't around, however, which immediately put me at ease. Everything happened so fast then.

Salomé invited us to stay at her villa by the sea, where she lives with her mother, eager to catch up with her niece and nephew. So we left the hotel, despite Léo and Amrah's incessant nagging; the pair had no interest in leaving the five-star establishment to reconnect with their family. I expected as much from Léo alright, being the hermit that he is, but Amrah? *Why wouldn't she want to see her mother and grandmother after all these years?* She too was stuck at the palace, after all.

It took me a while to understand that the Hakimi females had no idea about Amrah's presence at the resort, and I was shocked to hear they had never been in contact with her either after her tragic passing.

"Don't tell me you made this?" El cries.

His grey eyes roll with delight as he brings a slice of homemade sweet potato cake—*gâteau patate*—to his lips. He chews intently, his head bobbing at Juliette's grandmother.

"Are you sure you aren't a Michelin Star chef, *Mamie* Min?" he compliments.

Mamie Min (which directly translates to "Grandma Min") giggles, the thick wrinkles creasing her tanned face stretching tightly around her almond eyes and forehead.

If what I found in my research is correct, *Mamie* Min was the youngest of five siblings and one of the princesses of China before she was forced to relocate to Reunion Island to join its King—Karam Hakimi—in union. When Blanche Rivière was proclaimed queen of the island, King Daniyal took her family name to express his loyalty to France and gratitude for his marital partner.

Salomé was supposed to inherit the crown one day but her royal status was downgraded from 'high princess' to 'duchess' the moment she announced to her parents that she was to marry a commoner—Amrah's father. There was no way King Karam would have allowed a non-royal, even a powerful witch, to come to the throne. This, of course, created tension between Salomé and

Daniyal but I wasn't able to find much more about it online.

"Aren't you sweet, Elmas!" *Mamie* Min manages, patting him on the back. "Here, have another slice."

Her ageing fingers wrap around the table knife on the white-tiled kitchen counter to cut a generous chunk of cake for El.

I curse silently, wishing my competition away already. Vampires don't even eat non-bloody food. El is trying way too hard. It is pathetic!

Salomé and *Mamie* Min were sorry to hear about El's inability to function during the daytime, so they urged Juliette and Léo to join them as they performed a magical ritual on El's heirloom to heighten its protective performance. Hence the bane of my stay; El can now spend as much time as he wants with Juliette and her family.

"What about you, Féidhlim, do you want some cake, too?" *Mamie* Min offers.

I startle, dread invading my limbs at being detected. There I was, discreetly leaning against the edge of the windowsill on the far end of the open-plan living room leading to the kitchen area, hoping nobody would notice me as I thought of all the unimaginable ways to rid myself of El. I keep forgetting the Rivières (and Hakimis) are a family of clairvoyant witches—nothing gets past them—and *Mamie* Min is by far the strongest and wisest of them all.

100 Enchanted

"Don't waste your time, *Mamie* Min," El replies for me, wrapping a long arm around the female's tiny stature. "Éire prefers white potatoes."

Mamie Min's lips thin and she nods slowly, clearly disappointed.

But not on my watch!

"While that may be true, I have enjoyed every single Reunionese dish I've tried so far, and I have to say, the kitchen smells absolutely divine," I tell her, joining them by the counter and making a point of ignoring El. "I would love to try some of your sweet potato cake, *Mamie* Min."

Her frown turns upside down as she happily plants the knife through the squared sponge one more time and puts a generous slice of the dessert onto a pink-flower plate for me. I grin, biting into the delicacy like a starved male, which causes *Mamie* Min to giggle, delighted with my fervour. A rush of satisfaction washes over me the moment I catch El's eyes darkening, his arms crossing over his chest, unimpressed.

"You two boys eat without me," the wise female says, placing the rest of the cake on a tray, accompanied by a set of plates, napkins, and cutlery. "I'm gonna go and see if anyone else is hungry."

I nod and smile, and so does El, so I decide to show more teeth. He copies me, the muscles in his neck stretching to accommodate his facial features. *Mamie* Min frowns at us, swiftly disappearing down the sitting room and out onto the balcony, prompting our forced expressions to relax at last.

"What are you doing?" El hisses at me, nostrils flaring and jaw clenching.

"What do you mean?" I ask innocently, bringing the last bit of cake from my plate to my lips.

"Back off, already!" he barks, jostling me on his way out of the kitchen.

I find my balance, glaring at him.

"Watch it, Elmas, or—"

"Or what?" he taunts, turning back around to face me. "Or you'll tell on me?" he mocks, his bottom lip pouting.

"What's your problem?" I squint, the anger and frustration from the past couple of days stirring in my middle like a volcano on the verge of eruption.

"Clearly, *you* are my problem. You managed to keep Julie all to yourself at the hotel, but things have changed now. Now, *I* am around, so back off," El spits, the grey of his eyes obscuring, the lines of his face turning feral. "Go find another princess to harass."

"It isn't harassing when the princess in question likes it!" I retort, smirking evilly at him.

I watch as El's upper lip curls, revealing two pointy canines; I have struck a nerve. Good.

"Please… don't flatter yourself, Féidhlim. Julie's just being polite." He smiles fakely. "She wouldn't want to offend Éire's poor little prince. She is too nice to tell you the truth, but you're wasting your time. And hers! Why are you courting her again? Oh yeah!" His fingers snap. "Because your *daddy* made you."

He bursts out laughing, a genuine loud cackle that makes his chest puff and his stomach shake.

"Shut up, Elmas!" I roar, losing composure. "You know nothing about my situation."

My heart races, adrenaline kicking in like a drug.

"I wouldn't be so confident if I were you, Fé. You know, I had a *lot* of time to myself at *Fleur Fané* Resort," El announces casually. "It got me thinking. Why have you been fighting so hard to 'win this competition,' as you like to call it?" He quotes and unquotes my words. "So I decided to do some digging, and what I found out is gobsmacking, prince of Éire." He cackles. "I know what happened between you and that country female back in Éire three years ago," he goes on, an eyebrow arching triumphantly.

My features remain stern but my body stiffens. I don't say a word. I hold my breath while I mask the burning need to punch him in the face or make him choke on fae dust to make him shut up.

"What was her name again? Ah, yes! Aoife Burke," El carries on, his tone light and amused.

His grin widens and he takes a step closer, his mouth only an inch away from my ear.

"She named the baby after her grandfather, *Oisín*," he goes on under his breath.

My eyes suddenly grow glassy at the mention of the youngling, a lump forming in my oesophagus, cutting off my breathing and making my heart squeeze. I never knew his name.

Oisín.

Painful memories flash in front of my eyes, horror at my past deeds being revealed turning my brain into a hazy maze.

"Judging by the expression on your face, my PI earned her money," El adds, a light rumble echoing through his chest. "Stay away from Juliette, Féidhlim. I've never been good at keeping secrets."

I swallow with difficulty, my burning eyes meeting his as my mind battles to form coherent thoughts.

"I can't…" I manage eventually, gathering the strength I have left to use my words. "My father would never—"

"Tell him you'll try again next year," El cuts in, his tone icy.

I shake my head slowly when he holds a hand up to stop me, his palm invading my private space.

"Stay in my way, and the entire Rivière family will know about your bastard son," he threatens. "We'll see how King Daniyal treats you after hearing the news."

My inhales grow shallow, panic racing its way through my every cell, beads of sweat pearling my forehead at the thought of my deepest secret coming to light; my deepest fear coming to life.

"The dolphins are back!" I hear Juliette's voice echo from the balcony, and my heart shatters into a thousand pieces.

Juliette.

She can never find out…

What will she think of me?

"Féidhlim!" She hops her way in to join us in the kitchen. "Are you coming?"

I force a smile, hoping my face has regained its usual composure. My mouth parts when El answers for me.

"Sweet Julie, I'm afraid Fé isn't feeling well."

He fakes a frown.

Juliette's brown eyes rest on me, a genuine look of concern painting her face as she takes me in.

"Do you have a temperature?" She gently presses the back of her hand against my forehead, and I cringe at the sweat she collects on her skin.

"No, I—"

"He didn't like your grandmother's cake," El interrupts me, his shoulders casually shrugging.

"Oh…" Juliette's brow draws in, deception saddening her beautiful face. "That's okay. Just don't tell her." She smiles shyly. "You should go upstairs and rest, then, Fé."

"Yes, Féidhlim, you should go." El nods profusely before eagerly wrapping a hand around Juliette's arm. "I'll take Julie to the beach."

He winks at her.

"Well, maybe we should stay with Fé for a little while, just to make sure he's alright," she suggests kindly, patting me on the back.

"I don't think that's necessary, sweetheart," he argues, turning to me, his gaze dark and intense. "Do you?"

I clear my throat, my back to the wall.

"El's right, Jules. I'll be fine. I'll see ye later."

She frowns at me, the delicate lines of her face screwing up, so I look away, unable to hold her stare. My heart sinks as she nods and turns around at last to follow El.

"By the way, have you seen Léo and Amrah?" I hear her ask him as they step outside.

"I never see Amrah, love…"

"You know what I mean!" she deadpans.

106 Enchanted

He moves his hand from her arm to her hip, his fingers gripping her skin to keep her close to him.

"Léo went to a bar with K, I think," is the last thing I hear El say before they both disappear onto the sandy ground of the beach.

My head bows, defeated, and for the first time since my arrival on Reunion Island, I am uncertain how to proceed next.

Chapter 12
Juliette

"El, what are you doing?" I giggle as his fingers grip the edge of my green cotton hammock, dangerously making it sway from side to side under our weight between the tall filao trees in my aunt's garden.

The fresh sea breeze envelops us with the sweet scent of salt and the smoky aroma of grilled chicken, while younglings laugh and scream nearby as they dash into the sea, causing speckles of damp sand to dust away under their steps and seawater to splash all over.

"I'm joining you," he deadpans.

"But you can't," I argue, grasping the canvas bed tightly to stop myself from toppling over to the ground. "You're gonna make us both fall off it!"

I let out a squeak when El passes his right leg over mine to try and climb in beside me. The cords at both ends of the hammock shake, making my heart pinch in fear of meeting the hot sand below us.

"Come on, Julie, move over," he demands, heavily landing on top of me.

"*Umph.*" I grimace.

Though he is currently invading my personal space, it is refreshing to spend time with El in broad daylight for once. His skin doesn't tan, ever, no matter how long we stay under the sun, but his cheeks turn the faintest shade of pink, just bright enough to remind me that, although a vampire, El is as alive as the rest of us.

While I thoroughly enjoyed Féidhlim's presence at Fleur Fané Resort, I have to admit that I also missed El. It is nice to reconnect with my friend at last. I tried to spend as much with him in the evenings as I could, but a part of me was still ashamed I would rather be with Féidhlim.

A spike of distress hits my heart at the thought of the fae prince. Féidhlim has been avoiding me and I don't know why. I don't know what I did to make him stay away from me. I have tried talking to him, but he wouldn't let me in on his thoughts. He has been spending an awful lot of time in his guest bedroom at my aunt's, disappearing there when I am around or going for long walks or night flies on his own. If only he would talk to me, I would be able to rectify what I have done wrong.

"Why would you want to share my hammock when you can have one to yourself?" I remark, propping myself up onto my elbows to try and make room for the both of us.

"Why do you think?" El replies, his gaze meeting mine.

I swallow, uneasy at the need and affection in his eyes. The grey of his irises shines bright, his pupils minutely dilating as they roam my face.

Oh…

No…

"El, I don't think that we should be more than—"

"Let's go to Lithuania," he cuts in, his fingers gently wrapping around my waist as his tall frame presses against mine to make himself comfortable by my side.

"What?"

"Yeah, we should go to Lithuania. I know we don't have sharks to protect us there, but our Baltic coastline is stunning. You would love it. I could show you my country."

I look away, uncertain.

"I've never left this island," I remind him.

Though, this isn't the main reason why I don't feel comfortable going to Lithuania with him…

"There is a first time for everything, Julie," he tells me, leaning over me so I can't avoid his stare. "I can be your first for whatever you want."

"Oh…"

Is he talking about… sex?

"So, when is a good time?" he presses.

"For what?"

"For us to go to Lithuania."

"El, you can't be serious!"

"Oh, but I assure you that I am," he confirms with such conviction my stomach turns at the prospect of letting him down.

I know that El's agenda is still very much geared up for a union; a union that I know for a fact I only want with one person, and sadly it isn't him. I don't want to lead El on and waste his time. I value his friendship like no other and am perfectly satisfied with the way things are between us. I do not wish to take them further.

"Julie, I know you've been feeling down lately," he goes on. "I'm only trying to help. Maybe a change of scenery is what you need."

The virile fragrance of his cologne—sandalwood and cypriol— makes its way to my nostrils as another breeze swooshes our way. My heart stutters, an unexpected ache making my organ swell in my ribcage, robbing me of my breath for a split second.

Féidhlim.

I love Féidhlim's cologne… more so than I do El's.

But Féidhlim has been avoiding me for days now, refusing to look at me at the dining table or even talk to me when we are in the same room. His demeanour has grown defensive and icy, and I don't know why.

I feel the tears prickling the back of my eyes again, and I hate myself for feeling the way I do. It is the uncertainty and lack of understanding that forbids me from moving on, even when I get to spend my days with the handsome vamp sharing my hammock.

I am ashamed to say that I have shed tears over Féidhlim's distancing himself from me every night since he began building invisible walls between us. I thought Féidhlim and I had something. I thought we shared a connection. I thought… he liked me. I was wrong. And it hurts.

"Julie?" El calls, the sound of his deep voice a faint echo in the distance. "What is it?"

His thumb runs along the bone of my chin as his large hand cups my face, his dark eyes searching mine, full of worry.

My head shakes and I force a smile, my features regaining their composure. I may not be well experienced at all things romantic, but I know I shouldn't talk about Féidhlim with El.

"Nothing," I mutter, my tone more timid than I intended.

He stares at me, squinting, a smirk twitching from one of the corners of his mouth.

"Don't tell me you're anxious about our trip, love," he murmurs.

I shake my head in response, wishing for the lump in my throat to disappear. I have not shared my heartache with anyone—not even Léo. I doubt it will be well received by El. I tried to openly redefine my relationship with him after my aunt and grandmother upgraded the spell on his heirloom, but El has a knack for cutting me off every time I bring it up.

"I don't know that I can leave the island, El," I confess, hating the childishness in my tone. "Running away from the palace was a big step for me. I don't know that I am ready to leave Reunion altogether."

"It'd only be for a couple of days, Jules. I'm not asking you to move in with me… unless that's what you want."

He winks at me in that charming way he knows how.

Okay, let's try this one more time, I brace myself.

"El, I need to tell you something and I need you to listen," I blurt out, my heart racing dangerously loud in my chest. For once, he waits to hear the rest, though his jaw squares. "Féidhlim and me… we kissed… a lot." I wince, expecting El to jump up any second now from shock and horror, but he doesn't. "Well, we did more than just kissing, actually."

I look down, feeling the painful heat of shame burning my face. When El still doesn't react I frown, wondering if I misunderstood his intentions.

"I expected as much," he replies calmly. "Did you have sex with him?"

"Uhm…" I hum, taken aback by his shockingly serene demeanour and quiet tone.

"Are you still a virgin, is what I'm asking," he echoes.

"Yes," I rasp, my throat growing dry.

"Okay."

"Okay?"

"Yeah, okay," he repeats in that same detached tone of his.

"I don't understand," I murmur, my brain malfunctioning from the foggy veil of confusion. "Why did you ask me that?"

"I should've made my move long ago," he sighs, his eyes skimming the cloudless sky above us.

That still doesn't answer my question but I let it go.

"I don't know that it would've changed anything, El," I admit in a murmur, awkwardness tugging at the knot in my middle. "I… enjoyed Féidhlim's company," I confess, unable to look him in the eye.

He exhales heavily before wriggling to face me, making the hammock sway hazardously once again.

"El!"

"Sorry…" he apologises quickly. "So… Lithuania?"

I blink at him. At the ease with which he changes the topic of discussion at the snap of a finger.

"El." I roll my eyes, which earns me a chuckle from him.

"I'm starving," he announces unexpectedly, his most serious expression smearing his pale face. "Lunch?"

"Sure."

We carefully sit up, our bodies pressing against one another as the hammock dances in the air, its cords almost vibrating against the trees.

"What are you guys doing?" Léo's voice echoes beside us, full of revulsion and apprehension. "Are you two fucking?"

"Léo!" I cry, looking down at him, appalled. "No, of course not."

My brother shrugs, his honey skin shining under the sun. He runs a hand through his dark-brown hair and winces.

"K and I are going to a nude beach, wanna come with?" Léo offers casually, watching as K hops down the steps from the balcony to join us.

"No, thank you, little prince," El declines politely. "I'm having lunch with your beautiful sister. I'm taking her on a date."

Léo's brows skyrocket as he locks eyes with me. My cheeks flush a deep shade of pink.

"El... that's not what we agreed on," I jump in, frustration stiffening my muscles as I stare at him with disbelief. "We're just having lunch."

"I know, Julie, I know," he replies, his demeanour impossible to read. "I was only joking."

Only his tone didn't sound like he was.

Léo's stare remains on me, sad and pitiful, though I don't know whether he is feeling sorry for me or El. I eventually look away, embarrassed, hoping the scent of my discomfort doesn't linger in the air.

"Okay, so... K and I are gonna go alone then," Léo announces tentatively. "We'll see you guys later?"

I nod.

"You don't really want your big sister around anyway, do you?" I ask him next with a mischievous wink, changing the topic of conversation and forgetting about El's pushy behaviour for a moment.

My eyes dart to K, then back to Léo, whose face turns bright red.

Did he truly think I wouldn't notice the way he and K sneak away from our group every chance they get? The pair have been "secretly" dating ever since that day at the palace when K asked Léo to teach him archery. They couldn't have been more obvious about it. Plus, I know my brother well; he was, after all, my only friend until now.

Is it time I have a chat with K to make sure of his intentions toward Léo? I wonder. I am not too sure how these things work.

Knowing about their relationship is what stopped me from confiding in my brother about Féidhlim. Why would I stain his happiness with my sadness? Léo too was imprisoned by our parents. He deserves his shot at what a normal life looks like.

"Before I forget." Léo's fingers snap as he turns back around to face us. "Have you guys seen Amrah? *Tatie* Salomé and *Mamie* Min want to see her."

I frown, my head cocking.

"No, not since we left the hotel," I tell him.

He shrugs, leaving us to walk with K instead.

"How about we have dinner without them this evening?" El suggests, smirking at the pair as their forms shrink in the distance. "I'm sure they'd appreciate the privacy."

I bite my bottom lip.

"They would," I agree.

"I'll let them know after lunch not to wait for us this evening."

I nod, excited for my brother. Would it be his very first dinner date, I wonder.

"And, El, just so we're clear, it isn't a date," I feel the need to add.

He nods but doesn't say a word.

Chapter 13

Féidhlim

Mrs Burke was our head housekeeper at the royal palace for as long as I can remember. I have always known her as stark and practical, but her loyalty to my family made her indispensable once upon a time. She used to bring her daughter, Aoife, to the palace with her over the summer holidays, her marital partner too untrustworthy to mind a young one. My mother loved having fae my age on the premises. It was her way of ensuring I would grow up with plenty of healthy socialising, despite my homeschooling.

I can't recall my first encounter with Aoife. It was so long ago. But I remember how we used to race down the stony staircase leading to the forty-seven-acre gardens and dash along the path encircling the lake, her blond mane shining brighter than the sun.

"The last one to get to the mermaid statue (the one facing the palace) *is a rotten egg!"* we would cry.

Our laughter, innocent and jovial, would echo through the gardens, and the workers and assistants would watch us for a while, their heads bobbing in tandem at our livelihood. Aoife would play dirty, though, jostling me away when I got too close to her, sometimes even tripping me for fear I would win. But I didn't mind. She was my closest friend.

I dreaded the end of summer, knowing I wouldn't see Aoife for another year then. We would write and message each other throughout the colder months, but nothing beat our time at the palace together. Other members of the royal housekeeping family would bring their younglings over as well but I never bonded with them the way I did with Aoife. Everything was *fun* when Aoife was around, and I was happy.

Aoife is beautiful, tall, and strong like a warrior queen with bright blue eyes, soft fair skin, and plump rosy lips. But I didn't feel any kind of romantic attraction toward her back then, even when we shared our first experimental kiss. Being the same age, we discovered life together, our curiosity often getting the best of us both. Hence, she was my first for a *lot* of things.

We went our separate ways when we turned eighteen, however. After her leaving cert, Aoife went abroad to France to study culinary arts. She always had a passion for cooking, which I encouraged through and through since I always got to be her food taster for the summer. Everything this female touches turns into pure bliss and delight. She really does have a knack for cooking *and* baking.

She then built a cosy life for herself in Paris and even opened a restaurant there. I followed her success for a while, celebrating from a distance when she got her first Michelin star, and another, and another.

But life soon became more stern and rigid as my royal training kicked in, demanding greater focus and commitment from me if I were to take over for my father someday. And sure enough, after a while, I stopped answering Aoife's messages. At first, it was innocent, too tired to check my phone and engage in social interactions after a long stressful day shadowing my father in his affairs. But then, as time went on, I began ignoring Aoife altogether, and on purpose…

My father was never a fan of hers; she isn't royalty. He never thought she would be any good, or use, to me once crowned. He preferred—still does—to see me interact with people of my own rank and status. Aoife was alright as a distraction when we were kids but as I grew older, he started getting into my head. No matter how successful of a business person she is, we aren't from the same world. She grew up as a nobody when I did as the future king of Éire.

As a result, Aoife and I kept our distance from each other for several years, but I always had a thought for her every time I went down to the gardens to clear my head, or to the kitchen for a midday snack. When I saw her again, it was at my mother's funeral, three years ago.

While the kingdom took turns to mourn their late queen, gathering around her casket at the main hall of the palace, I retreated to my aisle, heartbroken and unable to keep my composure.

"Fé…" Aoife's shy voice echoed through the wallpapered corridor, striking my heart like never before.

I froze, tears rolling down my cheeks with relief.

Aoife.

The only person I could bring myself to talk to in that instant. My closest friend.

Her steps thumped quietly over the thick runner rug as she rushed after me, only stopping when the tips of her black heels met the back of my leather boots. Her arms wrapped around my back, her hands clasping over my long coat—one of the pieces of clothing belonging to my traditional gown.

"Breathe, Féidhlim," she murmured, her head resting against my shoulder blade.

So, I did.

I spun around to grip her tightly against me, my hands desperately clutching the one person I knew I could trust with my feelings in such a heartbreaking moment. I kissed her hair… her forehead… her cheeks… then her lips.

"Fé… I don't think this is a good idea," she whispered, pulling away.

"Why not?" I argued, taking a step closer, my fingers linking with hers.

Her skin was so soft and warm, her scent beguiling. I was under her spell.

"Because you're not thinking clearly," she pointed out. "You're grieving."

"I missed you… so feckin' much, Aoife," I murmured in her ear, my arms wrapping around her waist.

I should have listened to her, though, because she was right; I wasn't thinking clearly. I was looking for a distraction, a quick fix to put back together the pieces of my heart, an easy way to feel good.

I pressed my hips to hers, my dick swelling at the prospect of having her again after so long. One night. I just needed one night with her. One night of warmth and familiarity. Air seeped through her teeth, her cheeks flushing pink at my hardness rubbing against her pelvis over our clothing.

"You want it, too," I rasped, trailing my finger along the length of her arm.

"I'm not staying in Éire, Fé," she said.

"I know," I replied, my mouth finding her neck.

"I'm not looking to be in a relationship," she added, her eyes closing.

Me neither!

"I know," I told her. I bit her neck, the action reminding me of the cliché-scene non-magical beings like to reenact when pretending to be vampires. "I need you, Aoife."

One thing led to another, and she gave in to her primal needs, satisfying mine in the process.

Aoife subsequently decided to stay with me in Éire a while longer to help me get through my grieving. My father wasn't particularly happy about it, but he was too taken by my mother's passing to interfere. So Aoife and I were lovers for the short month that followed. We were happy and… in love.

Ignorance was bliss.

"I'm late," Aoife said dryly, her fingers anxiously running through her shoulder-length hair as she exited our en-suite.

"Late for what?" I frowned, swiftly getting out of bed to hug her.

"No, Féidhlim… I am late.*"*

Her eyes flickered to mine, holding my stare, and I flinched.

Aoife's fingers were wrapped around a white pregnancy test, two pink vertical lines visible on the small oval display.

"Oh," is all I could say.

I cringe reliving the scene because I know I should have said something else. Something warmer. Something comforting. But all I could think about was: "How is my father going to react?"

Dread began to course through my veins, fear closing my stomach into a tight knot.

My father's plans to expand our resources and power through a royal union were ruined. The minute the media found out about Aoife and our unborn baby, I would have to propose to her, sealing the fate of our nation for another generation. My father was going to kill me, or worse, strip me of my royal duties, denying me the throne forever.

"Féidhlim, you okay?" Aoife called, handing me a glass of water.

My eyes lowered to her flat stomach and, just like that, shame washed over me like a waterfall of mortification snapping me back to reality.

What had I become?

How was she the one caring for me when she was carrying our youngling?

How low did I stoop that I was prepared to put power and image before Aoife and the baby?

The answer snaked through my middle, suffocating and deadly; I had become my father.

So I got down on one knee in front of her and she burst into tears. She said yes to me that day, making me, Prince Féidhlim of Éire, the rightful successor to the throne, betrothed, with an unborn child at the age of twenty-seven.

The next morning when I woke up, Aoife was gone with our baby, her stuff missing from the bedroom and her mother fired from the palace. My father never spoke of it but I know it was his doing. My whole world shattered in the span of a nanosecond.

I travelled around the world for months in a desperate attempt to find Aoife and our youngling, but everywhere I went led to a dead end. She had left Paris; someone else was managing the restaurant in her stead. Aoife was truly gone, and our baby with her.

Knock.

Knock.

I hear the loud tap outside my room. I startle, dashing to open the door when I realise it isn't me the knocking was for but Juliette. I stop dead in my tracks, my muscles tensing as if playing a game of Red Light, Green Light—or *Un, Deux, Trois Soleil*, as they call it here.

"It's your turn, PJ!" K shouts behind her door before sprinting back down the stairs.

"Coming!" Juliette sings through the wooden frame.

The corners of my lips curl upward into a soft smile, my body relaxing at the sound of her melodic voice.

What would she think of me if she knew I had a son I never met?

If she knew I already have a successor to my throne?

But then my brows draw in because Juliette is caring and loving, more so than anyone I have ever met before. If I trust someone would understand, it has to be her.

My heart pounds against my ribs, bile rising in my oesophagus. I take a deep breath, wrapping shaky fingers around the brass knob to pull the door open. And there she is, standing in her white dress in the hall, barefoot, her curls falling over her nude shoulders like the princess that she is. She is breathtaking. My heart stutters when we lock eyes and she smiles at me shyly, her cheeks rosy, her gaze full of hope.

"Hi, Jules," I greet calmly, battling my every instinct to keep my composure impeccable.

I want to run to the beautiful female in front of me, hold her tight, and apologise for my absence and cold demeanour. But I don't.

"Oh, hi!" she cries, her brows shooting high, clearly taken aback.

I smile warmly, daring to take a step forward. My fingertips twitch, the pull to Juliette unbearable, but I refrain from touching her even when I pause only a couple of inches away from her. She looks up at me, her curls falling back to hover over her back, the sweet scent of coconut enveloping us. Juliette's bright brown eyes linger over my lips, making my heart ache because I too want to kiss her, but I can't. Not with El around.

"It's good to see you," I mutter, my gaze burning as I soak in her beauty, running over the soft features of her face over and over again, hoping to remember every single detail.

"Is it?" she asks, a hint of sadness softening her voice.

I swallow when her chest heaves, the motion making her generous breasts press against the seam of her décolleté. My cock bobs in my pants, the mouthwatering vision of Juliette in her red bikini flashing through my brain.

"Yes." I nod, my eyes finding hers.

Her lips part but no word comes out. My throat grows dry at the distress on her face, and I wish I was brave enough to tell her the truth and trust she wouldn't judge me for it.

"The boys and I are playing video games in Léo's room. Do you want to join us?" she offers, a shy smile lighting her face.

Yes, of course, Jules, you know I'm a gamer, too! is what I want to say.

"Another time maybe, but thanks," is what I tell her instead.

Her lips close in a thin line and her head bobs slowly, clearly disappointed with my answer. I curse myself for letting her down. *Again.*

"I'll see you later then," she murmurs.

She shrugs before turning around when my fingers wrap around her arm of their own accord.

"Wait!" I cry, surprised by my reaction. "There's something I need to tell you."

"What is it, Fé?"

Her eyes search mine, concern painting her face, her hand closing around my shaky fingers. I swallow, bracing myself, because I realise I do want to take a leap of faith and come clean. I no longer wish for secrets between us, and most of all, I need Juliette to know how I feel about her. I need her to know I don't like avoiding her, that I don't like ignoring her or being cold to her. All I want is to hear her laugh and hold her flush against me, kiss her and make her feel safe. I hate toying with her feelings. And I deeply miss her. My heart swells in my chest so I take a deep breath.

"Jules—"

But I pause when El comes up the stairs to join us in the hall, his grey eyes dark and threatening.

"Yes?" I hear Juliette's voice echo, unable to take my focus away from El.

When I tell Juliette about my past, it will be on my own terms, not his.

"Féidhlim?" Juliette calls me again.

I clear my throat, mechanically taking a step back from her.

"What did you want to tell me?" she presses, heartbreaking hope in her hazelnut eyes.

I glance around my room, racking my brain for something to say that will get El off my back and keep his mouth shut.

"Yeah, uhm, do you mind bringing this to the kitchen for me?" I chance, handing her an empty plate. She frowns, her jaw tightening, and I know I have pissed her off. "Since you're going downstairs—" I add, my tone softer.

"Bring your stupid plate to the kitchen yourself!" she snaps, abruptly turning around to stomp down the stairs. "I'm not your fucking maid, Féidhlim!"

My grip tightens around the plate, my knuckles turning white, urging me to shatter the feckin' dish against the wall out of frustration, but I don't.

Great. Now, the female I like thinks I am an even bigger dick. Well played, Féidhlim!

I swallow my anger back down, locking it away in the pit of my middle—the same cavity already filled to capacity—as I fight for composure.

Why on Earth would I ask Juliette to bring a feckin' dirty dish downstairs for me?

El clears his throat and spins back around to look down the stairs.

"Seven o'clock?" he asks Juliette, who temporarily stops in her tracks to nod.

I frown, puzzled, so El leans against the wooden railing, his arms crossing over his chest.

"She agreed to go on a date with me," he explains proudly, his voice a faint whisper.

I squint, furious, my eyes meeting his. An amused smirk twitches across his face, his perfect white teeth shining under the light, and… I lose it. I roar, slam my body against his, pin him down against the tiled floor, and land my right hook against his nose; weeks, months, *years* of frustration releasing at last.

Reunion Island Royal Palace

132 Enchanted

Reunion Island
Marché Forain

Samoussas

Emilie Ocean 133

Chapter 14
Juliette

I sit across the white-clothed table from El, smiling and nodding as he tells me all about his family back in Lithuania.

"And I know people are afraid of my grandfather, but Vilius isn't so bad once you get to know him, really." El shrugs, the muscles of his toned chest puffing slightly under his black shirt.

We meant to go out for dinner just the two of us last week to give Léo and K a chance to eat alone—my aunt and grandmother tend to do their own thing in the evening—but the universe had other plans. Hence my being here with El six days later.

As I look around, I can't help but realise that this dinner setting—although with a friend—is everything I have ever wanted for a first date: a secluded table under the white gazebo of the most romantic spot in town, fairy lights hanging down from the white marble columns and branches of the litchi trees, live violinists playing in the background, and delicious food with a handsome prince.

So I wonder whether El was the one organising this elaborate and formal meal layout, or if it was provided by the restaurant on a complimentary basis. Maybe every patron who reserves the secluded gazebo we are at gets to enjoy the romantic ambience the place has to offer. Though he said nothing about the love-filled setting, El told me he selected the private sitting area himself in case someone recognised us on the main, central floor, which I am grateful for. The last thing I want is someone alerting my parents of our presence here.

With that said, I can't seem to shake the feeling that something is missing. A selfish part of me wishes El hadn't brought me here; that I had waited for my first date to be somewhere this intimate with someone. But I shove the thought back down with a mouthful of deliciously steamed white rice.

"… and he never drinks from witches either. Anyone who says the opposite is a liar!" El goes on about Vilius before bringing his glass to his mouth.

I nod, feeling awful for being unable to give El the attention he deserves. Truth be told, I haven't been able to ground myself since Féidhlim attacked him a week ago. K had to jump in to get Féidhlim off him. El's nose was broken; a waterfall of dark blood splashed onto his top and pooled over the tiles under him. *Tatie* Salomé and *Mamie* Min had to use magic to patch him up for fear he would black out.

It was shocking to see Féidhlim in such a feral state; dilated pupils, ticking jaw, and flushed skin. He is usually so composed; never laughing too loud, never saying the wrong thing, never losing control over his person. What shook me the most, however, wasn't the rage emanating out of Féidhlim's pores, or the feral growl escaping his throat when he launched himself at El, but the unexpected burning sensation that settled between my legs at the sight of it all.

I could have stopped the fight or interfered in some way, but I didn't. I stood by the stairs, transfixed by lust at the sight of Féidhlim's dominance. He was strong, and impressive, and wild. He was utterly beautiful.

Shortly after K took matters into his own hands and separated the two princes, however, Féidhlim packed his bag and left. I woke up every morning hoping he would return but he never did. It has been six days.

"He's my grandfather but I was always told never to refer to him as such," El says. "I've always addressed him by his name, or title, or both."

"Why?" I ask, puzzled.

I would never be able to address my grandmother as anything but "*Mamie* Min." Anything else seems too cold and distant.

"Vilius likes strength, control, and power," he explains with a shrug. "Nothing screams 'weakness' and 'old age' like 'Grandpa Vilius.'"

I chuckle, agreeing with him.

I wonder what Féidhlim would call his grandparents if they were still alive.

"Have you ever introduced him to your girlfriends?" I casually make conversation, urging my mind to stop wandering off to where Féidhlim is and to remain here in the present moment with El instead.

El takes another sip of his drink, the red liquid—thick and bright—smears his lips like blood usually does, and his tongue swipes across to clean his skin. I try and refrain from wincing,

"No, I don't like mixing business with pleasure," he confesses, his eyes piercing as they lock on me.

I nod and smirk.

"Do you consider your family 'business?'" I quote and unquote the term.

"Don't you?"

I cock my head, thoughtful.

"I suppose I do sometimes... but never with Léo... or Amrah."

El watches me intently, his eyes squinting ever so slightly.

"Now that Féidhlim's gone, who do you think your parents will choose?" he wonders, changing the topic of conversation as his fork sinks into the blood sausage on his plate.

The question makes my heart stutter with discomfort. Although I hated the fact that Féidhlim was my parents' favourite, I grew to accept it because he was

Emilie Ocean 137

mine also. And I wanted to believe our love story was one of those that were just meant to be.

I was wrong.

And Féidhlim is gone.

"Well, I don't know," I reply dryly. "I haven't thought much about it."

A lie.

Of course, I have thought about it. How could I not? I have been agonising over it. I don't know what I will do when my parents choose another mate for me. K has been courting Léo, and I have grown to appreciate El's company the same way I do my brother's. Neither option seems appealing…

"If you had a say, who would you pick as your mate?" El asks, his eyes narrowing on me as he voices his thoughts out loud.

I smile softly, pushing the pain pulsating from my broken heart deep down where I can't feel it.

"The term 'mate' is overused, don't you think?" I reply, purposefully choosing not to answer his question.

"Go on," he prompts, sitting back in his chair, an eyebrow arched at me.

My cheeks flush at the sudden spotlight even though I am the one who asked for it.

"In ancient lore, someone's mate was their soulmate, their one true love, the person they couldn't live without," I recite. "It was never about political power."

"Things have changed, Julie," El sighs.

I nod, looking away. Tears suddenly prick the back of my eyes as a lump forms in my throat. Never have I ever felt more stupid.

Being stuck at the palace for over a decade allowed me to roam the library shelves to soak in the magic and enchantment provided by my beloved books. While I never dreamt of a knight in shining armour rescuing me from the château, I did hope many, many times to live a free life of pure bliss and happiness with my kindred spirit. I wanted what the stories in romance novels depicted. I ached for true love and happily-ever-afters despite knowing that in this day and age, soulmates almost never meet. But I kept dreaming because I was sure karma would have my back for the way my parents controlled my every move for so long.

Then, on my twenty-first birthday, they announced they would mate me with a prince of their choosing, and I lost faith. When I met Féidhlim, however, a glimpse of hope settled in my heart and I wanted to believe that the universe had sent him to me. That he was the one true love I was waiting for. But Féidhlim is gone—and my heart with him.

How innocent of me to have put my faith in him. If what El told me is true, Féidhlim never once saw our potential union as anything but a political deal. Where is the magic in that? Maybe our relationship wasn't as bewitching as I thought it was. Maybe it was all in my head.

I don't even know why I am sulking over Féidhlim's doings. I never wanted a union in the first place. Maybe this is the universe's way of giving me what I asked for; freedom. Though my clairvoyance has been at me from the moment El and I walked through the restaurant doors. I haven't been able to decipher what it is telling me yet, but I have the feeling Léo and I will be heading back to the palace soon.

With my heart in bits, I haven't been able to practise much magic lately. I hoped every day for Féidhlim's return but it isn't looking good. The tears in my eyes aren't new; no matter what I do to console myself, they keep coming back like an unwanted boomerang.

I am embarrassed to care so much about a male… I have tried to get up and forget about it all but I know my body needs time to process what I have lost; to feel the range of emotions attached to witnessing Féidhlim's departure. This is after all my first heartbreak. This is all so new to me.

Léo and I have always made fun of those silly females in books or television, who give everything they have to their partners only to have their bubbles burst ten minutes later. Now it seems I have become one of them at Féidhlim's expense.

I should hate him for it!

But hatred isn't an emotion available to me at this time…

"Julie?" El calls, leaning over the table to wrap his hand around mine. "Are you okay?"

I blink.

"Yes!" I say rather loudly. "Why do you ask?"

I force a giggle, well aware of my saddened facial expression.

"You seem… in pain," he confesses earnestly.

"Oh…"

What am I to say next?

I know I shouldn't talk about Féidhlim with El, but I don't want to lie either.

"The strap on my left shoe is digging into my skin," I tell him matter-of-factly, which is technically true.

I made the unfortunate decision to wear the new sandals I bought in town today when I went out shopping with my aunt. I hadn't done anything this frivolous with her since I was twelve.

"May I?" El offers and I nod. "Sit on the table so I can take a look."

"O-Okay."

I tentatively leave my seat to settle on the white tablecloth instead, biting my lip at the uneasiness spreading through me. El takes my left ankle to examine my shoe, where the buckle grazes the flesh.

"I'll loosen it up for you," he suggests and once again I nod. "Better?"

"Much!" I smile. "Thanks, El."

"Of course, Julie." He winks. "Anything to put a smile on your face."

"You're a great friend, Prince Elmas," I declare instantly without giving it too much thought.

His eyes snap away from mine, his upbeat expression dulling at the speed of light.

"I'm not, Julie…" he argues, seemingly disappointed.

"What do you mean?" I ask, defensive.

His head shakes, showing me a vulnerable side of his I didn't know existed. Suddenly, I am not so sure he is disappointed with me. He seems to be at war with himself.

"It's about Féidhlim…" he starts in a whisper.

My brows knit at the mention of the fae prince.

"What about… him?" I press, my pulse livelier than circus drums.

"I'm afraid you won't talk to me again if I tell you."

The sight of El's face, torn with sorrow, is a sharp nail to my breathing organs.

"El, you can tell me anything," I reassure him.

"I don't know, Julie… I can see how taken you've been by Féidhlim's sudden departure," he remarks, his fidgety eyes meeting mine. "I'm afraid to lose you if I tell you what I did."

"You won't lose me, El. I'll always be your friend."

"My *friend*…" he echoes under his breath, the start of a smile pulling one corner of his mouth before curling downward again. "Okay…"

With that, his head bobs forward as if falling from the weight of my words.

Chapter 15

Féidhlim

I flew back to Éire shortly after assaulting El, heartbroken and tortured, but most of all irrevocably disgusted with my lack of self-control over my anger.

He won.

No, I let him win.

So, now what?

I tsk at the pristine see-through glass of the window in the parlour as I gaze outside at the mermaid statue facing the lake. My thumb presses against my lips and I mechanically chew on the nail, something I rarely do but that always relaxes me.

"*Prionsa Féidhlim?*" (Prince Féidhlim?) I hear Máire, my father's adviser, call in Gaeilge.

I turn around to see the middle-aged female standing in the white double-door frame, her green blazer impeccable against her petite frame.

"*Ba mhaith le d'athair tú a fheiceáil sa seomra gnó,*" (Your father is asking for you in his business chamber) she announces.

My shoulders stiffen and I swallow, a heavy knot tightening my stomach. Apprehension runs through me like a deadly shiver.

"*Go raibh maith agat, a Mháire,*" (Thank you, Máire) I say nonetheless, my features perfectly composed.

She nods, her blond hair—tied into a tight bun—so fair it turns white in the bright light from the Galway crystal chandelier above our heads. She swiftly vanishes down the hall, the heels of her black pointy-toe pumps clacking against the cold tiled floor.

I take a deep breath, bracing myself to face my father.

"*Is amadán ceart é mo mhac!*" (My son is an imbecile!) my father, King Fionn of Éire, roars, the flat of his large hand smacking the front page of the newspaper on his mahogany desk.

The bright timber surface shakes under the impact, making me flinch.

"*Dúirt tú go raibh cúrsaí faoi smacht agat!*" (You said you had the situation under control!) he yells, specks of saliva escaping his mouth like white moths. "*Dúirt tú go raibh a cinneadh déanta aici!*" (You said she had made her decision!)

My brows draw in, my eyes snapping to *An Ghrian Ghaelach*, one of our most trusted sources for celebrity gossip. My heart sinks when I read the title in bold capital letters: *"RUGADH AR PHRIONSA ELMAS ÓN LIOTUÁIN LE BANPHRIONSA JULIETTE Ó OILEÁN REUNION."* (PRINCE ELMAS OF LITHUANIA CAUGHT WITH PRINCESS JULIETTE OF REUNION.) My gaze lowers, and there it is, a picture of Jules, her back facing the camera, sitting on a dining table, her ankle in El's hand. I glower at the vamp's smug face, remnants of the rage I felt at Salomé's house resurfacing.

"*Tá…*" (She has…) I manage with flared nostrils, fighting the tears prickling the back of my eyes. "*Tá sé thart.*" (It's over.)

"*An t-aon chúis leis sin ná gur chaith tusa do hata leis!*" (Only because you gave up!) my father snarls, glaring at me from behind his desk. "*Bhí tú ró-lag le dul i bhfeidhm uirthi agus mar sin rith tú abhaile mar chladhaire ceart!*" (You were too weak to make an impression, so you ran back home like the coward that you are!) His hands seize the paper, crumpling it until I can no longer discern Juliette from Elmas. "*Is mór an díomá mar mhac tú agus is tubaisteach mar phrionsa tú!*" (You are a disappointment of a son and a joke of a prince!) he spits his venom, his face now red with fury. "*Imigh leat as mo sheomra!*" (Get out of my chamber!)

I swallow the lump in my throat, only it doesn't go away. My heart is shattered into a million unrepairable shards, my head spinning as I try to make sense of it all.

Juliette and Elmas.

My Jules and El.

My tongue grows heavy in my mouth, bile rising to my oesophagus; my father is right. I should have stayed in Reunion and fought for her, but I couldn't. I was too afraid of her reaction if she found out about Aoife and… my son.

Oisín.

And just like that, my jaw ticks, my damp hands closing into fists. I hold my father's stare—something I have never done before—and he frowns, taken aback. Fury and hatred course through me, steaming out of my every pore like a volcano erupting.

"*Cá bhfuil siad?*" (Where are they?) I growl, hot tears making my vision blurry.

I have never cried in front of him before either, too insecure to take his mocking comments, but when the tears roll down my cheeks, they only fuel my wrath, making my bones buzz and my muscles clench.

"CÁ *BHFUIL SIAD!*" (WHERE ARE THEY!) I yell again, my hands smacking the desk the same way he did only a short moment ago.

My father takes a step back, his lips parting in horror at my rebellion, before his features darken and he regains his composure.

I freeze, not because I fear what he might do next, but because I hate what I am seeing. It is like looking in the mirror. I hate what I have become. No matter how hard I fight it, I am my father.

"*Cén fáth ar mhaith leat é sin a fháil amach?*" (Why do you want to know?) he asks, his hands clasping behind his back as he turns around to stare out the window.

"*Mar is mo mhuintir iad—*" (Because they're my family—)

"*Ná habair é sin arís!*" (Don't you dare say that again!) he retorts, his piercing blue eyes snapping back to me, his jaw squaring with indignation. "*Ní cheadóidh mé duit aon chlann a bheith agat ach clann ríoga. Ní shuífidh feirmeoir riamh i gcoróin. An gcloiseann tú mé?*" (The only family I will allow you to have will be of royal blood. No farmer will ever sit on the throne. Do you hear me?)

"*Ni raibh Maim ina banphrionsa go dtí gur phósaigh sí tusa—*" (Mother wasn't high princess until she married you—)

"*Comhartha ó chúirt Shasana a bhí i do mháthair, bronntanas a thug an comhaontas eadrainn chun críche. Ní raibh inti ach fichillín!*" (Your mother was a token from the English court, a gift finalising our alliance with them. She was nothing more than a pawn!) He cackles, his long blond hair swaying against the hunter-green jacket of his suit. "*Agus ní raibh maith ar bith léi lena chois sin…*" (And a useless one at that…)

The anger that only seconds ago raged through me calms down, sadness filling my fibres in its stead at the thought of my late mother. She was never happy here at the palace with my father.

My mother, Queen Felicity of Éire, was the king of England's niece. She was "ripe" for marital duties, my father said, when her uncle gave him her hand as a means to bring Éire and England together. Their high princess was already married and her two younger sisters had passed in a fire a couple of years prior. The closest relative to the English crown still available for a union was therefore my mother. She agreed to the proposal and mated with my father for her country's political power, making Éire one of England's strongest allies. Love was never in the equation.

She wanted to see the world but my father never enjoyed travelling. As it would have been improper for the high queen to roam the Earth without her mate, my mother stayed put, forgetting all about her lifelong dreams to keep up with the fake happiness the royal family had to portray at all times.

She wanted more younglings but, again, my father didn't. His logic was—is—that one perfect offspring would be better than a handful of disobedient heirs, who would only make the passing of the crown messier. She didn't agree with his views, of course, but there wasn't much she could have done about it. Once she had me, my father barely spent any time with her; she had fulfilled her marital duties.

My mother often told me I was her ray of sunshine in the darkness; the only reason why she would do it all over again. I never truly understood what she meant but the comment always made me feel special. It always gave me the morale boost I needed to live up to my father's ever-growing expectations. And now, after everything that happened, I can't help but wonder if she too is disappointed with my actions. With the way I handled things.

My father drags his office chair out, its legs rattling against the recently polished walnut herringbone flooring.

"*Imigh leat anois,*" (Leave) he orders.

"*Nílim ag imeacht go n-inseoidh tú dom cá bhfuil Aoife agus mo mhac—*" (I'm not leaving until you tell me where Aoife and my son—)

"*Ná bíodh focal eile asat,*" (Not another word) he cuts in, his voice a low rumble so stern and icy it slices through me like a honed *sgian-dubh*; a single-edged knife. "*Más mian leat mo mheas a ghnothú, téigh ar ais go hOileán Reunion agus tóg lámh Juliette. Mar a dúirt mé, ní ghlacfaidh mé ach le clann ríoga.*" (If you want to earn my respect, go back to Reunion Island and take Juliette's hand. As I said, the only family I'll recognise will be of royal blood.)

"*Sa chás sin, tá brón orm go mbeidh fanacht fada ort, a Dhaid,*" ("In that case, I'm afraid you will wait a long time) I argue, my nails digging through the skin of my hands as my fists tighten. "*Ní rachaidh mé sa tóir ar Bhanphrionsa Juliette riamh arís, agus ní bheidh garpháiste eile agat riamh. Caithfidh ár líne ghinealaigh brath ar Oisín as seo amach.*" (I will *never* pursue Princess Juliette again, and you will never have another grandchild. Our lineage will have to count on Oisín to survive from now on.)

The words leave my mouth before I have time to process them, and I silently curse myself for making such promises and shooting myself in the foot at the same time. Maybe I am being too hasty. I don't know that I can forget about Juliette but the look on my father's face is worth trying to.

I turn around to swiftly march out of the business chamber, my head high, my back straight. My heart races against my ribs as I expect my father to storm out after me, but he never does. So I stride to the gardens, keeping my composure intact as I meet housekeepers and assistants on my way. All nod at me in respect so I nod back, ensuring my steps are steady while my pace remains rapid.

I exhale heavily the second I reach the mermaid statue, knowing the palace is now too far behind me for anyone to witness my meltdown. My body collapses onto the fresh lawn beneath me, the sudden chill of the grass cooling me down. My fingers wrap around the green straws of the meadow, rich soil settling under my nails. And I scream a loud and raw roar until the vibrations in my throat make my vocal cords burn, and birds take off from their safe spots in the trees surrounding me. I take a deep breath in, my shoulders lighter though my heart is still fragmented. I bring my fingers to my eyelids next as my chest heaves and tears shed.

How did I manage to lose everything good in my life? They all slipped through my fingers like loose threads, one after the other, leaving me here with my father and his thirst for power. Always more power.

Buzz.

Buzz.

My phone vibrates in the pocket of my beige chino trousers, snapping me back to the present moment. I check the screen and I see red.

Elmas.

A part of me wants to march back to the lake and throw the device in the pond water so that I never have to see his name on the screen ever again. But I don't. I unlock my phone and click on the text message.

El: Sorry things ended the way they did. No hard feelings

My molars threaten to break at how hard I grit my teeth as I read his message. *Everything went down because of that piece of shit!*

El: 6 Banshee Rd, Bainbridge Island, Duwamish Land, WA 98110

Washington?

I met the Washington royal family a few years ago at a private event hosted by my father, but that was the only time I interacted with them.

I frown, reading the address again, wondering if the message was meant for someone else.

El: I hope you find them. Good luck

Chapter 16
Juliette

"Let me out!" I yelp in English, in case someone who doesn't speak Reunionese walks by.

My bruised fists hammer the thick double doors of my bedroom back at the royal palace, but they don't budge. I kick the wooden barrier and pull the handles, screaming from the top of my lungs, but the doors don't unlock, and no one comes to my rescue.

"*Jules... Aret, i serv a rien...*" (Jules... Stop, it's no use) Amrah tells me in our mother tongue.

Her voice is weak and shy, her brown eyes full of sorrow. She kneels in front of me in her usual bloodied gown, her hands reaching for mine despite the fact she can't touch me.

"*Cé out fot tou sa la !*" (This is all your fault!) I snap back, my glare causing her to take a step back.

My cousin is one of the few people with whom I am comfortable speaking Reunionese. My parents always made it clear my English had to be impeccable if I wanted my pool of suitors to be extensive. Thus, they have always only spoken English to me and forced my brother to do the same. My parents were wrong, though, language didn't make a difference because only three princes were interested in what I had to offer, and one of them is courting Léo!

"*La poukwé ou la parti rod mon band paren ? Ou té koné zot té sa ni pou nou. Ou té koné zot té sa ramen a nou la kaz...*" (Why would you get my parents involved? You knew they'd come for us! You knew they would bring us back home...) I bark as my voice breaks, hurt from the betrayal choking me.

I bring a hand to my throat, the pads of my fingers gently massaging the skin, hoping for my vocal cords to regain their strength. I glower at my cousin once again, the fact she is dead turning my anger into frenzied rage because now I cannot kill her myself.

"*Aret gard a mwin koma !*" (Stop looking at me like that!) Amrah snaps, hands over hips, eyebrows drawing in.

"*Aster ou lé 'offended' ?*" (Now you're 'offended'?) I roll my eyes to the back of my head, caring very little about mixing Reunionese and English. "*Ou la rodé. Ou la parti koz derier nout do ek nout band paren. Ou la traï a nou !*" (You brought this on yourself when you ran to my parents to throw us all under the bus!)

The memory of the king and queen trampling through the restaurant doors as El leaned over my ankle at the dining table, cutting our meal short to drag me to their carriage by the arm like I was a bold youngling, makes my skin crawl.

I didn't even get to hear what El had to say about Féidhlim.

When I think they have humiliated me enough, they strike again!

I was thrown against the seat of the pumpkin-shaped coach like a vulgar sack of rice, forced to watch as my father marched back to El to roar at him. The sight was actually quite hilarious when I look back. My father had to pathetically go on his tiptoes to almost be at eye-level with El. While the king's index finger waved at him, threatening, my mother was watching me, her jade-green eyes piercing and evil. I held her stare, the orange flame of my burning hatred turning blue.

"We locked you up for good reasons," she began in English as always. "Look at what you did the second you stepped out of the royal grounds. You degraded yourself and this family. You spread your legs wide for a… bloodsucker."

I flinched at the comment, not knowing whether to be insulted by her false depiction of my character or be appalled by her obvious prejudice against vampires.

A part of me wanted to clarify that nothing sexual or romantic happened between El and me; that he was simply helping me with the strap of my sandal, but I figured she wouldn't believe me so I remained quiet.

"I told your father it was a bad idea to have those creatures at the palace," she huffed, looking out the window toward El, a hand under her chin.

"I don't understand," I started. "I thought you wanted me to find a mate."

"Yes, ideally another witch."

"But none of them are witches," I managed, blinking at her. "You picked my suitors."

"The second best option was that male fae your father is so fond of," she said, dismissively waving her hand at me. "It doesn't matter who you unite with…"

She shrugged, staring out the window once again.

"You said we needed to solidify our political alliances to prevent the island from being swallowed by bigger nations," I recited, finding it hard to understand her behaviour.

She rolled her eyes, fed up with me already.

"Juliette," she sighed, "Reunion Island is one of the strongest nations in the Indian Ocean. We have enchanted the entire shark population around our coral reef to attack intruders. We have a very active volcano controlled by all the elemental witches the palace hires. We practically govern the weather and can hex our enemy in the blink of an eye," she listed casually. "Do you really think we need more power?"

"I'm confused," I admitted, wrinkles creasing the space between my eyes. "Why am I to be married, then?"

"Because you're too old to be single," she confessed, shame in her voice and disdain in her eyes. "You're twenty-four, for Gods' sakes. We need heirs. We need our lineage to keep growing. We need you to do your job as a royal female."

Something hard took shape in my esophagus at the way she described my "duties."

"I am not a cow," I grumbled, my eyes burning.

"What did you say?" she hissed, squinting at me. "How many times have I told you to articulate when you speak?"

I took a deep breath, though it did nothing to slow down my racing heartbeat.

"You're the one who locked me up at the château for, not ten but eleven years, Mother!" I dared remind her. "I was never going to find anyone to court there, was I?"

"Which is exactly where you're going back," she snapped, lifting her hands to build a magical, soundproof wall between us so she wouldn't have to continue listening to me.

Her childish use of magic was infuriating. I had more to say about her prejudiced views and behaviour and those of my father. From what I have gathered, they never once spent quality alone-time with El, who has been nothing but a good friend to me. If only they knew Léo was courting a werewolf!

I laughed silently, though I was also repulsed by the way they saw me. I was repulsed by their audacity. By the way they believed they had the right to tell me how I should be using my body. Mate or no mate, having younglings was never a thought I entertained. At twenty-four years of age, being a mother was—is—the last thing on my to-do list. Plus, it isn't like I had a reliable, motherly figure growing up. I wouldn't know how to raise a youngling if I had to.

My father entered the carriage, his gaze murderous. He said something to my mother, the tendon in his neck hardening as his eyes landed on me, but I couldn't hear it. Tears rolled down my cheeks when the winged horses took off, leaving El behind on the footpath. I watched him from the small oval window as his frame shrunk on the ground below us, feeling as hopeless as ever.

Now that I think about it, I should have rebelled. I should have used my magic to get away from my parents. To exit that ridiculous-looking carriage. But I stayed put, the unknown more frightening than the prison of a castle I grew up in.

When we landed on the beach, my parents' faces dropped at the sight of Léo and K cuddling on their sézi—a traditional rug made of vacoa—like two lovers under the stars.

"Léopold Rivière, what on Earth are you doing?" my mother shrieked, her eyes widening at the romantic setting. "Step away from the werewolf! Now!" She turned to my father. "Daniyal, go get him!"

My father obeyed, of course, swiftly stepping out of the carriage like his life depended on it. Léo argued with him *and even fought back, his hands clenched into fists, his feet bucking, and his magic—specks of dark purple lights—swirling around him to form a barrier, refusing to make his way to us. But my father bypassed his magical shield, caring very little for his own skin as it reddened and dried like sunburns when he abruptly grabbed my brother by the arm to force him into the carriage like he did with me.*

"Your sister's… suitor?" my mother bellowed to Léo in the carriage.

"Yes. And?" he barked back. "Juliette doesn't mind."

My parents stared at me, wide-eyed.

"You knew about this?" Mother asked me, bewildered.

"And you let it happen?" Father chimed in.

"I don't see what the problem is," I dared say. "K and I never courted."

Their eyes remained glued on me, sheer revulsion on both their faces.

"Is it because he is a male?" Léo barked at them, his purple magic creating rays of steam around him once again. "A werewolf? Or maybe it's because he's older than me?"

Our parents' silence continued as they processed what had just happened.

"Yes," the queen replied eventually, still in shock.

She locked eyes with the king, who spun around in his seat to order the driver to take off, neither one of them affected by Léo's display of poor magic control.

If it weren't for the royal guards following my parents closely, Léo would have put up a braver fight, but he knew it was pointless. What would he have done then? Flee Reunion Island with K? That would not have gone down well. It would have started a new feud; an international one.

"*Ma fé tou sa pou protèj a zot,*" (I had to protect you and Léo) Amrah tells me for the hundredth time, her head shaking.

"*Cé sek ou aret pa d'répété mé mi koné toujour pa cé kwé i ve dir, Amrah ! Mi pens plito kou lé jalou d'nou, a mwin ek Léo. Nou la gingy profit in peu pou in fwa. Cé akoz sa ?*" (You keep saying that but I still don't know what you mean, Amrah! I'm starting to believe you were just jealous that Léo and I got to enjoy life for once. Is that it?) I roar, getting back on my feet to stare out the window.

Guards look up at me from under the tree and I roll my eyes at them.

"*Poukwé ou la reni la kaz pou racont ladi lafé? Ou té fatigué domoun i té fé pa in cont ek ou ?*"(You were desperate for attention, so you came back here to cause drama, is that it?) I guess.

"*Bé non, té pa sa—*" (No, it wasn't like that—)

"*Danska di a mwin poukwé ou la traï a nou !*" (Then tell me why you betrayed us!) I turn around to face her, my nostrils flaring, my skin burning from the scorching midday heat, and my rage adding fuel to the fire. "*Mi aret pa réflechi é mi konpren pa poukwé ou la fé sa. Nou la atend onze zan pou sort isi, Amrah. Onze zan ! Poukwé ou la fé sa ?*" (Because I've replayed it in my head over and over again, and I can't understand why you would do this to us. We waited eleven years to get out of here, Amrah. *Eleven years!* How could you?)

"*Mavé peur pou out sécurité—*" (I was afraid for your safety—)

"*Nimport kwé !*" (Bullshit!)

"*Lé vré…*" (It's true…) she whimpers, her black curls swaying from side to side as her head bobs profusely.

"*In, ou koné kwé, alé bat karé, Amrah !*" (You know what? Just go away, Amrah!) I scream, grabbing my left shoe from the floor to throw it at her.

It doesn't hurt her, of course. It simply flies through her to bounce off the wall behind her.

"*Alé ant in ot moun,*" (Don't you have someone else to haunt?) I roll my eyes, arms crossing over my chest.

Her eyes fill with tears, her bottom lip pouting.

"*Mi ve pa ant in ot moun…*" (I don't want to haunt anyone else…)

I stare at her, my gaze softening against my will because I know just how strong Amrah's ghostly abilities are. She could have gone anywhere she liked over the past eleven years but she chose to remain *here*. With me. We went through long periods of time without making supernatural connections but I could always feel her presence lurking in the shadows. And it was reassuring to know I had someone on the other side looking out for me.

"Amrah," I say quietly, any trace of my fury vanished. "*Cé kwé la arivé ?*" (What happened?)

She rubs her reddened nose with the back of her hand.

"*Bé, kan zot la kit le lotel, mwin mi la rent la kaz.*" (Well, when you guys left the resort I came back here.)

"*Cé pa sa mi ve dir.*" (That's not what I mean.) I shake my head. "*Cé kwé la spasé le jour ou la… mor ?*" (What happened the day you… died?)

She doesn't say anything, only looks out the window, her arms crossing over her nightgown, her palms stroking her upper arms as if she were cold.

"*Ou la di ou té ve protej a mwin ek Léo,*" (You said you wanted to protect Léo and me) I go on, joining her with caution. "*Protej a nou de kwé ?*" (Protect us from what?)

"*Pa de kwé… mé de kisa,*" (Not what… but who) she corrects, her dark eyes locking on me, intense yet mellow.

A shiver travels up my spine, goosebumps erupting over the skin of my forearms.

"*Ou la été assassiné ?*" (You were murdered?) I gasp eventually in a weak voice, my own eyes growing glassy.

A sad smile curls upward from the corners of Amrah's pale lips and my hands grow rigid, my tongue drying in my mouth.

The question has burnt my lips for years but I always held my tongue, afraid of the answer. I suspected the cause of her death wasn't natural; how could it be? But I could never bring myself to ask her about it, and she never opened up either.

The entire family agreed it was an illness that couldn't be cured, so I went for the cowardly option and listened to them. I never asked questions although I knew something was off. My clairvoyance was screaming at me but I ignored it. I pretended everything was fine because I could still see Amrah. I could still talk to her, hear her, and feel her presence within the walls of the palace. It was easier that way.

"*É ou koné cé ki out lassassin ?*" (And you know who did it?) I dare to prompt, a mixture of curiosity and fear making my heart thump loudly in my ears.

Amrah nods but her lips don't part. I watch her for a moment until something icy envelops me; my clairvoyance. It is telling me something. So I close my eyes, focusing on the message, a turmoil of feelings and sensations tornadoing in my insides. Splashes of red, yellow, and black flash behind my eyelids before my lungs squeeze tight and I am knocked out of oxygen. I collapse to the floor, fat tears cruising down my face as I battle for air, though my respiratory system won't listen.

And then I see it. All of it. I see shapes, hear voices, smell herbs. I feel a sharp pain constricting my oesophagus before it all goes black.

When the vision passes, I sense Amrah kneeling in front of me and, for a split second, I *feel* her touch. Her hands are cold but gentle as they wrap around mine, her thumbs stroking my knuckles. My heart warms, love spreading through my veins and making my muscles relax. I gasp, able to breathe again at last, my chest heaving as I greedily inhale oxygen to fill my burning lungs.

"*Ma vu a el…*" (I saw her…) I manage, my eyes flying open, red and dilated. "*Mavé jamé vu dan le pasé…*" (I never saw the past before…) I go on, inhaling deeply. My gaze darts to my cousin, flickering and urgent. I grab her by the shoulders, my grip rougher than I mean it to be. "*Amrah, té ali sa… té el mem ke la fé sa… ma vu a el…*" (Amrah, it was her… she did it… I saw her…)

I bring my hands to my mouth, muffling my distress as I burst into tears on the floor. Years of doubt and fear confirmed under my eyes while confined between the four walls of my bedroom. And for the first time since my parents dragged me back to the palace, I am thankful to be here.

Chapter 17

Féidhlim

The grip of my fingers tightens around the leather handle of my gear bag as I exit the ferry terminal to find a taxi. The passengers hustle me out of the way when I stand in the middle of the bridge leading outside, my heart racing so fast in my ribcage that I find it hard to breathe.

"Get out of the way, you idiot!" a male rudely yaps at me, his protruding belly hanging down from his stomach under his grey-and-black basketball top.

Of course, he doesn't know who I am. No one does here.

"Sorry," I mutter, my head bowing, my baseball cap casting a shadow over my tired features as I start moving.

I didn't want to fly to Duwamish Land on our private jet or use a magical carriage. I wanted to do this my way. So I bought a plane ticket, flew over the Atlantic Ocean in economy class, and then got the ferry to Bainbridge Island.

Modes of Transport in Duwamish Land are hybrid-built. They display the perfect blend of magic and modern technology. Most of the Duwamish population are werewolves but the non-magical community still represents a solid quarter of the country. I personally like the way the state of Washington was able to marry magical and non-magical advances in a seamless fashion. Mechanical engines are mostly fueled by spells and enchantments while requiring a mechanic to assemble the parts to make the final product usable.

The cool breeze from the waters of Puget Sound runs through my blond curls, my hair longer now than it was in Reunion. I should have gone for a haircut—and a shave—before showing up here unannounced. *Thank Gods, I, at least, brought fresh sets of clothes with me on the journey.*

Moisture settles over the palms of my hands and for a brief moment, I think of running back to Éire, where the known feels safe. But I shake my head at the absurd thought because I know I can't keep running forever. I need to face the music. *I need to see my son.*

I pick up the pace and nod at one of the taxi drivers impatiently waiting for work. The middle-aged male swiftly unlocks his car, allowing me to slide into the backseat, my gear bag resting on the black leather spot beside me.

Everything seems more… practical here. Less enchanting. Or maybe it is just the anxiety keeping me company that casts a dim glow over my surroundings.

"Where to?" the driver asks, his bulbous eyes staring at me through the rear-view mirror.

"6 Banshee Road," I recite Aoife's address, the one that has been echoing in my mind on repeat ever since El's text.

He turns on the engine and the car takes off. I stare out the window as we pass by the town centre, and I take a mental note of the hotels and restaurants I see on the way. I should have made a reservation for the night somewhere before coming here, too, but in all the excitement and nervousness I didn't think of it.

What am I gonna say when Aoife asks me where I am staying?

If I tell her I didn't book a hotel room, she will feel obliged to offer me a room for the night, which might lead to an awkward situation for us both. A knot tightens in my middle as I start overthinking my meeting with her. Showing up on her doorstep unannounced and out of the blue no longer seems like a good idea after all.

"Actually, please stop the car. I'll get off here!" I blurt out, fear suddenly getting the best of me.

Because what if Aoife doesn't want to see me?

What if she ran away of her own accord?

What if my father did her and Oisín a favour?

My breathing grows shallow, my fingers suddenly numbing at the thought I might be looking for someone who doesn't want to be found.

"Here?" The driver frowns at me through the rear-view mirror.

"Yes. Thank you."

I pay and swiftly exit the car, my heart drumming against my ribs and apprehension coursing through me. The second my feet touch the footpath, I inhale deeply, forcing my lungs to open up to welcome the air I am sending there. My muscles relax and my heartbeat slows down, allowing me to take in the town. There is a café to the right of me and a three-star hotel on my left.

Okay, that will do.

Hotel room first, coffee after.

I enter the building and head straight to reception, where an elderly male welcomes me, a kind smile smearing the toffee features of his aged face. He enters my details—and *fake* name—into his computer before handing me the electronic card to my room. A grin creeps its way across my lips as I stare at the rectangular piece of plastic, flashbacks of Juliette losing her *Fleur Fané* key card on the beach and then dropping mine on the road moments later zooming through my mind. My heart aches in my chest at her memory but I ignore it, shoving the pain down and hurrying up to my room instead.

I will never pursue her again…

What am I saying?

Even if I did want to fight for her, Jules is with El now, and I doubt she would leave him for me after witnessing my childish outburst at her aunt's. I cringe as I relive the scene, cursing myself for the hundredth time for losing composure.

I sigh, my features suddenly darkening. Regardless of what Juliette thinks of me, my father will never have the satisfaction of having a grandchild of noble birth. It is a promise.

And yet, as I access my room, leave my stuff on the bed, and enter the shower, the delicious image of Jules' naked body lying in bed beside me at *Fleur Fané* Resort camps in my brain. I exhale heavily with frustration, irritated at the blood rushing to my cock despite my desire to forget about her. My erection bobs under the hot water steaming the bathroom, pre-cum pearling its crown.

Fine, if this is the only way to get Jules out of my system, so be it!

My soapy fingers wrap around my shaft and I pump hard, jerking off to the memory of Jules' shapes; that tiny little red triangle bikini top that barely covers her tits, those thin string bottoms of the same colour that get lost between her ass cheeks, and… that naked dance she did for me that night at the hotel to make it up to me after the truck drove over my key card. I groan, ejaculating jets of cum against the shower wall, my frustration taming at last. But something tells me, those memories of Princess Juliette of Reunion Island will continue to haunt me for a long while, if not forever.

Two hours later, refreshed and buzzing with caffeine, I swiftly exit the coffee shop across the road from the hotel and jump into a taxi. This time, I stay put until we arrive at my destination, my nervous system on high alert but my head and heart approving.

"We're here," the driver announces after a mere ten-minute journey, pulling up in front of a Craftsman-style two-storey house. "That'll be ten dollars."

I hover my phone over the machine to tap and reluctantly exit the taxi, my legs heavy. I stare at the property from the footpath, taking in the low-pitched gable roof, the white tapered columns supporting the covered front porch, and the window panes on the ground floor through which I see shapes move inside the house.

My heart pinches; they are home.

I brace myself, gathering all the strength I have left in me to walk up the steps leading to the porch. The tip of my index finger rings the doorbell, and my blood grows cold inside my veins as the chimes echo through the house. I breathe out an exaggerated exhale, debating whether I should leg it and never turn back, or stay.

"*Maim!*" (Mama!) I hear a toddler cry behind the door.

My legs freeze under me, no longer responding to my brain, so I stay, my ears pricking up.

"*Fan, a Oisín,*" (Wait, Oisín) Aoife's familiar voice replies, which makes the corners of my lips curl into a soft smile.

Keys cling as they turn in the cylinder and soon the door swings open, Aoife's always-so-radiant grin smearing her friendly face. She stops dead in her tracks when she sees me, her smile dropping, her eyes growing glassy. Her rosy lips part but no sound comes out.

I have imagined this moment a thousand times in my head, and yet every rendition pales in comparison to the actual thing.

My heart swells against my ribs as I take Aoife in. She hasn't changed one bit. Her blond hair, although longer, still shines brighter than the sun; her cheekbones sit as high as ever, just like when we were kids. She stands tall and strong in front of me like the warrior queen I always knew she was, only now she wears cardigans and loose jeans. It suits her.

"*Maim?*" (Mama?) a youngling with blond curly hair, bright blue eyes, and similar high cheekbones mumbles, his little hands wrapping around Aoife's calves.

He looks up at me and my heart sinks, shame and guilt tightening a knot in my throat.

"*Dia dhuit,*" (Hello) he greets me in all innocence and bliss.

I smile internally; Aoife raised him bilingual, of course. She wouldn't have allowed Oisín not to be in touch with his own culture despite the fact that they live in Washington.

I bring the pads of my thumb and index finger to my eyes, drying the tears before they fall, my heart heavy. I take a deep breath to compose myself when Aoife places a hand over my shoulder. She pats me there gently, like she used to, until I am able to meet her gaze again. She smiles softly, kneeling behind the toddler.

"*A Fheidhlím, seo Oisín,*" (Féidhlim, meet Oisín) she tells me calmly, running her fingers through his curly mane. "*A Oisín, seo Féidhlim, cara dó Mhaim.*" (Oisín, this is Féidhlim, Mama's friend.)

The little fae cracks me the sweetest of smiles, baby teeth showing and all. I smile back, the most genuine expression of happiness I have allowed myself to show since I left Reunion Island. I kneel in front of him to shake his tiny hand.

"*Haigh, a Oisín, tá sé an-deas bualadh leat faoi dheireadh.*" (Hi, Oisín, it's so nice to finally meet you.)

Chapter 18
Juliette

After finding out the identity of Amrah's murderer, I began to hammer the double doors of my bedroom like never before, only stopping when the bones inside my fists ached and the flesh was bruised and raw. But no one came. So I sent Amrah to go get my parents. She wasn't keen on it at first but obeyed nonetheless when I threatened to break the connection between us forever.

"You're my beacon here," she articulated in English, hurt by my words. "If you break our connection, it won't be as easy for me to make myself seen by other witches."

"I know," the two syllables came out of me a tad too cold.

Amrah froze, squinting at me for a moment, the expression on my face showing her just how serious I was. So she passed through the walls and wandered across the palace to fetch my parents. They eventually came to get me after a while, frantic about the vision I had.

"Mais, on ne voit pas le passé !" (But we don't see the past!) my mother cried in French—her mother tongue—which was a first, her head shaking so profusely it could have flown off her body altogether.

The use of her first language was enough to tell me she was distressed by my news.

"Tu *ne vois pas le passé, mais moi si,*" *(*You *don't, but I do)* I replied, defiant, cockiness adding venom to my words.

Her face fell, obvious jealousy turning her blood green in her veins. And I grinned because, in all honesty, my mother has made my life a misery ever since she realised my clairvoyance was stronger than hers. She made it very clear throughout the years that it was unfair for me to display such power when I didn't need it in the first place.

Soon after they freed Léo, I initiated a family meeting, summoning my parents, my father's siblings, and his mother to the palace. The king and queen weren't eager to allow his family to roam through the walls of the château again, but they conceded in the end as I wouldn't give them more information about Amrah's murder until I had everyone in one room.

"I'm not stupid, I know you know something was off about her death," I spat to my parents as we waited for the rest of the family to join us, impatience making my brow tick. "Why would you banish your own family from the château so suddenly? You know it was one of them!" I blurted out, my stare coldly holding my father's.

He remained silent, his dark eyes snapping away to look outside the floor-to-ceiling window in the parlour. And that reaction in itself was enough to confirm my statement.

After all these years, it seemed the magical veil surrounding the royal grounds had been implemented to keep both Léo and me safe; imprisoning us for eleven years just so happened to be one of the ramifications our parents were ready to live with. Unlike us, they were free to travel in and out of the estate.

Moments later, my grandmother, aunt, and two uncles—who I have no doubt were summoned to the palace in the rudest manner possible—marched through the doors leading to the parlour to meet the five of us.

So here I am, watching as my parents enter a staring contest with my father's side of the family, everyone on edge already, despite only being here five short minutes. The herbaceous scent of white sage spreads through the room, although it does nothing to diffuse the tension.

Léo sighs, his eyes rolling to the wedding-cake ceiling as he surreptitiously turns around to whisper in my ear, "You better be right about this, or you'll start another war…"

I nod, swallowing with difficulty because he is right. Pressure weighs tons on my shoulders, and I suddenly wish I never had that bloody vision in the first place.

I glance at my mother on the divan closest to the door, her stare venomous as she glares at my grandmother.

Maybe she was right…

Maybe I don't deserve to have a clairvoyance this powerful if I am not able to bear the consequences. I now wish I could crawl under a rock and disappear until the storm has passed. Maybe my mother should have been the one with the ability to see the past. But the second that thought formulates in my mind, the right corner of my lips lifts into a smirk.

What am I even saying?

That would be detrimental to our family and nation. One of the perks of seeing the future is that my parents can sense when a political deal is shady even when it doesn't seem like it. Sometimes my mother would have visions of the future or summon the dead to help her make difficult decisions regarding the welfare of the island.

I don't know why I ever thought my joining together with a prince was necessary to the development of my country. I soaked in my parents' words without thinking twice despite knowing better.

My eyes rest on each individual in the room and my heart fills with happiness and warmth. I love my father's family. I want them all to be happy, and this reunion will only help bury the hatchet.

My uncles stand at the far end of the parlour, opposite each other, their backs facing the sideboard along the back wall, where pastries and fresh fruit await. I can't help but notice the resemblance between them and my father. My uncles, *Tonton* Ayan and *Tonton* Zain, are slightly taller and fitter-looking but they have the same curly salt-and-pepper hair, the same dark-brown almond eyes, and the same dark olive skin tone. Anyone would know the three of them are brothers just by looking at them.

My aunt, on the other hand, is more Amazon-like than the rest of us. While her brothers' features are soft and their build smaller than average—just like their mother's—my aunt's physique is tall and sturdy. I cock, watching as she settles on the divan opposite my mother's. I wonder if *Tatie* Salomé shares my grandfather's physiognomy. I never met him—he died when I was only a toddler—and the black-and-white photos of him I found in old albums don't do him justice.

My grandmother, *Mamie* Min, approaches me carefully, the cold saggy skin of her hands wrapping around mine.

"Cé kwé *nou fé ici* ?" (What are we doing here?) she asks me in a whisper in Reunionese.

My eyes lower to her, sad and heavy, as I inhale the familiar scent of rose soap floating around her. My lips part to respond when I hear my uncle, *Tonton* Zain, clear his throat loudly.

"Daniyal, what gives you the right to summon us here against our will?" he exclaims in English, which only means one thing: business. "Some of us had to fly over to be here."

His tone is stark as he glares at my father across the room.

Tonton Zain left Reunion Island shortly after Amrah's tragic death to marry the high queen of Madagascar, fortifying our island's position within the Mascarenhas Archipelago. He has two younglings whom I have never met before, and whom I am sure have never set foot on our soil, which is a real pity considering our islands are practically neighbours.

Though Zain and my father don't see eye to eye ever since my paternal family was banished from the palace, the two brothers regularly attend business calls and meetings, both of them being kings; hence the use of English in today's setting.

Tonton Ayan is the only Hakimi sibling who never got married or had younglings, despite being in his late 50s. Even though the Duke of Reunion South (the island was divided into four domains when my grandfather passed, each one of his children receiving an equal piece of the country), Ayan is never home. He likes to delegate his duties to his counsellors and personal assistants while he tours the world.

"We have far more important matters to tend to than to be at your disposal whenever madness strikes you," *Tonton* Zain goes on, squinting at my father.

"Do you really think I want to be here? Take this up with your niece. She's the one who insisted we have a family reunion," my father replies, his disapproving stare snapping to me next.

English it is, I guess.

My limbs grow rigid, my heart stuttering at the sudden spotlight as all eyes are now on me. The incessant low chatter from my family's babbling grows non-existent. *Tonton* Zain's gaze softens.

"Juliette, what's this about?" he asks, his demeanour calmer now that he is talking to me.

My breathing grows shallow, however, and my eyes anxiously roam the room for Léo's in search of a pillar to centre myself, but it isn't enough. I need to somehow convey confidence and assert my authority for these people to take what I am about to say seriously. So I mimic… *Féidhlim*. I puff my chest out, straighten my spine, and gain composure. And when I clear my throat, positioning myself in the centre of the parlour, the room patiently waits for me to say my piece.

"I had a vision…" I announce in English, opting for the political language of choice so as not to upset Tonton Zain, although I suspect he wouldn't have minded the use of Reunionese either if it was from me. I stand tall as I take another step forward, my clammy hands clasped behind my back so nobody notices them. "… of the past," I add. "I had a vision of the past."

Eyebrows draw in, lips roll, and heads cock, which is the exact reaction I was expecting them to have.

"*Juliette, mon gaté, nout fami i vwa pa le pasé,*" (Juliette, sweetheart, our family doesn't see the past) *Tatie* Salomé reminds me, unafraid to go against her brothers and switch to Reunionese. Her head shakes in confusion before she turns to my mother next. "*É la vot, Blanche?*" (And yours, Blanche?)

"No, we don't," she replies with disdain, switching back to English while crossing a leg over the other on the divan.

This back and forth of languages is giving me a migraine; as if choosing one over the other will assert dominance in the room.

"Our family's magic gets stronger every year we stay on this island," *Mamie* Min explains in English, which surprises me as I thought she would want to support my aunt over my parents.

I guess, the lines are blurred now since *Tonton* Zain was the first one to speak in English.

Mamie Min squeezes my right hand tight in hers and says, "Our ancestors probably thought it was time to grant one of us more powers." Her lips stretch into a proud grin and I smile sadly. "What did you see?" she asks me, curiosity brightening her tired eyes.

I shift my stance, moving my weight from one hip to the other. It is time to face the music.

"Amrah?" I call, scanning the room carefully. "Please, join us."

No answer.

"*Amrah lé la ?*" (Amrah's here?) *Tatie* Salomé asks in a hurry, jumping up from the divan.

I nod.

"*Li la reni in pe apré nou la ariv out kaz,*" (She came back shortly after we came to visit you) I tell her in Reunionese despite the glower my mother casts at me for using one of my mother tongues.

My aunt's eyes grow glassy and I can't help but notice the way her brothers look down to their leather sandals, clearly affected by her distress. *Who would have thought that after eleven years of ghosting each other, they would still care about their sister; the poor woman who lost her only youngling?*

"Amrah, please," I beg, hands now over hips.

I should have known she would be a no-show. I sigh heavily, my head bowing to the pristine marble-tiled flooring with disappointment.

"*Lé pa out fot, mon gaté,*" (It isn't you, sweetheart) my aunt tells me, her voice weak. "*Cé mwin li ve pa vwar.*" (It's me she doesn't want to see.)

She looks up at the ceiling, past the chandelier, as if she can tell her late daughter is listening from the room just above the parlour.

"*Amrah, mi lé désolé pou sek la ariv a ou...*" (Amrah, I am so sorry for what happened...) her words get lost in her throat, her sobbing taking over.

Tatie Salomé sits back down on the divan, her face burying in the palms of her hands, her back and shoulders heaving as she allows her vulnerability to show in front of her family. *Tonton* Ayan silently joins her, wrapping an arm around her deflated frame.

We all stare at one another, waiting for my aunt to regain her composure. Léo squints, the features of his face expressing that familiar concern that silently screams *"What is going on?"* at me. I shrug because I am honestly not sure.

"Sal, cé kwé ou la fé ?" (Sal, what did you do?) *Tonton* Ayan asks his big sister, gently patting her on the back.

Her head shakes profusely, her curls bouncing sideways around her shoulders.

"Mi té koné pa... sinon sa mi loré jamé fé sa..." (I didn't know... I would never have...) she starts before pausing to sniffle.

My uncle locks eyes with his brothers but remains quiet. *Tatie* Salomé looks up again.

"Amrah, ma chérie, mi loré jamé fé sa si mavé su—" (Amrah, darling, if I had known, I would never have—) she starts.

"Ou loré jamé fé kwé ?" (You would never have done what?) Amrah's murderous voice resonates through the room, although her body is nowhere to be seen, the temperature in the parlour suddenly dropping. *"Killed me?"* she roars, choosing to say it in English for dramatic effect.

"Kwé la fé !" (Wait. What!) my father and his brothers exclaim in unison, on the same wavelength for once, their heads turning to their big sister so violently their necks threaten to snap in half.

Amrah believes the Duchess of Reunion West—her own mother—to be a murderer and therefore a threat to the nation, is what I gather.

A gust of icy wind tornadoes through the four walls of the parlour, peeling off the antique *vieux* wallpaper in its way.

"*Amrah, aret ek sa!*" (Amrah, stop it!) I yelp, panic seizing my insides.

My cousin has never displayed such anger before, and I don't know how far she is ready to go.

"*Amrah, ou enten a mwin ou la?*" (Amrah, do you hear me?) I add.

But food and drinks get tossed onto the floor from the sideboard behind my uncles, while the wooden legs of the divans scrape the tiles as they are pushed away toward the double-doors. We all gather in the centre of the room, my mother, aunt, and uncle swiftly jumping off their moving seats to join us.

"Amrah!" Léo barks, hooking an arm around me.

Plates and glasses fly off from the sideboard, the wind only getting stronger by the second. Léo and I duck, barely avoiding being smacked in the face by a pink saucer.

"*Amrah, tan manman!*" (What the fuck, Amrah!) he hisses, glaring at the chaos around us.

Lights flicker and the floor-to-ceiling window opens wide, hitting my father in the head in the process. He growls, his body heavily landing on the floor in a hefty *boom*. We all stare at him in shock, eyes wide.

A part of me is evilly satisfied at seeing the king in such a precarious position, but I don't take the time to explore it, preferring to focus on my cousin instead.

The natural disaster happening inside the parlour immediately ceases.

"*Eskuz a mwin !*" (I'm so sorry!) Amrah cries, her ghostly figure materialising in front of our frightened eyes to hover over my father.

She hands him a hand out of force of habit, forgetting he cannot touch her. His brows draw in at her vain attempt before he effortlessly pulls himself up onto his knees.

"*Ma pa fé expré,*" (I didn't mean to) Amrah squeals, referring to his minor accident.

"I'm fine, Amrah," he manages, his worried eyes scanning his niece's face. "Are *you*?"

Her lower lip quivers and she turns around, tears rolling down her pale cheeks. She takes a couple of slow steps toward her mother and pauses once before her, her ghostly hands fisting the bloodied material of her nightgown.

"Why did you kill me?" Amrah sobs, clearly unable to pick a language and stick to it under the pull of her emotions. Her chest heaves as she battles for oxygen before she yelps, "*A koz ?*" (Why?)

"*Oté, mon gaté…*" (Oh, my dear…) my aunt breaks, her tortured gaze resting over her daughter at last. "*Mi té koné pa…*" (I didn't know…)

"*Mentèr!*" (Liar!) my cousin screams, her body floating in mid-air again. "*Juliette la vu a ou dan son vizion!*" (Juliette saw you in her vision!)

My aunt bursts into tears once more, her eyes now bloodshot, her nose and cheeks flushed. Her head shakes and her mouth parts but she isn't able to form coherent words, only gibberish sounds.

"*Sal, lé vré?*" (Sal, is this true?) my father breathes, his face contorted in an expression of shock and horror.

"*Oui!*" (Yes!) Amrah answers for her. "*Juliette i pe confirmé!*" (Juliette will confirm it!)

They all turn to me and my heart swells in its cavity at the weight of my cousin's statement. They wait for me to talk, impatient and alert like ravenous dogs expecting their dinner. I swallow with difficulty, mechanically taking a step back. Debris crunches under my flip-flops, urging me to stop in my tracks and face the room.

"*Non, Amrah, lé pa out momon ke mi la vu,*" (No, Amrah, your mum isn't who I saw) I confess, trepidation causing my pulse to hammer my eardrums.

I lock eyes with my aunt, whose head cocks sideways, clearly as shocked as her daughter to hear me come to her defence.

And why is that? I wonder. She should know she isn't the one from my vision.

"*Mi kompren pa,*" (I don't understand) I admit, massaging my temples with the pads of my fingers. "*Dan mon vizion, mi lété out kaz dan out kuizin,*" (In my vision, I was at your villa in the kitchen) I tell *Tatie* Salomé, who nods profusely, fat tears rolling down her cheeks. "*Mé mi la pa vu a ou.*" (But I didn't see you.)

No, I saw my grandmother, her back arched over the white-tiled kitchen counter, a straw tote bag—or *tante*, as we, locals, call it—beside her by the sink. She reached into the bag, her gloved aged fingers carefully wrapping around some kind of greenery, which she placed in the granite mortar in front of her. She then grabbed the pestle and, with a force I had never seen her use before, battered the leafy greens until they turned into a thick, dark paste. And this is what I tell the room.

"*Mi navé okun idé ke navé la pwazon dan out smoothie, Amrah,*" (I had no idea your smoothie was poisoned, Amrah) *Tatie* Salomé cries, falling to her knees in front of her daughter. "*Ma jamé souèt out maler. Mi aim a ou!*" (I never once wished you harm. I love you!)

My cousin turns to me, her brown eyes full of distress, and I know she is wondering if I am telling the truth.

"*Ou koné ke mi inventré pa tou sa kan mem,*" (You know I wouldn't make all of this up) I tell her softly, a weak smile smearing my face.

Léo grimaces, his head shaking disapprovingly, a tad like our father.

"*Ou sa Mamie Min la pasé ?*" (Where's *Mamie* Min?) he asks gravely.

We all look around the parlour, but *Mamie* Min is nowhere to be seen.

Chapter 19

Féidhlim

I stayed in Bainbridge Island a little longer than I had originally intended to, but it was worth it. I needed to spend time with Oisín and get to know him. I am aware one month is nothing in someone's lifetime but it is a start. Aoife agreed to let me watch him while she went to work; she opened another restaurant in the town centre last year. So I got to stay at hers with Oisín, minding him like I should have done this past year-and-a-half.

I expressed my regret to Aoife more than once, making sure she knew I had never forgotten about her and the baby. That I left Éire shortly after she was gone to try and find her to no avail.

"*Chuir d'athair iallach orm—orainn—bogadh go tír eile gach mí ar feadh bliana iomláine…*" (Your father forced me—us—to move country every month for an entire year…) she confesses in Gaeilge as we sit under her front porch, sipping wine. "*Bhí eagla an domhain air go n-aimseofá sinn.*" (He was terrified you'd find us.)

I pinch the skin between my eyebrows with my thumb and index finger, forcing my lungs to fill with air.

Any mention of my father makes my blood pressure soar and my heart rate skyrocket.

"*Cén fáth ar éist tú leis?*" (Why did you listen to him?) I ask Aoife, my gaze meeting hers at last.

"*Mar, a Fhéidhlim, beidh tusa i do rí lá éigin, agus níor theastaigh uaim a bheith i do bhealach.*" (Because, Féidhlim, someday you will be king, and I didn't want to be in your way.)

My mouth drops, gobsmacked by the genuineness of her tone and expression.

"*A bheith i mo bhealach?*" (Be in my way?) I repeat, brows now drawing in. "*Céard atá i gceist agat?*" (What do you mean?)

Aoife adjusts her position on the bench, turning sideways to face me.

"*An lá a rinne mé tástáil le haghaidh toirchis thiar in Éirinn, bhí a fhios agam nach raibh saol ríoga i ndán dom. Níor theastaigh uaim a bheith i mo bhanphrionsa ná i mo bhanríon. Theastaigh uaim a bheith saor chun mo chuid gnó féin a stiúradh agus gan a bheith freagrach d'aon duine eile. Is breá liom a bheith i mo chócaire agus mo bhialann féin a bheith agam, Fé,*" (The day I took that pregnancy test back in Éire, I knew royal life wasn't for me. I didn't want to become a princess or a queen. I wanted to be free to continue running my own business and report to no one. I love being a chef and having my own restaurant, Fé) she explains, her eyes glittering with joy as her lips stretch upward into an innocent grin. "*Mar *sin d'imigh mé liom mar níor theastaigh uaim go leanfá mé i gcoinne thoil d'athar. Teastaíonn uait a bheith i do rí. Teastaíonn ó Éirinn tusa a bheith i do rí."* (So I left because I didn't want you to follow me and go against your father. You want to be king. Éire needs you to be king.)

I force a smile, a lump growing in my throat.

"Ach céard faoi Oisín? Is mise a athair." (But what about Oisín? I'm his father.)

"Bhí orm tús áite a thabhairt dó." (I had to put him first.) Her head shakes. *"Ní fhéadfainn ligean dó fás aníos mar 'gharpháiste tabhartha' rí na hÉireann. mar a thug d'athair air…"* (I couldn't have him grow up as the 'bastard grandchild of the king of Éire' as your father put it…)

My mouth parts, my eyes widening.

"Dúirt sé é sin leat?" (He said that to you?)

She nods slowly, hurt twisting her features into a grimace.

"Is cuma liom cad a cheapann sé fúm, mar is eol duit, ach ní fhéadfainn ligean d'Oisín fás aníos in atmaisféar diúltach den sórt seo. Ní fhéadfainn ligean dó éisteacht leis na rudaí uafásacha a bhí le rá ag a sheanathair dó ná ní fhéadfainn a fhéin-mhuinín a nimhniú," (I don't care what he thinks of me, you know that, but I couldn't have Oisín grow up around this kind of negativity. I couldn't have him listen to all the horrible things his grandfather had to say to poison his self-esteem) she manages.

Tears roll down her cheeks so she swiftly dries them with the back of her hand. I look into the distance, sighing heavily.

"*Míle buíochas as é a chosaint,*" (Thank you for protecting him) I tell her in a whisper.

It took a lot of convincing but Aoife eventually agreed to come back to Éire with me on holiday. After our conversation under her porch, I knew my father was going to be a problem, so I made sure to keep Oisín away from him. And yes, it is selfish of me to bring them here, but there is so much I want to show my son; everything Éire has to offer, the palace, the gardens, Aoife's family home, the beach…

The beach…

The dolphins…

My heart constricts, a pinching ache cutting my breathing short.

Juliette.

How am I not over her yet? I have everything I could ever wish for—or almost—and yet my mind keeps reverting to Juliette every chance it gets, and against my will at that! She was a good distraction while I had lost everything, but I am back in Éire and have Aoife and Oisín now. And Juliette has El.

I am a male of my word; when I told my father I would never go after Jules again, I meant it because the look on his face was priceless. But something doesn't sit right with me.

"*Féach, a Dhaid!*" (Dada, look!) Oisín exclaims as a red admiral butterfly settles on his forearm. He giggles, excited, and the bug's wings flap before taking off again. "*M'anam!*" (Wow!)

I smile softly, my son's glee contagious. My arms rest over my bent knees, Aoife and I keeping an eye on him as he plays in the gardens with his toys; yellow trucks, red cars, and fae action figures. We watch him attentively from the cool lawn, the green grass tickling my ankles when the breeze dances through the short leaves.

"*A Oisín, an eitleoidh tú do Dhaid?*" (Oisín, will you fly for Dada?) Aoife encourages out of the blue, her fingers running through her blond hair.

I turn to face her, surprised.

"*Tá sé ábalta eitilt cheana fein?*" (He can fly already?) I cry, eyebrows arching.

"*Tá. Nach bhfuil sé ar fheabhas!*" (Yes, isn't he great!) she giggles, nodding proudly. "*Féach air.*" (Watch him.)

Her head bobs, her chin proudly pointing toward our son. Oisín stands up, his hands tightening into small fists, his eyes squinting. Soon, sparkling dust-like light—golden and silver, just like my own—envelops his tiny frame before his runners leave the ground. I jump up to my feet, the widest of grins twisting across my face with pride and excitement.

Amazing!

"*Maith thú, Baba,*" (Well done, Baba) Aoife rejoices, getting up. Her arms straighten, inviting. "*Tar anseo.*" (Come 'ere.)

And so he does!

Oisín uses his arms and hands to propel himself through the air as if he were swimming in water and lodges himself in his mother's embrace.

"*Tá tú chomh tapa!*" (You're so fast!) she compliments, depositing a big smooch on his shiny blond hair.

"*Tá sé sin iontach, a Oisín!*" (That's amazing, Oisín!) I agree, the palm of my hand petting him on the head.

He giggles, delighted with himself. Aoife puts him down and he happily returns to his toys, where an action figure awaits by a yellow truck.

"*Tá an-obair déanta agat leis,*" (You've done such a great job with him) I tell Aoife in a murmur, our eyes locking. "*Go raibh míle maith agat. Ní fhéadfainn cúiteamh a dhéanamh leat riamh.*" (Thank you so much. I could never repay you.)

Sadness fills my chest at the years I have missed. I wasn't there to support her throughout the pregnancy; I wasn't there to help during labour; I wasn't there to mind Oisín at night; and I wasn't there for my son's "firsts", including flying. I want to be there with them for everything else. I *need* to be by their sides.

"*Nílim ag iarraidh cúiteamh a fháil, Fé. Tá áthas orm go bhfuil tú páirteach ina shaol anois..*" (I'm not looking for repayments, Fé. I'm just glad you're in his life now.) She smiles kindly.

"*Agus i do shaolsa,*" (And yours) I add swiftly, holding her stare.

"*Gabh mo leithscéal?*" (Sorry?) She frowns, puzzled.

"*Bheadh sé ciallmhar dá mbeadh an bheirt againn ar ais le chéile arís, nach mbeadh?*" (It would make sense if we got back together, wouldn't it?) I start hesitantly. Her eyebrows draw in closer. "*Sin an chéad chéim loighciúil eile le bheith inár gclann ceart le chéile.*" (That's the logical next step to be a real family.)

"Féidhlim…"

"*Ba mhaith liom a bheith páirteach ina shaol, a Aoife,*" (I want to be in his life, Aoife) I cut in, anxiety making my eyes flicker, my gaze now unsteady.

"*Is féidir leat a bheith ina shaol.*" (You can be.) She nods slowly, her gaze holding mine.

"*Ach chuige sin, caithfidh tusa agus mise—*" (But for that, you and I—)

"*Fé, nílim ag iarraidh páirtí a bheith agam anois … agus fiú dá mbeinn, ní tharlódh sé toisc go bhfuil se 'lóighciúil',*" (Fé, I'm not looking for a partner right now… and even if I were, it wouldn't be because it's 'logical') she mutters, her face screwing up and my heart stuttering in my chest.

"*Céard atá i gceist agat?*" (What do you mean?) I wonder, completely oblivious.

"*Táim ag súil fós mo mhuirnín dílis a aimsiú lá éigin,*" (I still have hope I'll find my one true love someday) she confesses, a shy smile smearing her face.

"*I ndáiríre? Tusa?*" (Really? You?) I can't help but exclaim.

I had no idea Aoife was a romantic. She always seems so carefree and independent. I never thought she would be the type of person to believe in true love.

"*Sea, tá a fhios agat, catamas ar nós 'grá ar an gcéad amharc' agus mar sin.*" (Yeah, you know, all that love at first sight bullshit.) She shrugs casually, a light giggle escaping her lips. "*Sin atá uaim.*" (That's what I want.)

I nod, reflecting on her words. I think I want that too actually. But I also want to be in Oisín's life.

"*Ar aon nós, cé hí Juliette?*" (Besides, who's Juliette?) Aoife asks next, a cheeky smirk stretching across her face. "*Chuala mé tusa agus d'athair ag caint fúithí ina sheomra gnó an lá cheana.*" (I heard you and your father talk about her in his business chamber the other day.)

My eyes widen at the mention of the name. My mouth parts but I remain silent, unsure what to tell Aoife because, frankly, I don't know who Jules is to me at this stage.

She is this beautiful princess from that paradise island; the female I tried to seduce but failed miserably; the one I can't stop thinking about but cannot have.

When I got back to Éire with Aoife and Oisín, my father called me into his office for another one of his impromptu confidence-smashing meetings. He was beside himself that I brought back "guests" from my trip to Washington without his approval, which prompted me to yell back that Oisín and his mother were family. Again, King Fionn reminded me that the only family he will accept will be of noble blood before urging me to return to Reunion Island to win Princess Juliette back. I exhaled heavily and retorted Jules and I would never cross paths again. I then marched out of his office without waiting for an answer and slammed the door behind me.

Oisín is yet to meet his paternal grandfather, which I hope never happens.

"*Pé scéal é, is cuma faoi sin.*" (Anyway, it doesn't matter.) Aoife casually chases the air with the flat of her hand, clearly uninterested in my love life. "*Is féidir linn clann* ceart *a bheith againn fiú nach bhfuilimid le chéile, Fé. Beidh tú in ann teacht ar cuairt aon am—*" (We can still be a *real* family even if we aren't together, Fé. You can come visit whenever—)

"*Teacht ar cuairt?*" (Visit?) I repeat, shocked by her proposition. "*Á, a Aoife, tá níos mó ná sin ag teastáil uaim. Teastaíonn uaim Oisín a fheiceáil gach uile lá..*" (No, Aoife, I need more than that. I want to see Oisín *every day.*)

She stares at me like she would a circus animal before sighing heavily, her gaze softening. Her head shakes, her arms crossing over her beige cardigan.

"*Ní thuigim conas a n-oibreodh sé sin…. mura mbogann tú go hOileán Bainbridge?*" (I can't see how that'd work… unless you move to Bainbridge Island?) she suggests, her lips closing into a thin line.

"*Nó b'fhéidir go bhféadfaidh sibh teacht abhaile? Ba chóir d'Oisín a bheith gar dá dhúchas Éireannach,*" (Or maybe ye can come home? Oisín needs to be close to his Éireann roots) I offer, apprehension making my heart race against my ribs. "*Ach seans nach mbeadh sé sin oiriúnach toisc go mbeidh m'athair ann.*" (But that mightn't be ideal with my father around.)

"*Ní bheadh, ní bheinn compórdach leis sin.*" (No, I wouldn't feel comfortable with that.) She shakes her head, adamant. "*Ní theastaíonn uaim go mbeadh Oisín gar leis.*" (I don't want Oisín near him.)

My head bows in disappointment; I know she is right. I would never want my son to grow up like I did—with a demanding king whose expectations are unachievable—and the weight of the world on his frail little shoulders. I cannot risk having my father disrespect him and shatter his confidence as he did mine.

"*Tá an ceart agat. Tá brón orm tagairt a dhéanamh dó fiú,*" (You're right, I'm sorry for even mentioning it) I tell Aoife as I force a sad smile.

She pats me on the arm before urgently gesturing to the stone staircase leading to the palace behind us with her chin. I turn around, following her gaze when I see a couple of cars from *An Garda Síochána*, our police force—white vehicles with yellow-and-blue livery that silently hover over the ground thanks to fae dust—parking in front of the main entrance of the palace. The loud siren from a yellow-and-green ambulance sings through the gates next, joining the *Gardaí* in a hurry, before a group of paramedics rushes inside.

"*Fan anseo le hOisín!*" (Stay here with Oisín!) I order in a panic, already leaving Aoife's side to go investigate.

Chapter 20
Juliette

I close my eyes and inhale deeply, my fingers fisting the black satin of my royal gown, the soft material crumpling under my touch. The back of my head rests against the cushioned padding of the pumpkin-like coach, my curls draping over my shoulders. I exhale, my eyes fluttering open again. I look out the window to enjoy the exhilarating sensation that buzzes through my body at the white clouds and clear blue sky surrounding us.

I love flying!

It reminds me of Féidhlim. He showed me what he could do with his magic—though fae don't call it that; they refer to their magic as *fae dust*—on the beach in Saint-Gilles. I remember the decadent golden and silver tones in the lights emanating out of his almost-naked body as his strong arms wrapped under my knees and around my back so that he could lift me into the air. We momentarily hovered over the water, our gazes locked on one another.

"Can we go higher?" I asked, unable to take my eyes off him.

He nodded and a second later we were a solid 50 metres above the sea. The pearls of water on our skins glowed under the sun, the gentle breeze of the late afternoon caressing our faces and swooshing through our curls. With the orange hues of the setting sun behind him, Féidhlim looked more handsome than ever. He was god-like. I never wanted that moment to end.

I clung onto him, my hands moulding around his muscles, and lifted my head for our lips to join. His grip around me tightened as his tongue slipped inside my mouth.

"Ready?" he asked in a murmur.

I frowned, wondering what he meant. We then began moving through the air at such a fast pace my eyes widened.

"Where are we going?" I gasped.

"Over there," Féidhlim said, pointing at the above-water coral large enough to accommodate both of us.

He carefully placed me down on the rocky ground, its surface covered with green moss. The feel of the algae tissue usually repulsed me, but that day I was happy to see it. It provided us with ample cushioning to lie down on the piece of coral, away from the shore.

Féidhlim's lips took mine. His sturdy build was hovering over my body as his hands framed my face and his knees spread my legs. His pelvis pressed against mine and I moaned, the delightful touch of his covered erection awaking the nerves in my clitoris.

He slid the red triangular piece of clothing away from my right breast and popped the nipple in his mouth to suck it between his teeth. I hissed with pleasure, my hips rocking under him for more friction, my own juices adding moisture to my pussy. Though my bikini bottoms and his swim shorts were made of thin, stretchy materials, the layers were still too thick between us for my liking. I wanted more. So much more.

"Can we..." I managed, my fingers hooking around the seam of his swimwear—the only garment he had on. "Can we... do more?" Féidhlim left my nipple alone for his eyes to meet mine. "I want more, Fé," I begged. "I'm ready for more."

He held my gaze for a silent moment, his expression unreadable.

"Your first time needs to be special," he replied dreamily, stroking my cheek with his thumb. "It can't be on a rock in the middle of the ocean."

"Why not?" I breathed, kissing his neck. "Nobody can see us here." Another peck. "I'm free." And another. "And I want you."

He seeped air through his teeth, his mouth claiming mine with such strength my head lowered back to the mossy ground.

"I don't need to be inside you to make you come," he rasped, his hands gripping my bikini bottoms. "Can I?"

"Yes."

I wriggled a little to allow him to take them off. His breathing grew shallow as his eyes rested on my bare cunt; I opened my legs wider, voluntarily exposing myself to him. He pressed a kiss to my pussy and I smiled, eager for the rest. But Féidhlim pulled away from my sex to plank over me instead, his right hand stroking his length.

"I thought you said not today," I murmured against the pull of lust.

He gave me a crooked smile in response as he continued to look down at me, his fisted fingers roaming up and down his cock.

"I know," he said, lowering his pelvis to mine.

His mushroom head collected the moisture at my entrance before sliding through my lips—never entering me—his shaft stirring his crown upward toward my clit. I gasped when his dick added friction against the sensitive nub, his hips thrusting slowly as if we were doing missionary.

"Oh…" I moaned under him, surprised to be feeling so much pleasure when no penetration was involved.

"How's that?" he asked through hooded eyes filled with want.

"Yes." I nodded profusely, overwhelmed with the elation his body provided mine with, before realising I hadn't answered his question. "I mean, it's… yes!"

Féidhlim let out a quiet chuckle, his lips so delicious-looking when they rolled like that. So I kissed him again and he dived into the touch, his fingers entangling in my curls as he leaned closer. My legs wrapped around the muscular cheeks of his ass to close the gap between us. He exhaled heavily when my heels gave him more momentum to thrust through my lips—now swollen and hot with a constant pool of my own juices lubricating his shaft—to rub my clit.

My breathing soon turned laboured and I could feel the raw heat gathering in my pussy; the one that told me I was about to come.

"You're close?" Féidhlim guessed but I couldn't talk.

My eyes squeezed shut and my legs clamped around his hips as the familiar sensation of relief spread through me, only this time it was much more intense than when I use my finger in bed at night. I am pretty sure I moaned, my chest heaving to catch my breath as I played with my nipples to add abrasion to my orgasm.

When my eyes opened again, Féidhlim was stroking himself. Hard. I had never seen a male touch himself like that before—masturbation being such an intimate practice—and Féidhlim looked beautiful. Every muscle in his arm pulsed as he kneeled before me, his gaze greedily exploring my naked body. The motion of his wrist suddenly grew brisk and he grunted, warm jets of cum splashing against my thigh.

Féidhlim kissed me tenderly and helped me up, keeping me cradled in his arms like I was something fragile he needed to protect.

"Let's go for a swim, Jules," he said, eyeing his ejaculate on my skin while holding my bikini bottoms in his left hand.

We carefully neared the edge of the coral, sat there with our feet in the late afternoon seawater, and waited.

"Is everything okay?" I asked, noticing the worry lines making his features frown.

Anxiety kicked in then because I was sure he regretted touching me the way he did. Maybe it wasn't as enjoyable for him as it was for me. Maybe I hadn't expressed my gratitude enough. Maybe—

"Are there sharks here?" Féidhlim queried, the nervousness in his eyes reminding me of a child. "I mean, we're so far away from the shore…"

I stared at him for a moment, surprised to see this vulnerable side of his for the first time. His defences were usually up, forbidding him from showing too much weakness, but that day he let me in.

"They're everywhere," I confessed with an apologetic frown, "but as long as you stay with me you'll be safe. They don't attack the natives."

"Are you sure about that?"

"Yes, a thousand percent, Féidhlim," I told him, entwining our fingers. "Maybe we should make this a little bit more exciting, though."

I removed my bikini top and urged him to take off his shorts, which he had pulled back up to cover his cock again. I jumped into the water, splashing him in the process.

I hide a smile, excited and very much looking forward to reaching our destination, even though I know I shouldn't be. I should be focusing on more pressing matters, but here I am up in the air in an enchanted carriage, giddy at the prospect of seeing Féidhlim.

My family and I searched the entire island for *Mamie* Min to no avail. She vanished off the surface of Reunion.

Where could she have gone?

And why would she leave so suddenly?

All we wanted to do was talk to her. Understand why she did what she did. Amrah has so many questions still… Surely, *Mamie* Min didn't think my parents would arrest her without hearing her side of the story. Surely, what she did to Amrah was an accident. Surely…

My family didn't want to get the authorities involved because *Tatie* Salomé isn't going to press charges anyway. Amrah agreed, declaring she was more than happy to wait for our grandmother's passing—which would be anytime now, considering her grand age—to confront her on the other side directly. She waited eleven years to find her true murderer's name—so what is another three? Another five?

When I began relaxing and enjoying life at last—because our parents lifted the magical veil around the palace, allowing Léo and me to come and go as we please going forward—we were struck by another crisis, so to speak. King Fionn of Éire—Féidhlim's father—had died of a sudden heart attack. Royal leaders and their families were thus promptly invited to the Emerald Isle to attend the funeral, which is where we are heading now.

My aunts, uncles, and cousins from Reunion Island and France are on their way there, too.

Although I should be devastated for Féidhlim right now, a genuine fat grin keeps creeping its way onto my lips, making me look like a sadistic witch, revelling in the misery of others. I press the pad of my thumb against my mouth, prompting it to compose itself right this second before my parents and Léo notice it.

My heart stutters at the thought of seeing Féidhlim again after months of being apart. I washed and wet-plopped my hair to give my curls the definition they needed to impress; I plucked my eyebrows and waxed; I even applied a light layer of make-up and sprayed this brand new vanilla-and-coconut perfume I bought for the occasion. But despite being satisfied with my looks, sweat settles on my palms, and I wonder if I am trying too hard. I frown nervously.

"K and El said they'll meet us at the gate," Léo announces, locking the screen of his phone beside me.

I turn to him, a soft smile relaxing the lines of my face. I nod, regaining my calm at the mention of our group reuniting.

"Are you still in touch with them?" my father asks, his arms crossing over his chest, disapproving.

"Yes, why?" Léo deadpans.

My parents lock eyes, and the king clears his throat, uneasy. I watch my brother roll his eyes to the egg-white ceiling of the coach, unimpressed with their attitude. Now that they have shown their true colours, Léo and I can't help but despise them even more. Our values simply don't align.

Soon, the sky turns grey, the once-light-and-bright clouds forming heavy patches around us before the rain pours down, thick droplets snaking down the windows.

The pilot tries her best to voice something through the transmitter attached to the wall above my parents' seats, but her words get cut off. I guess what she is trying to say is *we have arrived.*

Éire
Royal Palace

Emilie Ocean 209

Éire
Mermaid Statue

210 Enchanted

Chapter 21

Féidhlim

I am not alone.

I have Aoife and Oisín.

Then why do I feel this unsolicited emptiness in the depths of my pit? Like a punch in the gut that never ceases.

I keep staring at the unlocked screen of my phone, hoping I would receive a text from *her*. From Jules.

Guilt has been hard to swim away from in all the darkness that fell upon the palace this past week. My father had a heart attack seven days ago and was brought to the nearest private hospital in the same half an hour that followed. He was in a coma for four days without any sign of awakening. I should have gone to see him, but I didn't. I couldn't bring myself to visit him and have my actions analysed by the journalists stationed outside the building—one could have easily broken into the premises and snapped unwanted shots of me and my father.

I have never shone away from the media—I grew up with cameras pointed at me all my life—but I could not bring myself to let the nation see me in that state. Smiling instead of crying. Thankful instead of mourning. I feel guilty because I know I should not be experiencing relief and glee when my father is gone.

I had Máire, his assistant, stay with him at the hospital while he was unconscious. I couldn't bear having to pretend I cared when I didn't. Plus, Máire was genuinely taken by his health condition from the moment he collapsed in his business chamber. It was she who got in touch with the Gardaí and the ambulance. She wanted me to stay with him on his way to the hospital but I declined, pressing a hand over my lips, pretending to be in shock when in reality I was trying to hide a grin.

Suddenly, I could see a flicker of hope in the obscure nightmare that living under the same roof as King Fionn had been. So, instead of wishing for my father's recovery, I prayed for his death. That is when the guilt began gnawing at my bones. My mother raised me better than to wish ill on others, but I couldn't reverse the way my mind was swirling with happiness.

If my father died, Oisín would never have to grow up the way I did. He would never meet his horrible grandfather, the man who openly despised his grandmother and mentally and physically abused his father. Oisín and Aoife would finally be able to come home for good. I would get to be in my son's life and witness his upcoming firsts.

I could… mend my relationship with Juliette. Or is the promise I made to my father still valid in the afterlife?

I check my phone again, wary, and glance out the window in the parlour. Royals from all over the world have been sporadically arriving at the palace for King Fionn's funeral, but there is still no sign of the Rivières.

Still no text from Jules.

Have her parents taken away her methods of communication or has she moved on already, forgetting me as a friend and a lover?

Four days after my father was brought into the hospital, our family doctor, who had gone there as soon as he got the call from Máire, told us his verdict: King Fionn was still unconscious and his state was unstable. Dr Fahy also let us know that we would be "lucky" if my father survived the night. Máire broke into an uncontrollable sob while I had to walk away so nobody would notice the relief on my face.

Freedom was calling. It was just around the corner and I could not wait to lay hands on it.

No more degrading sermons from my father.

No more impossible tasks to complete.

No more hiding my true colours.

No more shame about my family.

I would never have to live in fear again, because there would be no more physical punishments for crossing my father.

One summer, as I would rather spend my free time with Aoife in the royal gardens to play instead of training with some of the males in our army, my father whacked me so hard across the face with his decorative dragon-wood walking stick that I toppled over and crashed to the ground head first. I passed out instantly.

When I woke up again I was in my bed with royal healers around me, chanting their magic away to help me recover faster. I was only ten, but I knew then never to disobey my father again.

Aoife told me later that summer that my mother had rushed to me in the gardens and placed herself between my father and me. She too got a whack that day for going against the king.

I never viewed my father the same after that. Growing up I often wondered how many times my mother had to endure his authoritarian tantrums, and sometimes I would go as far as wondering if her sudden death truly was an accident. Did she truly fall down the stairs after tripping on the hem of her dress? Surely, being raised as a duchess, she knew better than to walk on her own royal gown.

My father did many, many horrible things to me, but the memory of his dragon-wood cane smacking me so hard across the cheek everything went black is the one that stuck.

After living on eggshells all my life, how could I not be anything but relieved and excited at the prospect of enjoying being *me*, worry-free?

"King Féidhlim?" Máire calls from the door.

I startle, not used to the title yet.

Máire's new intern—the aide the English court sent us as a means to express their regrets for my father's passing—quietly stands behind her. Since she doesn't speak a word of Gaeilge and Máire is to train her, English it is.

"What is it, Máire?" I reply, composing myself.

"We received words that a couple more flying carriages would be here in less than an hour."

I spin on my heels to face her. Máire's eyes are bloodshot from all the crying, darkened bags hang under her eyes from her lack of sleep, and loose strands of hair float around her pale face. Of all our employees, Máire is the most taken by my father's passing.

She has—had—been his assistant since I was five years old. She spent more time with him than any of us ever did. She knew all his secrets and made excuses for his behaviour the entire time she worked for him. Máire isn't the warmest of females, but I could never understand why she would put herself through my father's tyranny without ever complaining about it. Surely he treated her as badly as he did our other staff.

"Flying carriage from where?" I ask, hope blooming in my chest as I take another glance at my phone.

Still no messages from Juliette.

"Madagascar and…" she looks at the notepad in her right hand, "Reunion Island, Your Majesty."

Yes!

Surely King Daniyal and Queen Blanche are bringing Juliette and Léo with them.

"Very well," I say with poise. "Please let the welcoming committee know about our next guests so they don't get lost when they arrive."

"Already done, Sire." Her head bows deeply. "Also, Prince Elmas from Lithuania and Prince Kai from Spain, who landed two hours ago, generously offered to show Princess Juliette and Prince Léopold around upon their arrival." She flinches when I lock a pair of cold eyes on her. "I, ahem, of course, told them it wasn't necessary, given we have staff for this sort of thing, but they insisted. Prince Elmas doesn't want to interrupt your busy schedule seeing as you are now king, and it is my understanding that Prince Kai has entered courtship with Prince Léopold."

I fight the urge to roll my eyes at Elmas being the forever thorn in my side and decide to focus on the fact that Máire didn't say anything about Jules and El courting. If she deliberately mentioned the relationship between K and Léo, why would she omit the one between my Jules and that vermin of a prince?

El tried to make up for blackmailing me by giving me Aoife's address in Duwamish Land. I should be able to move on, but I cannot. While I am thankful to have reunited with my son at last, I will never be able to forget the way El did his best to get me out of the picture in Reunion. I was so ashamed of myself for losing my temper and attacking him in front of Juliette that I could not bear to face her again. I had to flee. I could not bring myself to stay there and hear her voice out loud her disgust toward me for harming her other suitor.

Other suitor…

The phrase leaves a sour taste on my tongue so I shake my head, hoping to dismiss the thought of Jules and El together right this instant.

"So, that is a 'no' then," Máire says, ticking something off her list.

I blink at her.

"My apologies, Máire," I rasp, willing my mind to focus, "what was that last point you made?"

"Prince Elmas offered to book rooms at the closest hotel for the Rivières, the Hakimis, and his own people, the Andrises, were they to extend their stay," she repeats blankly.

Hotel rooms?

Does he take me for an *eejit*?

"Please express my sincere gratitude to Prince Elmas and his clan," I tell Máire, "however, considering my time in Reunion Island, were Princess Juliette and Prince Léo in need of accommodation while in Éire, they are more than welcome to stay here at the palace. After all, their family's hospitality was most pleasant when I was on Reunion Island myself. It is only normal and expected that we do the same for them." Am I trying to convince myself or Máire? "I doubt Princess Juliette and Prince Léo's relatives will want to spend the night, but if they do, they can stay here, too."

Máire clears her throat.

"And... what about Prince Elmas?" she asks carefully.

"El can stay at the hotel down the road if he wants," I reply bluntly.

Máire's cheeks flush as she scribbles something down on her notes.

"Very well, Your Majesty," she breathes.

"Is that all, Máire?" I query, dying to go back to my chamber to get ready for Juliette's arrival.

"I'm afraid not, Sire," she says apologetically. "Your aunt and uncle, the queen and king of England, are soliciting your presence in the reception room. They would like to introduce you to English diplomats who travelled with them."

I exhale quietly and glance at my phone again. Juliette will be here in less than half an hour.

With my father gone, I feel stronger and more confident. It can take whatever criticism Jules has in store for me. I will listen and let it all soak in before begging her to reconcile. If I can't have her romantically, then her friendship is the second-best thing I can hope for. I will tell her everything; about Aoife, Oisín, my father, and even El. I will have no secret for my princess.

Feck.

Oisín and Aoife.

I have been gone too long.

"First, I would like to ensure my son and his mother don't need anything," I tell Máire, marching past her and her trainee.

"They are fine, King Féidhlim," Máire confirms, matching my pace as we make our way down the hall. "The little prince just had his lunch with his mother. Our chef made them a picnic. They are currently outside on the lawn by the mermaid statue, enjoying the sunny weather while it lasts, Sire."

"Oh," I exclaim, coming to a halt. "That's... perfect."

"The queen and king of England are waiting in the reception room, Your Majesty," Máire reminds me before glaring at her trainee, who inadvertently bumps into her as we pause in the hall.

"Lead the way, Máire," I exhale, suddenly feeling deflated again.

Chapter 22
Juliette

Amrah stands between Léo and me, using her ghostly abilities to form a transparent veil of magic above our heads to protect us from the rain. Ever since her outburst in our parlour, she has been able to perform magical tricks with the weather, like summoning wind or moving rain droplets out of the way.

A smirk twists on my lips as I catch my brother and K holding hands on my right. The couple was dying to reunite. After Léo and I unceremoniously got locked up in the château again, K went back to Spain and El to Lithuania, but not a day went by that my brother wasn't in touch with his lover. They haven't announced their courting to the press yet, K's parents being against same-sex courtships—just like our parents are—but it is clear as day K and Léo are in love.

"This is a funeral, Julie, you should be listening to the druid," El whispers in my ear, his grey eyes solely focused on the casket ready to be buried only a couple of feet ahead of us.

I glance at him, my index finger pressing vertically against my lips.

"*Shhh*," I shush him swiftly.

I see his mouth twist into an amused smile but he remains quiet.

Another shiver—the third one since my feet touched the Éireann soil—drums up my spine to settle at the nape of neck, leaving a cold trail of gooseflesh on my arms despite my skin being fully covered.

"Are you okay, Jules?" El asks in a murmur, his brow knitting.

"Yes… just another shiver."

"Maybe you're coming down with something," he mocks and I roll my eyes at him.

Witches are human, which means that unlike the rest of the magical community, we too are prone to the common illnesses that affect non-magical beings.

"Stop talking and listen to the druid," I tell El, my gaze locked on the fae priest near the casket.

I am glad we are in a good place, El and me. After he went back to Lithuania, we kept in touch, of course. He didn't come clean right away about the part he played in Féidhlim's leaving—my parents giving him an out when they invited themselves to our dinner to publicly humiliate me—but he did eventually, guilt killing him. While I was relieved to hear I wasn't the reason that drove Féidhlim away—not directly anyway—I was disappointed in El. I didn't know he had it in him to use blackmail as a means to an end. I thought he and

Féidhlim were friends. I am still unsure of the compromising information El held over Féidhlim's head but whatever it is, I am ready to accept it with a non-judgemental heart were he to ever share it with me someday.

I spent long nights in bed, debating whether to distance myself from El after what he did to Féidhlim, but decided against it in the end. El is my friend. And he knows he fucked up. I made sure to express my disappointment so he wouldn't think I didn't care about what happened between him and Féidhlim, but I also told him how much our friendship meant to me. I was telling the truth when I said El was one of my closest friends and I liked him like a brother. I would hate to lose him.

The casket enters the hole dug in the ground, the pillow-box side facing west as per tradition, before Féidhlim steps forward to deposit soil on the wooden surface, prompting his late father to return to nature.

My eyes eagerly take him in; the wet strands of blond hair falling over his forehead, the perfect composure of his face, his straight spine and confident stance. Even on a day like today, Féidhlim is as handsome as ever in his traditional royal clothing; a long emerald-and-gold coat that should be fastened at the front but isn't, which reveals the simple white shirt tucked into a pair of black leather pants. Black leather boots complete his outfit—if one doesn't take into consideration the shiny crown made of pure gold that sits on his head.

Was Féidhlim close to his father at all? I wonder as I observe the lack of emotion in his eyes. I can't remember.

Regardless, my heart softens in my chest as I watch him. I follow his every move like a hawk—or a stalker—wishing I could give him the tightest of hugs to show him he isn't alone.

The crowd begins to move around us, leaders (my parents, aunts, and uncles included) keen on adding soil to the casket to show their support. K, Léo, El, Amrah, and I thus decide to get out of the way and retreat to the palace's parlour to warm ourselves up.

As I leave our group to head to the bathroom to fix my hair—all this rain and humidity are making my curls frizz like a bloody alpaca—a little youngling runs into me, his chubby little body bumping against my legs before he falls backward onto the tiled flooring.

"Oh Gods, are you okay?" I cry, kneeling beside him to help him up.

He nods, taken aback, his bright blue eyes resting on me with an innocence I have never seen before. I smile kindly, my heart warming at the sight of him; blond curly hair, pointy ears, rosy cheeks, and little sausage fingers that wrap around mine as he finds his balance.

"Is this yours?" I ask, handing him a yellow truck, the toy the same size as his palm.

"Yes, thank you," he replies in an accent I don't recognise, his words all mashed together in that adorable way babies talk.

He smiles back at me as his round head nods eagerly, his hand closing over the miniature replica of the road vehicle.

"What's your name?" I wonder, glancing down the hall for his parents.

"Oisín," he tells me, kneeling to make the tires under his truck roll over the tiles.

"Oisín? What a lovely name!" I exclaim happily, which only makes him giggle, his cheeks flushing red at the compliment. "Are you here alone, Oisín?"

"No." He shakes his head. "Dada."

He looks around, his blond brow drawing in when he doesn't see his father.

"I'll help you find him, okay?"

He nods again, so I wrap my hand around his to lead him down the hall, making sure he doesn't leave his truck behind. As we approach an intersection, I hear the angry voices of a couple arguing around the corner.

"What do you mean you don't know where he went?" the female cries through gritted teeth, frustration making her sigh loudly.

"I was shaking hands with diplomats. One minute he was here, the next he was gone," the familiar voice explains, defending himself. "Can we not speak English, please?" he asks in a hurry. "They are still looking."

"I'll speak whatever language I want, thank you very much!"

"Fine," he grates.

My heart pinches in its cavity.

Is this…

"You said *you* were watching him," the female goes on.

"I'll have the entire palace help us find him, Aoife," he reassures her, although he too sounds nervous.

I can hear it in his tone.

Oisín and I hurry up, reaching the end of the hall to come face-to-face with the couple. I hold my breath, my eyes instantly finding Féidhlim's. He drinks me in, blinking with surprise as he loses composure for a second before his gaze drops down and he sees the youngling beside me.

"Dada!" Oisín rejoices, dashing to… *Féidhlim.* The babe turns to the blond female on his left next. "Mama!"

My gaze jumps from Oisín to Féidhlim to the beautiful viking warrior hugging the child, and my mouth drops as does my heart.

Féidhlim has a family.

Chapter 23

Féidhlim

"Juliette, wait!" I cry, rushing after her as she swiftly turns around to walk down the hall. "Wait, please."

But she picks up the pace, dashing through the wallpapered corridor where portraits of my ancestors hang over the walls. I follow her closely, never quite catching up to her purposefully, my gaze mesmerised by the soft black satin veil of her dress as it flows around her tanned legs. I need to talk to her away from the crowd and gossipy ears so, in a sense, it is a good thing she is running away.

Of course, I knew she was at the palace. I had assistants notify me the second the Rivières' carriage landed, and I watched as Jules' feet touched the Éireann soil in my gardens for the very first time. And I continued watching as her long curly hair blew in the wind and her dress got wet under the rain. I wanted to sprint outside with an umbrella and a warm blanket to protect her, but I didn't. I couldn't with so many people watching my every move like their lives depended on it, waiting for me to do the wrong thing to then gossip about it later. Because I

226 Enchanted

know I should be mourning my late father, not drooling over a beautiful princess.

As cold-hearted as it sounds, I still feel nothing about my father's passing. If anything, I am more *relieved* now that the burial ceremony is over and King Fionn's body is locked underground, where it cannot escape. For the first time in my life, it is confirmed—the heavy burden of pleasing him has been lifted. I can fill my lungs with the fresh Éireann air and feel my shoulders soften as I exhale. I no longer need to worry about hiding Oisín from the world. I am a free man.

So when El joined Juliette in my stead—a fancy black, windproof, polyester umbrella in his hand—and pulled her into his arms to cover her shoulders with his jacket, my blood boiled in my veins, steam flowing out of my pores, threatening to melt the glass from the window in its tracks. I wanted to be the one to welcome her here. I wanted to be the one protecting her from the rain. And I wanted to be the one with an excuse to hold her close.

"Jules, stop!" I exclaim as we reach the top floor and she wanders down my aisle of the palace. "Stop…" I repeat, my tone softer as my hand snatches hers. "Please," I murmur, taking a step toward her, our fingers interlocking.

I dare to come closer and she lets me, her back sinking into the wooden panelling behind her, the one on the other side of my bedroom wall. My forehead rests against hers, my eyes fluttering shut as I inhale the sweet scent of coconut and… vanilla. My stomach twists, my cock bobbing in my trousers, because she isn't a fragment of my imagination. This time she really is here, standing in front of me, in *my* home. The home I am rebuilding to erase all traces of my father's tyranny.

And so, before I can even process what is happening, I kiss her. Our lips meet, and I can't believe my luck when her mouth parts, offering me her tongue on a silver platter. I eagerly mimic her, my hands cupping her face, my thumbs stroking the soft skin of her cheeks as the rest of my fingers bury in her curls. Our kiss deepens, and I revel in the fresh taste of strawberries and chocolate.

I smile against her, picturing her excitement at a bowl of fresh berries and warm chocolate sauce.

Gods, I missed her!

I know I made a promise to my father, but it doesn't matter right now, as long as I have her.

"Come with me," I breathe, guiding her toward the door on my left, never breaking our kiss.

My hand pats the wooden surface behind Juliette's back to find the doorknob and twist it open. I lead her through the room as she walks backward, her mouth sucking in my tongue, which only sends a delicious bolt of electricity down my spine. Impatience and lust make my movements hasty, her tongue now applying the right amount of pressure to mine. So I close the door behind us in a rush, pinning Juliette to it next, my hands roaming freely over her enticing body.

"I've missed you," I manage in a whisper, my lips pressing against the gentle flesh of her neck.

She fists my hair, mewling the second my fingers cup her breasts, my mouth following closely, my teeth latching onto her peaked nipple through the back satin.

"I... missed you, too... Fé," she pants, pressing her pelvis to mine.

Her eyes fly open as she feels my erection; hard and eager with pre-cum settling over its head to form a wet patch through my trousers. Her cheeks flush, her chest heaving rapidly. Then it is my turn to rasp as she grabs my hand, urging it to slide under her panties. I almost lose it when I feel her. When I feel her cunt dripping wet around my digits for *me*.

My thumb finds that sweet spot of hers before drawing circles all around it. Her fingers grip my back tightly, her nails fisting my coat. I bring my lips to hers in a rough kiss, our teeth clacking together in the process as I once again slurp her tongue into my mouth. She squeals against me when the pad of my thumb presses against her clit, swollen with want already, to flick it.

"Féidhlim..." she breathes, her knees giving under her.

If it isn't the sweetest sound I have ever heard!

"That's right, princess, and I'm gonna make you say it louder!" I urge, dropping to the floor to kneel in front of her.

I pull down her panties, taking them off her altogether and swinging one of her legs over my shoulder. I inhale the appetising scent of her femalehood, my mouth watering as I approach her pussy. I kiss it softly, once, twice, three times. And when my eyes find hers, I allow my tongue to dive right through her folds. Her legs tremor around my cheeks, placing a smile on my face. My fingers grip the juicy flesh of her ass, securing her pelvis against my mouth.

As I plunge through her folds to properly tongue-fuck her, however, I can't help but notice how tight and narrow her entrance still is. My cock uncomfortably presses against my zipper, dying to be let out, but I leave it alone. I could touch myself, releasing us both in one go, but I don't do that either. Juliette deserves my full attention, nothing less.

My lips latch onto her bundle of nerves next, and I suck it hard between my teeth. I watch as her cheeks flush brighter, a heavy panting escaping her parted mouth. Seeing her like this is breathtaking.

"Féidhlim... I... I'm... close," she manages through hooded eyes, her fingers closing over my hair, her pelvis rocking back and forth against my mouth.

So I keep up the good work while driving my index finger inside her. Her velvety walls are warm and... so fecking wet!

Fuck me!

I need to make her come.

I need to show her just how much I have been waiting for this to happen.

I need to show her that she is my dream come true.

Soon, I hit a thin layer of tissue that I didn't feel with my tongue earlier, and it dawns on me that Juliette is still a virgin.

"Féidhlim!" she squeals my name again, this time louder, before her thighs press against my ears and all I hear next is the thumping of my own heart beating for her.

Juliette rides her orgasm in my mouth and I greedily collect her juices, drinking every last drop like a thirsty male on his last breath. When the shaking in her legs calms down and her body relaxes, I get back up, cupping her face in my hands to look her in the eye. I bring my lips to hers for a tender kiss so she leans in, her frame moulding perfectly to mine. And I know it probably isn't the right time, but I need to ask. I need to know…

"Jules?" I whisper her name, my lips brushing the shell of her ear as my arms wrap around her, the flat of my hand stroking her dark hair softly.

"Uhm?" She looks up at me, a satisfied smile painting her face in the most charming way I have ever seen.

"Are you and El together?" I wonder, hoping I don't ruin the moment by mentioning my rival.

"No, we're just friends," she announces in a small voice, instant relief washing over me like a hot, relaxing shower. But then, she holds my gaze and my heart sinks at the sadness and hurt on her face. "And *you* have a mate… and a son."

I frown, taken aback, and in the blink of an eye she pulls away from my embrace, pushing past me.

"What? No, Jules… I mean, yes—" I pause, gathering my thoughts and forgetting about my erection to effectively lay out the situation to her.

But I stop, watching as she mechanically puts her panties back on and adjusts her dress around her chest and thighs before taking in my bedroom.

The space is pretty standard for royalty, I suppose. Nothing she hasn't seen before in her own palace; a solid mahogany Chippendale desk with a matching chair, a floor-to-ceiling glass door leading to a balcony, an en-suite, and a walk-in closet. But when her gaze rests over my super-king size Ottoman bed I am unable to read her thoughts, which only causes anxiety to suffocate me from the inside.

"I'm not married, Jules. I never was," I blurt out, panic tightening my chest, my breathing suddenly growing shallow.

Her eyes search mine as if wondering if I am telling the truth. I swallow nervously, dread invading my mind and any rational thought I once had in its way. That is when realisation strikes me like a lightning bolt; I am afraid to lose her.

I can't lose her. *Ever.*

Friendship will never be good enough.

Not anymore.

This is it; I can stop the search. I have found her. I have found the female I want to spend the rest of my days with.

Princess Juliette of Reunion Island.

My Jules.

"And Oisín?" she asks next, her facial expression perfectly composed, her features still surprisingly unreadable.

"Yes, he's my son," I confess earnestly through glassy eyes, sensing her slipping away from me. "But Aoife and I aren't courting."

"Why not?"

"Th-They live on a different continent—"

"Oh…"

She breaks eye contact, her head nodding slowly.

"But we wouldn't be together even if they lived here!" I go on, feeling the need to back up my own point. "Aoife doesn't like royal life, so—"

"I see."

She forces a smile and walks past me, her head high and her spine straight. I stare at her, alarmed to see her leave and frantic at her composure. *When did she learn to do that?* Back in Reunion, she enjoyed my presence and I could read her like an open book; anyone could. I continue watching her, anguish enveloping me in some

Emilie Ocean 233

kind of thick veil of darkness the second she opens the door to step out onto the landing.

"Jules, wait!"

"Don't… follow me. Please," she orders without looking back. "I am sorry for your loss, King Féidhlim. Our deepest condolences. Know that you have Reunion Island's support."

And then she is gone.

My legs freeze under me, an ever-growing knot in my stomach, smothering and heavy, preventing me from chasing after her. So I stand there like an *eejit*—a real fool—alone in my empty bedroom, her words a wake-up slap in the face. Juliette is here out of courtesy because my father passed away, nothing more.

How presumptuous of me to think she would want me back. And even if she did, the promise I made to my father is a promise a prince cannot break. Only, I am no prince anymore.

I am king.

And I want my queen back.

Chapter 24
Juliette

I rush down the stairs, my heart swollen and battered once again. I am mortified and embarrassed I let my arousal dictate my actions. *Was it good? Yes, of course!* But I didn't run up to the top floor for Féidhlim to give me head. I went there to find somewhere quiet to confront him, away from the greedy eyes that have been watching him all day. But when Féidhlim grabbed my hand and kissed me, all the animosity I felt toward him for having a secret family dissolved into a rush of adrenaline I wasn't expecting to feel. So I gave in to my fantasy materialising itself in front of my eyes.

I am a fool, though.

When will I learn my lesson?

I saw her. Aoife, he called her. And she is gorgeous. Shiny blond hair. Tall. Skinny. Fit. Beautiful. *How could I ever compete with her? Oh, wait, I cannot.* She is the *mother* of his youngling. And Féidhlim said it very clearly: they aren't together because Aoife and Oisín live far away, and she doesn't want to be a princess.

But what if they lived here, in Éire?

What if she changed her mind and wanted to be a royal after all?

Féidhlim is no longer a prince; he is a king, and this changes things. What if Aoife fancies life as a *queen*?

I let the tears shed down my cheeks and bring the back of my hand to my mouth to muffle my crying, heartbroken. My fingers twist over the black satin of my dress, fisting the garment where it covers my hurting organ.

I should have stayed in Reunion, where everything feels safe and familiar. But my head shakes at the absurdity of the thought, my curls swaying against my back. This is what I wanted. *Freedom.* I am no longer obligated to choose a marital partner; not that Féidhlim ever was truly interested anyway.

My parents revoked the union after they caught El and me at the restaurant, and Léo and K on the beach, that fateful evening. *Temporarily* revoked courting process, that is. They deferred it by one year to give them time to iron out our family… issues. Which means I have an entire twelve months to myself. I can do anything I want, see anyone I like. This is my dream come true. I should be happy right now. And yet, here I am, chasing after one of the very princes my parents chose on my behalf.

This makes no sense.

None of this does.

"Julie?" El exclaims, frowning as he takes me in. "Is everything okay? What happened?"

I startle in the hall, swiftly turning around to wipe my tears with the backs of my hands.

"Hm-hm," I hum in a small voice, nodding profusely when facing him again. "All good."

He arches an eyebrow, not buying it. And that is alright because it is El. I don't need to put on a mask with him; I can just be myself. So I rush to him, clasping my hands together around his slender waistline and burying my face in his strong chest.

"Oh, *mieloji*..." (Oh, sweetheart...) he says softly. "What is it?" My head shakes, so he gently strokes my hair with the palm of his large hand. "Who does K need to beat up?" he whispers when I don't reply.

I chuckle against his black suit, unable to keep my seriousness and gloominess in check at the thought of K being sent on a revenge quest.

"I need to talk to Léo," I mutter, looking up to lock eyes with him.

He winces.

"He went for a ride with K. They said they needed to get out of here. 'Too many old grumpy males,' or something like that." He shrugs casually before smiling again. "But you can talk to *me*." He winks, but I remain silent. "Is it Fé?"

"How did you know?" I cry out.

I pull away, my eyes wide with surprise.

"I saw him go after you down the hall," he explains. "What happened?"

My cheeks flush magenta, my sex clenching as I revisit our encounter. I should have stopped him, but I didn't. It felt way too good to be touched by Féidhlim. It was everything I had been dreaming of, except this time it was all real; his soft lips, his warm breath, his spicy cologne, his strong body. He was real. I feel my panties getting drenched again at the thought of Féidhlim and the things his mouth did to my body. Until my eyes grow glassy because I am not *her*.

"He has an Aoife," I tell El under my breath, my heart aching in my ribcage.

"A what?" He grimaces, rummaging his pockets for a tissue. "What's an 'ee-fah'?"

"She's his…" I grab the soft piece of paper and blow my nose, caring very little about my image right now "…his baby mama."

"Oh, yeah, I talked to her and the young one earlier," El says matter-of-factly, handing me another mint-scented tissue. "They're not together, though. You know that, right?"

My head shakes, a sob taking root in my throat. The image of Féidhlim's bed flashes in my mind. Is that where they did it? Where Oisín was conceived? Disgust pinpricks my insides, revulsion sending bile up toward my oesophagus. Another icy shiver follows suit and my teeth clack.

"But he said… they weren't a thing because… *she* didn't live here, and *she* didn't want this life," I sniffle, ignoring my over-the-top body reaction at Féidhlim and Aoife having a past, a present, and most definitely a future. My shoulders heave as my hands wave at the space around us. "Not because *he* didn't like her," I complete my sentence.

"Oh, Julie, I wouldn't read too much into it if I were you. Males aren't that complicated, you know."

He shrugs, a smirk curling upward from the corners of his pale mouth.

"But, what if—" I start.

"Will you stop already? I didn't step down to watch you throw it all out the window," he cuts in, grabbing my shoulders and leaning down to be at eye level with me. "They aren't together. The only reason why Féidhlim left Reunion was because he was afraid of your reaction when you found out about his son."

My face screws up at the absurdity of the comment.

"That's ridiculous. Why would I hold that against him?"

"Because Oisín is now next in line to the Éireann throne," he explains, holding my stare.

I frown, then look away, my thoughts going haywire inside my brain.

"Were you to become Queen of Éire, your younglings would probably never get the chance to govern," he goes on.

I lock eyes with El, a hard swallow gliding down my throat as I let the information sink in.

"Jules, are you okay with that?"

Another shiver.

I walk around the royal gardens, El's black umbrella in my hand to protect me from the mist. I wish Léo was back from his spin already. I need to talk to him. My brother is only twenty—and was locked away between the four magical veiled walls of the royal grounds in Reunion, just like me—but somehow he has got more experience than me when it comes to matters of the heart. He often engaged in romantic (and consented) pursuits with our staff throughout the years and was never afraid of getting caught.

I sigh heavily when the hem of my dress clings to my ankles, the wet ground soaking the fabric and causing it to stick to my bare skin. I should have stayed inside until the sun came back out, but after checking the forecast I realised the weather was going to be this miserable all day to match my mood. So I decided to go for a stroll. I needed the fresh air. The palace was getting stuffy with all those diplomats around.

I expected my family to leave Éire the moment King Fionn's casket was interred, but they stayed and have been in deep conversation with the monarchs of France and England ever since. I spotted *Tatie* Salomé in the reception room with the royal Spanish clan on my way out of the palace, and *Tonton* Zain with the Mexican leaders near the main entrance. Politicians are everywhere.

I sit on the stony bench by the lake, where the statue of a mermaid faces me. Sometimes I wish I could breathe underwater and swim with dolphins all day. Life would be so much more enjoyable then. I have yet to meet an actual mermaid, though, but it would be interesting to know what their thoughts are on wild sea life.

"Hello," a high-pitched voice exclaims beside me.

I look down, surprised to hear another being around in this weather. A soft smile paints my lips as I recognise Oisín, his big blue eyes sparkling with joy.

"Hi, Oisín! What you doing here?" I ask, brows arched as I look past him.

Aoife, who swiftly joins us, waves at me, her mouth stretching into a shy line.

"For you," Oisín tells me next as if prompting me to revert my attention to him. So I glance down at him to see a bright yellow-and-orange marigold flower in his right fist. "Pretty," he adds swiftly, a quiet giggle escaping his rosy lips.

"I guess someone has a crush on you," Aoife laughs, her blond hair swaying from left to right as she watches me accept the present.

I smirk at her and turn back to her son, grateful.

"Thank you so much, Oisín. You're very kind!"

The little fae giggles louder, showing me all his baby teeth in the process. And I can't help but chuckle at his cuteness, innocence, and liveliness. I never got the chance to spend much time around younglings, understandably, but I already know Oisín is the loveliest little one there is. The type you just want to hold tight against you like a teddy bear to shower him with kisses.

"Be careful, Baba," Aoife starts, bending down to brush his blond hair away from his eyes with a pair of long and gracious fingers. "You don't want to make Dada jealous." She winks at me, and I go red like the brightest of flowers on a flamboyant tree. "Juliette's courting Dada."

"Oh?" His bright blue eyes sparkle, his thin brow shooting to his hairline.

My eyes widen with embarrassment; I no longer know where to look, so my face screws up.

"Oh, no!" I cry, the palms of my hands facing away from my chest. "I'm not… we're not… it's not like that."

Aoife chuckles.

"May I?" she asks calmly, pointing at the free space beside me with her chin.

"Yes, of course!" I say a tad too loud, anxiety coursing through me like an electric spark, short-circuiting my brain.

Her laugh eventually dies down into a smile. She casually takes her seat on my right and hands the familiar yellow truck to her son.

"Here, Baba."

Oisín grabs it, eager, drops down to his knees, and silently begins to play with the toy on the lawn. I follow the motion of his little arms as they skim the ground to make the vehicle slide from point A to point B, and I hope my features don't show just how uneasy I feel with his mother right here next to me. I mechanically roll the green stem of the marigold between my thumb and index finger to make the flower dance back and forth, all the while racking my brain for something to say.

"Is it your first time in Éire?" Aoife breaks the ice.

She stretches her long legs in front of her and presses the palms of her hands onto her knees.

"Yeah." I nod profusely.

"How do you like it so far?"

"Uhm…" I frown at the grey sky above our heads, which causes a sudden burst of laughter to erupt out of her.

"You must miss the sun and the heat," she guesses at last, tucking a strand of golden hair behind her ear. "But I'm sure you'll get used to the Éireann weather eventually. And if not, you and Féidhlim can always spend the colder months in Reunion. That's an option too, isn't it?"

My eyes jump from the flower to Aoife, and I can't help but grimace at the comment.

"I don't want to sound awkward because I'm not sure what he told you, but Féidhlim and I aren't courting," I make a point of correcting her.

"No?"

Her brows hike in a genuinely surprised expression.

"No." I shake my head.

"Why not?"

My cheeks flush at her directness so I look down at my knees to regain my composure, while my fingers continue to twist around the flower stem.

What does she expect me to say? That I don't believe I can compete against her?

"Is there someone else?" she goes on, curiosity adding a charming glow to her stare. "El, maybe?"

My head shakes again, an amused smile now smearing my lips.

"No, we're just friends."

"Good," she nods, satisfied with my answer, "because Fé really likes you."

My gaze snaps to hers, my eyes flickering with excitement at the statement.

"He… does?" I manage in a small voice, my heart racing in my ribcage as I so desperately hope she is telling the truth.

Because, of all people, *she* would know.

Another giggle from Aoife.

"Yeah, he sure does," she confirms, adamant. "Now, keep that to yourself. Don't go telling him I said anything, or he'll be mad."

She dramatically rolls her eyes to the back of her head.

"Of course," I promise, unable to hide the grin of relief and happiness that stretches across my face to light up my features. My brows knit again within seconds, however. "What about you and Féidhlim?" I ask in a small voice.

"What about us?"

"Don't you two have a history?"

She observes me through pensive eyes, her head cocking as she works on her answer.

"We do," she replies earnestly, "but all we share now is Oisín's well-being. Nothing more. I am not a threat to you, Juliette. I promise."

Maybe not right now; but what about in six months' time when she realises that she made a big mistake?

"Right." I swallow. "I don't know that one can forget all about their first love, though."

She smiles sadly.

"I was never in love with Féidhlim," she confesses timidly. "And I don't think he ever truly loved me either."

That isn't what El told me.

"I was his best friend once upon a time and he was mine, so the lines often got blurred, but I can assure you he never looked at me the way he looks at you," she adds, patting me on the hand. "Don't turn him down on my account. I have no interest in going after Féidhlim."

I watch her for a long moment, and I think she is telling the truth. In fact, my clairvoyance is confirming she is telling the truth. I believe her.

Aoife was never in love with Féidhlim.

Féidhlim was never in love with her either.

She doesn't want to be a royal—be it a princess or a queen.

She is only here because of Oisín.

"Alright then," Aoife exclaims, getting back to her feet. She extends an open hand to her son. "Come on, Baba, let's go back inside. It's almost time for your tea." She turns back around to face me. "Nice talking to you, Juliette."

I nod.

"You too, Aoife."

They walk off, hand in hand, while Oisín hops over the puddles he finds along the way as he pretends to be a rabbit, his yellow toy in his little hand.

I smile warmly, relieved the red flags I thought I saw were just in my head, when my clairvoyance screams at me by sending another shiver rolling up my spine.

Open your eyes, Juliette, it hisses.

Chapter 25

Féidhlim

After his tea, Aoife brought Oisín to my business chamber so she could head back to her room for a shower. She made me promise to keep my eyes on him at all times to avoid repeating what happened earlier today when Jules found Oisín alone in the hallway. Aoife also made it clear she would not forgive me if I let our son wander around the palace unattended again. She glared at me one more time, pressed a kiss to his rosy cheek, and exited the office.

"Vroom, vroom," Oisín sings over and over as he makes his yellow truck run over his action figure for the fifth time.

I watch him, cosily set up on the floor on a soft rug between the door and the bookshelves, from behind my father's desk—my desk—the lines of my face pulled into a frown. I shake my head when the youngling giggles, proud of himself as the fae toy in his hand moves slightly under the impact.

Is this what children do nowadays? Pretend to kill people with their wooden toys?

I file the question away to be revisited with Aoife later when she is done being annoyed at me.

I tried hard to keep an eye on Oisín earlier after the burial ceremony was over and everyone retreated to the palace, but I only have two eyes and two hands. Kings, queens, dukes, and duchesses were flocking my way like a gaggle of geese; each one of them more eager than the previous monarch before them to shake my hand and present me with their condolences. They could all see I was busy minding a youngling, but none of them cared. They wanted to be seen by my side on "such a tragic day for my nation." If I didn't know any better I would say they were trying to get in my good books to ensure there would be no disruption in the Éireann trade with their respective countries. It is all political and tactical.

Even Jules came here for politics…

Princess Juliette…

I pinch the bridge of my nose, my tired eyes squeezing shut just long enough to collect myself.

She thought I was courting her while having a secret family waiting for me back home. She is only half wrong; Oisín was a secret for a long time, but with my father gone I have been keeping him by my side every chance I got. While I haven't introduced him to the world properly, I am planning on doing so as soon as the commotion for my father's wake dies down. Aoife has already agreed for me to do so, confirming that keeping Oisín away from his royal duties now might become problematic in the future.

Back in the day, when my parents were only younglings, royals were required to attend boarding school with other monarchs to prepare them for the tedious tasks of governing their own nations; the demanding responsibilities they would have to live with for the rest of their lives. The tradition became obsolete, however, when most royals opted to have their offspring homeschooled. I haven't talked to Aoife about Oisín's education, but I doubt she would want to send him away to a boarding school. It wouldn't make any sense; I did not get back into my son's life to enrol him in a fancy school across the globe.

I glance at Oisín, who is now making his fae doll kick the yellow truck so hard it goes crashing against the wall. I expect to hear the booming bang of the impact but it never comes.

"Dada?" Oisín calls, his head cocking to one side as he keeps his eyes trained on the small vehicle.

The truck…

The yellow truck… floats in thin air in front of him, no fae dust involved.

What the heck?

I frown, carefully getting off the office chair to make my way around the desk. Oisín, intrigued by the magic trick, brings his index finger up to press it against the side of the flying toy. It stops moving for a moment before collapsing to the ground in a quick thud, toppling over to lie on its roof on the parqueting floor.

"Huh?" Oisín exclaims, standing up to examine the toy, puzzled.

It is safe to assume he did not make that wooden vehicle float the way it just did. I have seen Oisín use his fae dust to manipulate objects before and I can safely say that the way that toy flew through the air did not look familiar.

"Dada?" Oisín cries when the truck wriggles at his feet like a possessed object.

"Stay behind me, Oisín," I order, grabbing him by the arm.

I have just enough time to pull him aside when the toy is launched at him with such force and speed no youngling could dodge even if they tried. The sharp edge of the vehicle digs into the thick layer of my coat sleeve before collapsing to the floor once again.

"*Argh*," I growl, kicking the toy away from us with the tip of my boot.

It hits the hard mahogany of the desk and breaks into pieces; pieces that magically get back together with a mind of their own to form one complete truck again before my shocked eyes. I turn around to see that tears have formed in Oisín's blue eyes, his little lip quivering as he can't stop watching the animated toy reinventing itself across the room.

What is going on?

In a hurry, I look around the chamber for something to destroy the wooden truck with. I settle for my father's walking stick—the same dragon-wood one that knocked me unconscious all those years ago.

As the toy levitates again, readying itself to strike, I close the distance between us and swing the cane at the tiny vehicle. Once again it breaks into pieces at my feet, which is when the door behind me swings open. Both Oisín and I spin around, startled. A flushed Juliette and a terrified Aoife paint the doorway.

"Mama!" Oisín cries, holding his hands up to urge her to pick him up.

Aoife rushes to him, kneels to the floor, and holds our son flush against her. His little arms wrap around her neck so tightly it makes my heart squeeze. Our little baba is terrified. Oisín breaks into a high-pitched wail; one piercing enough to match a banshee's.

"It's okay, Baba," Aoife whispers in his ear, her own eyes now glassy, too. "Mama's here, lovey."

I swallow, my gaze finding Jules' across the room. She looks… horrified. Like she just saw a ghost.

"Jules, what's going on?" I ask under my breath, utterly lost.

"Don't. Move," she grits, her legs bucking under her.

I grimace, slowly placing the cane down on the desk.

"Jules, I can explain—"

252 Enchanted

"If you think I came alone, you're wrong," she cuts in, her glare steady. "There are at least two dozen witches in this palace, ready to take you down."

"What?" I breathe. "Jules—"

"Féidhlim, stop acting the maggot and get over here!" Aoife yells at him as she retreats behind Juliette.

I flinch but obey nonetheless. As I hurry to join them, I realise Jules' glower never leaves the spot I was in only seconds ago. She continues to stare at the desk, on high alert.

"I know you," she says after a moment. "You're… King Fionn."

My eyes widen, my lungs stilling for a second as I forget to breathe.

Juliette is talking to the dead.

She is conversing with… my father.

"You just passed," she whispers, her voice growing weak. "How are you able to harvest this much strength already," she eyes the broken toy, "when you only died two days ago?"

She swallows as she listens to his answer.

"What's he saying?" I ask in a rush, wrapping a hand around her arm.

Juliette's face bleaches and she shakes her head so profusely that the scent of coconut and vanilla diffuses in the air.

"No," she tells the invisible ghost. "You can't."

"What did he say?" I echo, panic flooding my nervous system.

"He wants to 'right a wrong,'" Juliette replies, taking a step back toward Aoife and Oisín.

Right a wrong?

He wants to get rid of Oisín.

The blood in my veins freezes at the realisation, and rage thunders in my ears.

"Show yourself, you coward!" I roar at the room, placing myself in front of my family to protect them.

"He can't," Juliette explains. "He doesn't have that ability yet. All he can do for now is possess objects."

On cue, the wooden shelving unit by the door begins to tremor. Books float in the air next, aligning themselves to be supernaturally flung at… not me, or Juliette, or even Aoife, but at Oisín.

"Watch out!" Juliette squeals as the first heavy tomes cut through the space in my son's direction.

Aoife does a fine job of avoiding the first one, Oisín safely tucked in her arms. A second book, then a third, and a fourth are thrown at them, and I do my best to deviate them with my fae dust. The fifth and sixth tomes, however, I don't see coming, but Juliette does.

"Amrah!" she screams, opening her hands wide in front of her to summon her cousin.

A protective gust of wind blows a natural shield around us, reversing the trajectory of the evil manuscripts to their invisible sender.

"Amrah, no!" Juliette says next, her face flushing pale again.

I squint at the empty space before us, my eyes narrowing at the open books decorating the carpets on the floor. I cannot see, hear, or sense a thing. I have no idea what is going on on the other side.

"Jules, what is it?" I urge, eyes now wide with panic.

"You angered him!" she manages, her words directed at Amrah.

With that, the wallpaper peels off the walls, the lights flicker, and the glass window behind the desk bursts open. A loud, ghostly woosh sound echoes in the chamber before it rumbles like thunder.

Chapter 26

Juliette

I spin around and fold forward to add another layer of protection over Aoife and Oisín. My eyes squeeze shut as I wait for the impact of the wooden bookshelf to hit, but it never comes. When I look up again, my hands still gripping Aoife's shoulders, her son safely tucked against her chest, I see both Féidhlim and El before us, acting as living shields between us and the ghost of King Fionn.

El's grasp over the shelving unit is strong and steady as he uses his super-strength to toss it aside like a vulgar piece of paper with the help of Féidhlim, his fae dust glowing at his fingertips like sparkles.

Behind them, Amrah has Fionn stuck in a giant bubble of air, its gusts swooshing around the chamber to disrupt the organised order of the office. Chairs topple over, documents crash to the floor, lights flicker, and the glass window trembles. With my hair in my eyes I get back to my feet—seeing that Aoife and Oisín are fine—and join Féidhlim and El.

"Jules!" Féidhlim gasps when I am close enough, the warm palm of his large hand instinctively cupping my cheek. "Are you alright?"

I nod, though my brows are still knit with worry.

"I'm fine," I breathe. "Are you?" I ask, rotating slightly to include El in our conversation. "Thank Gods you both caught that bookshelf!"

"It was nothing, Julie," El says humbly.

Nothing?

Aoife, Oisín, and I would've been dead by now without them. My clairvoyance is useless in this kind of situation.

"Oisín!" Féidhlim cries, retreating to Aoife now that the attack has temporarily ceased.

He cradles the youngling in his arms, locking glassy eyes with the mother of his child, all three of them in shock.

"My family?" I ask El urgently.

"Gone," he replies. "They left the palace an hour ago."

"What?" I squeak, horrified.

They left without saying goodbye?

"Léo and K are on their way," he goes on. "I had Féidhlim's assistant look for them."

"Thanks, El," I say softly, grateful for his help.

Earlier today, as the cold shivers running up and down my spine continued, I decided to return to the guest bedroom Féidhlim had reserved for me. On my way there I grabbed a couple of candles from the kitchen—I reckoned King Fionn enjoyed proper candlelight dinners with himself—so I could perform another one of my rituals. I needed to meditate and retrospectively reflect on what my clairvoyance had been trying to tell me ever since our carriage landed in Éire. And while doing so, I felt compelled to play with elemental energies for a clearer message, hence the use of fire to symbolise purification and enhance the power of my consciousness. I also had a small glass bowl of water before me for clarity and intuitively.

    I couldn't believe it when the hissing voice of my clairvoyance showed me flashing pictures of King Fionn haunting the walls of his castle, frantically looking for Oisín, his grandson. With the preparations for his funeral and the political leaders' attendance at it, the late king never had the opportunity to strike without drawing attention. The last image that zoomed through my mind was of Féidhlim and his son alone in Fionn's business chamber. So I ran down the hall, panicking, and inadvertently bumped into Aoife who was on her way up to her bedroom for a shower. I told her everything my clairvoyance showed me, and together we hurriedly made our way to late Fionn's office. We found El in the hall outside it. Seeing the expression of dread on Aoife's face and hearing the panic in my voice, he swiftly volunteered to get witchy reinforcements to banish the poltergeist back to the afterlife realm.

    "Uhm, a little help would be nice," Amrah growls over her shoulder.

258 *Enchanted*

Her hands, extended in front of her, continue to hold Fionn's ghostly form inside the air bubble. Amrah's magic must be different from mine since she has passed because as far as I know, elemental magic isn't of any use against the dead.

"What can I do?" I ask, on the verge of a breakdown. "What can any of us do to stop him?" I swing the full length of my arm around me.

Three fae, one vampire, and one witch, and none of us has the ability to fight the dead.

"Let's get Oisín out of here," Féidhlim suggests, hopeful.

"If your father breaks free, he'll follow you anywhere you go," Amrah tells him, though he cannot hear her. "He'll haunt Oisín for the rest of his life."

"It'll only delay the inevitable," I summarise for the rest of the room, "but yes! Go somewhere safe, we'll hold your father off."

"We will?" Amrah cries.

On cue, Fionn roars at the door leading out to the hall, and just like that it shuts on its own in an ear-piercing boom that makes my bones vibrate. Féidhlim dashes to the doorknob and twists it again and again, but it doesn't budge.

"No… What do we do now?" Féidhlim asks in a weak voice, eyes wide. "We can't let my father…"

But I'm no longer hearing him because Fionn is talking to me, too.

"Juliette..." he rasps.

I swallow, turning around to see a crooked smile on his lips. Fionn's eyes are feral and his skin is sickeningly pale, but his bleached hair is perfectly combed to the side and his attire is immaculate. Though dead, he remains a king. Much like Amrah, his body isn't translucent; the only thing that gives away he is a ghost are his feet floating above the ground.

"Why fight me, Juliette, when I can solve all your problems in the snap of a *neck*," Fionn purrs.

Amrah grimaces at his poor choice of words. Breaking a toddler's neck... how horrendous.

BANG!

BANG!

BANG!

We all jump again.

"Open the fucking door!" I hear Léo growl from the hall, his fists battering the wooden barrier between us.

"Let me try!" K offers.

BOOM!

"'Fuck's sake..." K groans.

BOOM!

260 *Enchanted*

"*Oomph…*" K breathes. "Why are doors in Éire so fucking strong!"

"Fé's dead dad did some ghostly shit to it," El tells them, pressing the flats of his hands to the door.

"Fools!" Fionn hisses.

I revert my attention to him, eyes squinting.

"How would assaulting a youngling solve anything?" I manage in a shaky voice.

I take a step forward despite the shaking of my bones to join Amrah. I offer her my hand so she can use me as a beacon to strengthen the air bubble around our common enemy. We might as well keep him locked up until we figure out a way to defeat him.

"I know you like my son," Fionn tells me, his eyes squinting at Féidhlim as he helps Aoife up, Oisín now in his arms.

"And how would you know that?" I croak, glancing at Amrah from the corner of my eye.

"I saw what ye did in his room after *my* burial ceremony," he explains, unimpressed.

What the hell…

He is referring to Féidhlim giving me head.

"You… watched us?" I cry, disgusted.

"What were you doing in there with Féidhlim?" Amrah queries, at a loss.

I shake my head at her and revert my attention to Fionn.

"I can kill the youngling for both of us, Juliette," he offers, "then your firstborn, the one you'll have with my son, will be next in line for the throne. Your child, who will be of noble blood, can be crowned one day."

Amrah's worried gaze finds mine and my brows furrow.

"No," I respond, appalled by his logic. "I don't want that."

"You don't want to be queen of Éire?" he yells back, his ghostly fists bouncing off the windy walls of the bubble, sending Amrah and me a few steps back. "You don't want a union with my son?"

He strikes another blow against the airy ball, this time more violent. Amrah stays put but I fall backward like someone kicked me in the stomach, breaking the beaconing link with my cousin.

"Julie!" El is by my side in the blink of an eye, an arm over my shoulders to help me up.

"Juliette, are you okay?" Féidhlim joins us, on his guard.

I nod, accepting their help to get back up, my gaze all the while fused to Fionn's inside the magical bubble growing too thin around him. Amrah is struggling to keep it up. Soon her ghostly feet and legs sink into the parqueting floor while her upper body fights to remain in control of the prison.

"What did my father say, Jules?" Féidhlim asks, wary, his hands gripping my shoulders. "What is he going to do next?"

But I don't get the opportunity to answer; Fionn's arms lift once again with more momentum this time. A wave of plasmic energy unfurls within the business chamber, another gust of wind creating a mini tornado as Amrah's form disappears from our realm and Fionn frees himself. The rest of us topple over. I hear a loud bang and a wail behind me and my heart misses a beat.

Oisín!

I twist from where I am lying on the ground, Féidhlim on top of me and doing the same, to see that El managed to make his way to Aoife and her youngling on time. He has his arms wrapped around them, keeping them safe from the sharp debris under them, while his back is uncomfortably stuck between the sturdy wall and a broken chestnut cabinet. Féidhlim swiftly gets on all fours and makes sure I am not injured before running back to his son.

"It's okay, Fé," Aoife reassures him, sitting up with a wince. "We're okay." She locks eyes with Oisín. "You're okay, Baba, aren't you?"

His little head bobs forward, though his innocent blue eyes are full of terror. Féidhlim sighs as he hugs Oisín firmly.

"Thanks, Elmas," he says next, giving the toddler back to his mother.

He helps El up, grateful for his presence in the room and assistance to his family.

"Don't mention it," El replies with nonchalance, aiding Féidhlim as he hooks a hand under Aoife's arm to help her too.

"Juliette, is it over?" Aoife asks me, our eyes meeting across the chamber. "Is he gone? Is Fionn gone?"

I shake my head, frantic as I examine the room. Fionn is nowhere to be seen but I can still sense him. The ghost I can no longer feel, however, is… Amrah.

"Amrah!" I scream, tears prickling my eyes. "Amrah, where are you?" I continue to look around the dilapidated office, my veins frozen under my flesh. "Amrah!"

The door swings open, making us all jump one more time, to reveal a furious Léo and a worried K.

"I can't feel her presence," Léo gasps in lieu of a hello. "Jules, I can't sense her anymore!"

"Me neither," I cry and sniffle, holding a hand out to him as he crosses the warzone to get to me. "You don't think she is… do you?"

"She can't be!" Léo argues, his chestnut irises as dark as coal.

"Amrah!" we call her in unison—still nothing.

My heart breaks and so does Léo's, I feel it in my pit. My throat swells, tears rolling down my cheeks. My brother looks away so as not to let his emotions transpire, though he allows himself to hug me for comfort.

I don't know what happens to ghosts on the other side when they use up their plasmic energy. And that terrifies me. Is Amrah… gone?

"Fionn's still here," Léo says grimly, confirming what I already knew. "It's not over, Jules."

I nod, pull away, and dry my tears.

"No, it's not," I reply, steeling myself.

If anything, we need to win this fight in honour of Amrah.

K remains by the door, a trained look on our friends.

"Let's get everyone out of here while we can," K suggests, a hand against the door to keep it open, the other waving at Aoife and Oisín.

El guides them out, his arms wide open to block an eventual attack from Fionn. And he is right to prepare for the worst because the second Aoife crosses the threshold, Fionn reappears, more menacing than ever; eyes bulging out of their sockets, fingers stiff like claws, and body dangerously floating toward them.

"Amrah!" Léo shouts out of instinct, his focus on finding our cousin to stop Fionn.

I try to do the same when someone else calls for me on the other side. My gaze snaps to Féidhlim who has spun around to face us, his eyes searching the chamber to block the upcoming threat and protect Aoife and their son.

Juliette, the voice—as gentle as a warm breeze at dawn—says, *let me in!*

Again, my stare is drawn to Féidhlim.

Okay, I reply urgently.

I don't know what I am doing so I let my body dictate my movements. I hurry to Féidhlim and clasp my hands around his, holding them tightly. He flinches, brows hiking and face screwing up at the unexpected contact, but he doesn't back away.

"Jules?" Léo exclaims behind us, at a loss. "What are you doing?"

Let me in! the voice echoes.

"I'm trying!" I scream back, tightening my grip over Féidhlim.

"What?" he asks, confused.

"Who is that talking to you?" Léo barks, on the defensive already. "Another fucking ghost? Show yourself!"

I wince, and so does Féidhlim, as I gather my physical strength to make my grip firmer around him while my mind goes haywire to summon the new ghost. For a

266 Enchanted

reason unbeknownst to me, I need Féidhlim to summon her.

I just need one more push of my mind…

Pressure constricts my temples, my eyes squeezed closed, and my head bowed against Féidhlim's chest. I expect Fionn to strike at any given moment but he never does. Somehow, he has grown surprisingly quiet.

A moan from the splitting headache caused by my growing attempt at summoning a new ghost escapes my lips.

"Good job, dear," the spirit tells me once she materialises herself before Léo's surprised eyes in the centre of the chamber.

Chapter 27
Juliette

Queen Felicity's ghost launches itself at Fionn, a deafening screech bursting out of her lungs as she nears him. I can hear the years of repressed anger in her voice and see the rage taking over in her eyes. Queen Felicity is magnificent when her hands close around her late mate's throat and squeeze, her jaw squaring to reveal the meticulous concentration in her movements.

A pair of dark, sturdy horns proudly crown her head, giving away that she is a dark fae. Though I knew that already, I never pictured Féidhlim's mother this way. They look nothing alike; in that regard, he is his father's son through and through.

Long platinum strands of hair gather over Queen Felicity shoulders like a curtain of moonlight covering her pointy ears. The white gown she has on is probably what she was buried in a few years prior. I cannot see through her body, which confirms that Queen Felicity's ghostly abilities are as powerful as Amrah and Fionn's.

Amrah.

She is still nowhere to be seen, and if I am being honest, I know she is gone.

"She's beating the shit out of him!" Léo cackles, back to his usual laid-back demeanour.

Floating near the swinging chandelier, Felicity has Fionn trapped in yet another air bubble, except this one is of the next level. She was able to conjure thunder inside it to electrocute him.

"Jules, is the situation under control?" Féidhlim asks, joining us inside the chamber.

After summoning his mother, he left in a hurry to ensure the safety of his family.

I nod.

"Aoife and Oisín?" I query.

"Safe in the parlour," Féidhlim tells me. "Guards are with them, and so are K and El."

"Good."

"Fuck me…" Léo chuckles. "Your mum is a bad bitch, Fé!"

"She is?" he repeats, taken aback. "What did I miss now?"

Léo cheers as Felicity's air bubble retracts, forcing Fionn to fall to his knees in his makeshift prison.

Now, I get it!

It isn't just an air bubble; it sucks the plasmic energy out of the ghost trapped inside it. Fionn is growing weaker by the second. Felicity must have been watching us from the moment the fight broke out to know exactly where Amrah had left it off.

"Fé, I don't know that it is safe here for you," I admit, holding his right hand in mine.

"I'm not going anywhere, Jules." He interlocks our fingers, "I'm staying right here with you… and your brother."

"Thanks for making me feel like a third wheel, Fé," Léo sighs, rolling his eyes at him.

I giggle before composing myself again.

"Fé, I summoned your mother, and she is doing a great job at weakening your father," I say, "but maybe Léo and I can get more ghosts to pass through the invisible gates restraining access from the other side."

I lock eyes with my brother, who instantly offers me his hand to join forces.

"Let's do this, Jules," Léo agrees, determined.

"What will I do?" Féidhlim asks, stepping forward.

"You sure you wanna help?" Léo raises an eyebrow at him.

"Yes, little prince!" he confirms, adamant.

"Then stand here in case we need more magical energy," I tell Féidhlim. "You'll be our emergency beacon. We'll tap into your fae dust."

Féidhlim nods, and Léo and I join hands, focusing on the spirits harbouring the royal palace. And Gods, I am shocked to realise that hundreds of them have been watching the commotion, impatiently waiting to step in. Every single person—now dead—that Fionn crossed in his lifetime is here, begging to cross the threshold between the other side and our living realm to get their revenge. So Léo and I keep the passage open to allow them to float through and assist Felicity. In the blink of an eye the chamber is filled to the brim with ghosts like a haunted manor.

Fionn folds into a ball, high-pitched wails escaping his vile mouth as he tries to chase away the horde of wild spirits wishing for his demise. They all carry miniature air bubbles in their hands, which they stick to Fionn's body to steal his plasmic strength all at the same time. He squirms like a worm, pleading with his aggressors but the torture never stops. His form is covered from head to toe with translucent balls nibbling at his raw flesh. He cannot bleed but his skin cracks like fissures, swells like third-degree burns, and peels off like that of a lizard. His torment keeps going until he barely has enough energy to keep his ghostly eyes open. Felicity is the last spirit to strike; she brings her own bubble of air to his heart and shoves it past his ribcage for his last drops of deadly vitality to be shattered from the inside.

Fionn's frame slowly vanishes into thin air, just like Amrah's did. The army of spirits nods at us in tandem, satisfied to have been given a chance to right their wrongs. I ready myself to order them to regain the other side when they start marching in a neat row of their own volition. Once everyone is gone, Felicity pauses in front of us.

"Thank you," she murmurs, full of gratitude.

Her gaze rests over Féidhlim, loving and caring, a single tear cruising her pale cheek.

...

Féidhlim

According to Juliette, Mother is right here in front of me but I cannot see her. I cannot hear her or feel her. It is like talking to the wind. Léo left shortly after my father's spirit was depleted of its energy to give us privacy. Juliette offered to stay and act as a translator or interpreter (I am not sure of the correct term in this kind of situation if I am being honest), though it doesn't make any difference. No matter how hard I concentrate, my mother is still absent. With that said, however, every time Juliette relates thoughts and memories shared with her by my mother, my heart warms.

"... now that it's been established that she's been watching over you ever since she passed," Jules goes on with a shrug, "you know she'll always be by your side no matter what."

I nod.

"Thanks," I murmur to the both of them.

Jules stares at the vacant spot on her left and listens to what Mother has to say next. This used to annoy me when it was Amrah, but now that I know she is talking to my mother, I cannot help but be thankful for being in the same room as my two favourite females.

"Really?" Jules exclaims, which is meant for my mother. "To Reunion?" She pauses. "And what did you think of it?"

I watch her have a conversation I can't fully comprehend with a late host I cannot see, and smile. They seem to be getting on well even though they are strangers. Then again, Jules was the one helping her get her revenge on my father. Without her, my mother would still be watching us from the other side, powerless. Without Jules, my father could have seriously injured Oisín. I could never forgive him for that. Hatred is ugly but after what he did to my son, it is the only emotion he deserves me to feel toward him.

"Fé?" Jules places a gentle hand on my arm. "Are you okay?"

"Yeah, ahem, just a bit…"

"Queasy?" she finishes for me.

"Yeah…" I frown. "I'm sorry. I know you're exhausted, too, Jules. Being here playing translators is probably the last thing you want to do."

"Not at all." She shakes her head. "I cannot believe I am talking to Queen Felicity of Éire," she adds, grinning at my invisible mother. "I know I've already said it, but it is such an honour to be in your presence."

"I don't know what she's saying—"

"She is so proud of you Fé," Jules interrupts me, tears welling up in her eyes.

"She is?" I echo faintly. I face the empty space beside Juliette. "You are?"

"She's nodding," Jules describes, "and now she's coming closer to you. She is right... here."

Her hands wave where my mother is standing, only inches away from me. I lift my fingers to try and touch her, but again I cannot feel a thing.

"Mother, I wish I could see you," I tell her genuinely. "And I wish you could meet Oisín, too."

"Oh, she loves him!" Jules announces with a giggle. She waits, nods, and says, "Your mother's been in Bainbridge Island with him and Aoife the whole time."

"Really? Thank you," I reply. "Thank you for being there for them when I wasn't, Mother."

Juliette is staring at me but I don't have the heart to lock eyes with her. I am still deeply ashamed of my past behaviour, a behaviour she knows nothing about yet.

"She said that she'll always be there for you and Oisín," Jules adds. "And Aoife..." A pause. "And me? Why me?" she giggles.

My cheeks flush red. If Mother came back to Éire with us after my stay at Aoife's on Bainbridge Island, then she knows how I truly feel about Juliette. She perhaps witnessed my outbursts in my father's business chamber, or my vain attempts at writing explanatory letters to Jules, or even heard the thoughts I expressed out loud when I trusted I was alone.

"What's she saying?" I ask nervously.

"Uhm…" Jules' lower lip folds between her teeth and she mechanically tucks a dark curl behind her ear, unable to look me in the eye. "Nothing."

I frown.

"Mother, if you think you're helping, you are not!" I blurt, my stomach uncomfortably twisting at the fact I cannot hear their conversation.

I cannot believe that even as a ghost Mother is trying to play matchmaker!

Juliette shakes her head at her, then locks eyes with me before looking down at the hem of her black dress, her cheeks flaring like they were on fire.

What on Earth is Mother telling her?

The cheek of her to talk about me with Juliette right under my nose!

This goes on for at least another fifteen minutes, no matter how much I try to break it off. When Mother is satisfied with her doing and Juliette can no longer look at me, her cheeks resembling ripe tomatoes, she announces she is ready to regain the other side.

"Will you continue watching over us, Mother?" I ask, suddenly sounding like a youngling.

My throat closes at the thought of her leaving me—leaving us—again so soon, even though I cannot communicate with her.

"Always," Jules replies for her.

I nod profusely, bringing the pads of my thumb and index finger to my eyes to dry the tears that have settled there.

"Thanks," I manage to say to the both of them.

Juliette is quiet for a moment. When I chance a glance at her, once my eyes are dry, I see that she too is crying; only her tears are ones of happiness.

"Oh… thank Gods," she murmurs, the flat of her hand against her chest.

"What is it?" I ask, curious.

"Amrah…" she sighs, relieved. "Your mum just told me that Amrah is fine. Your father stole her plasmic force, but she'll be okay. She'll come back when she's ready."

"That's good to hear," I say earnestly. "Mother, please thank Amrah for me. She restrained Father long enough for Aoife and Oisín to escape. I'll forever be thankful for her help." I grab Jules' hand and bring the back of it to my lips. "Thank you, Jules, for everything."

Her face lights up, her features breaking into a breathtaking smile.

"Féidhlim…" she breathes, her brown eyes shining as they dive into mine.

So I bring the tips of her fingers to my mouth to kiss them, longing for more. So much more. How could I ever live the life of a king without her by my side? She is everything I could ever wish for and more. She is… perfection personified, sent to me by the Gods themselves. I need her.

I take a step closer when she says, "We're alone." I blink at her. "Your mother… she's gone back to the other side."

My smile saddens, wishing I could have talked to her directly, hugged her, and seen her face one last time, but the interaction—although unconventional—Jules facilitated will remain rooted in my heart forevermore.

"Thank you, Juliette," I say again, wrapping my arms around her to pull her flush against my chest.

Chapter 28

Féidhlim

I am on a mission.

The pace around the palace is slowing down at last. Leaders and diplomats, horrified to hear about my late father's attack, are finally leaving Éire with their families. The cleaning crew is taking their job seriously, scrubbing every corner of the castle like their lives depend on it. And after hours of reassuring our staff that the perimeters of the estate are safe, the tension around my royal court is starting to dissolve.

Léo convinced Juliette to stay put for another couple of days, using it as an excuse to be supportive of my kingdom, escape their parents, and visit the country. From what El told me, Juliette wasn't keen on prolonging her stay at first. She wanted to give Aoife, Oisín, and me privacy, which we do not require. Not from her, that is. After all, Juliette is the reason why we are all still alive. She was the one who warned Aoife about my father; she protected Oisín as best she could; she used her witchy gifts to summon reinforcements; and… she got me to spend time with my late mother. I will forever be grateful for all that she has done. So I asked Léo for a favour. I needed him to persuade his sister to stay in Éire a little while longer. I would have talked to her myself, but I was snowed under with energy-draining bureaucracy about my father's passing that I could not ignore. Juliette eventually agreed to extend her stay, eager to give her brother and K another chance to catch up.

This is my time to shine and rectify the situation between Jules and me for good. I need a grand romantic gesture to win her back, and it so happens that I know exactly what to do. Not that I needed it, but I am glad I received everyone's approval.

Aoife couldn't have been more encouraging, claiming that Juliette's warm and loving nature was required to balance out my cold demeanour; the one I spent hours practising and mastering. She is right, of course; Juliette helps me get out of my shell. She puts me at ease, which allows me to trust the world and the people in it. She is the glimmer of hope that brightens my thoughts when they go dark.

Léo and I never interacted much in Reunion but we both deeply care for Juliette, a mutual understanding that helped me win him over. Apparently, he had never seen his big sister happier than when she was with me.

"Or maybe it was just the high of being freed from the palace?" he felt the need to add almost instantly as if sensing my excitement, which made me want to throw an eye roll at him. Either way, I was there, and Léo witnessed it.

I have been walking on eggshells around El, still not a hundred per cent certain where he stands. How could my number-one rival switch sides so suddenly? El said it himself, he liked Jules. When I asked him about it, he simply shrugged and told me they weren't meant to be. I knew that, obviously. I nodded, playing dumb, and shook hands with him even though he wasn't a good sport and I haven't forgiven him for it.

So the last person I needed to talk to was Oisín, and that was a piece of cake. It turns out my son is quite fond of Jules already. I couldn't help but chuckle when Aoife told me he had a crush on her. But hey, how could I blame him? He has good taste, I have to admit!

"He'll grow out of it, don't worry," Aoife reassured me, and we simply laughed it off.

My heart warms in my chest because it is clear I am on the right path doing the right thing. I am not used to having this many people supporting my actions and decisions. It is refreshing to feel as though I belong to a circle for a change. What a boost to my confidence to know others have my back. Strangely, I don't feel the need to fake it until I make it anymore.

"*A Rí Fhéidhlim, is mór an onóir dúinn gur tháinig tú ar cuairt ar ár nUisceadán,*" (King Féidhlim, what an honour to have you visit our aquarium) the owner of Galway Aquarium exclaims as I walk through the entrance door.

The man stands straight, his arms and hands rigid along his thighs as his head bows deeply, thin strands of salt-and-pepper hair falling in front of his round glasses.

"*Is liomsa an onóir, a Úasail Uí Laoghaire,*" (The honour is mine, Mr O'Leary) I reply kindly. I extend a hand and he eagerly grabs it before shaking it a little too roughly. "*An bhfuil gach rud in ord don tráthnóna?*" (Is everything in order for this evening?)

"*Tá, a Mhórgacht, tá gach rud curtha in áit i Roinn an Aigéin san Uisceadán,*" (Yes, Your Majesty, everything has been set up in the Ocean Zone of the Aquarium) he confirms, his most professional expression smearing his proud features. "*Ar mhaith leat teacht isteach agus féachaint air?*" (Would you like to come in and have a look?)

"*Ba mhaith, le do thoil.*" (Yes, please.)

Mr O'Leary swiftly turns around, his portly figure leading the way toward the admission door and beyond, where a vast variety of sea animals await behind glass displays. The lights are dimmed and the air is cool as we pass by a tank full of clownfish.

The corners of my lips can't help but curl into a childish grin. My mother used to bring me here on Saturdays when my father was stuck in meetings and couldn't make our weekly family get-togethers. The place has changed a great deal in twenty years but the energy around remains the same.

I can't help but notice how clean and shiny the floor is, the fresh scent of lavender perfuming the spacious room.

"*D'iarr mé ar na hairígh na háiseanna a ghlanadh ó bhun go barr tar éis duit glaoch a chur orainn ar maidin,*" (I had our caretakers dive through a deep cleaning of the facilities after your call this morning) Mr O'Leary explains as if reading my mind. He grins proudly. "*Ní fhéadfainn dul sa seans go mbeadh an ócáid um thráthnóna ina phraiseach de bharr staid an uisceadáin.*" (I couldn't risk this evening's event being a fiasco because of the state of the aquarium.)

I hide a smile.

"*Go raibh maith agat. Is mór agam do dhíogras, a Uasail Uí Laoghaire.*" (Thank you, I appreciate your diligence, Mr O'Leary.)

I walk past him, recognising the blue walls with painted white fish on them.

"*An é seo é?*" (Is this it?) I ask, my stomach twisting with excitement.

"*Is é, A Rí Fhéidhlim. Díreach isteach na doirse seo, le do thoil.*" (Yes, Your Majesty. Right through these doors, please.)

His body bends in half into a deep curtsy, then his head leans toward the floor, and the flat of his right hand indicates the space ahead of us.

There it is, the Ocean Zone, where floor-to-ceiling glass walls showcase rocky-looking wreckfish, gilthead bream with shiny silvery scales, and blue-fin bass. I glance up, satisfied with the view; the ceiling too is made of see-through glass, sea creatures swimming above our heads to reach the other side of the room. It is as though we are underwater, surrounded by the magical sea life of the ocean. I look around the room next, and I am pleased with the turquoise reflection of the water over the floor and table. Fairy lights are entwined around the rare pieces of furniture surrounding us to recreate the fantastical element that is fae dust.

The door opens behind us to invite staff members of the aquarium to stroll in with bouquets of roses in large plant baskets, white ceramic pots, and glass vases in their arms, ready to decorate the naked floor.

"*A Rí Fhéidhlim, ar mhaith leat sraith peiteal róis chomh fada leis an mbord b'fhéidir?*" (King Féidhlim, would you like a trail of rose petals leading to the table maybe?) Mr O'Leary queries, his eyes brightening up.

"*Ba mhaith, más é do thoil é, ba mhaith léí go mór é sin,*" (Yes, please, she would like that very much) I confirm, nodding with conviction. "*An bhfuil a fhios agat? Scaipfimid peitil róis thar an urlár ar fad! Dearg agus bán!*" (Actually, you know what? Let's cover the entire floor with rose petals! Red and white!)

His eyebrow shoots to his hairline at my request but he chuckles loudly, his palm pressing against his round belly.

"*Ceart go leor!*" (Alright!) He turns to his team, his hands clapping impatiently. "*Ar chuala sibh An Rí? Cuirfimid peitil róis bhána agus dhearga timpeall an urláir ar fad, seo anois, ar aghaidh linn!*" (Did you hear His Majesty? White and red rose petals all over the floor, come on, let's go!)

Buzz.

Buzz.

I eagerly grab my phone from the pocket of my royal blue suit jacket and anxiously check the screen, my heart in my throat. I take a deep breath in as I read Léo's message, mechanically smoothing the fabric of my white shirt with my free hand.

"*Tá sí anseo,*" (She's here) I announce to the room, my composed demeanour shifting to something more agitated.

"*Ná bí buartha, A Mhórgacht, beidh na peitil curtha ar an urlár againn i bhfaiteadh na súl,*" (Don't worry, Your Majesty, we'll have the petals on the floor in two shakes of a lamb's tail) Mr O'Leary confirms, his expression nothing but seriousness. "*Ní bheidh a fhios aici siúd a bheidh inár mbanríon lá éigin go rabhamar anseo!*" (Our future queen won't know we were here!)

The organs in my middle twists at his words, stress and anxiety coursing through my blood as my fingers bury in the pockets of my wool suit trousers to wrap around the jewellery box I hid there.

What if she says no?

I would die of embarrassment and sadness and would have to give Oisín the throne sooner than expected.

I shake my head, chasing the dark thoughts away, urging my legs to walk me back to the entrance of the aquarium. The soles of my brown leather shoes clack against the flooring in rhythm with the thumping of my heart. Never have I ever felt such uncertainty—or *cared* so much—about a female's feelings toward me. I thought being king would grant me more confidence but it turns out, it doesn't make a difference. If Juliette turns me down tonight, I will die as miserably as I would if I were a prince.

I brace myself and push open the admission door to step into the reception area when my eyes meet Jules'. I falter, mesmerised by the magnificent angel standing in front of me in her white flowy dress. I take her in; her beautiful dark curls frame her face to rest against her back while her innocent brown eyes shine with timidity at the new setting. Her rosy lips twist into a shy smile. She is sheer perfection brought to me by the Gods; I said it before and I will say it again and again.

I swallow hard, unable to hide my contentment as my gaze skims her breasts first—the V-neck showing me more than enough to know she isn't wearing a bra—and her tanned legs second—the light material of her dress coming down as far as her mid-thighs. My mouth waters, visions of our time together in my bedroom and on the beach resurfacing, my cock uncomfortably straining in my pants.

Juliette's fingers twist around the golden strap of her handbag as she begins to walk toward me.

"Hi," she greets me in a small voice once close enough for me to smell her coconut-and-vanilla perfume.

"Hi," I murmur, my hands itching to pull her flush against me to hold her tight in my arms. "You came," I say instead, my eyes glued onto her.

"You asked me on a date, King Féidhlim," she replies, taking another step forward, her enticing bust now only an inch away from my racing chest.

"Is that why you're here? Because I'm king?"

My eyes search hers as I hold my breath with apprehension.

"I don't care what you are, Fé," she tells me, my gaze instantly lingering on her lips and back up to meet her eyes. "I came because I couldn't stop thinking about *you*—"

My fingers wrap around her waist, pulling her to my chest as my mouth presses against hers into a ravenous kiss. The bulge in my pants hardens, and she must notice it, too, because she moans, pressing her pelvis to it, her fingers running through my short curls. She goes on her tiptoes, her tongue darting past her delicious lips and into my mouth, the sweet taste of cherry exploding on my taste buds like the most coveted of treats.

"Wait, not here... let me take you inside," I manage against her mouth, reluctantly pulling away from her.

"Okay," she breathes, a mischievous smirk darkening her features.

Chapter 29
Juliette

My mouth drops open in awe as I take in the Ocean Zone unfolding before me. This is surreal; Féidhlim and I are surrounded by a thick floor-to-ceiling glass barrier, encompassing the walls and ceiling that showcase a beautiful family of fish as they swim around us and above our heads. A soothing turquoise light shines through the water and onto us, boreal-like waves dancing on the floor at our feet.

What on Earth?

My eyebrows shoot to my hairline when my gaze eventually lowers to see red and white rose petals decorating the pebbled gravel floor. Bigger flower pots, baskets, and vases filled with generous bouquets of roses smile at us everywhere I look. The fresh floral scent suddenly invades my nostrils and I can't help but grin at the most spectacularly romantic view I have ever seen.

"Is it too much?" I hear Fé ask, unneeded uncertainty in his voice.

I snap out of my reverie to turn to him, my curls bouncing from the shaking of my head.

"It's *perfect*," I mutter, warmth crowding my chest at the obvious care and effort he put into our date.

Féidhlim sighs with relief, the flat of his hand pointing at the candlelit dining table ahead of us. Subtle fairy lights provide the area with the brightness it calls for without ruining the magic.

I can't believe he did all this for me.

This is everything I ever wanted, but never have I thought someone would be attentive enough to my needs to guess what a perfect date would look like to me. Let alone a *king*!

"Are you hungry, Jules?" Féidhlim wonders softly, a hand wrapping around my hip to guide me to my seat.

But I pause as he leans closer, something hard pressing against my back. Electricity seizes my stomach, making my insides quiver and my pussy clench.

"I'm ravenous," I confess, pressing my chest flush against his as my fingertips get a hold of the belt tied around his waistline.

He looks down at me, his eyes lighting up and his lips parting. And when I open the button of his suit trousers and slide the zipper down, he nervously glances around the room as if expecting the aquarium staff to barge in any second. Though his brow arches at the door, my heart races delightfully in its cavity, the fear of getting caught adding to my excitement.

I grin mischievously, dropping down to my knees to pull open his pants and free his cock. And there it is; his dick bobs under my eyes in all its glory, thick and hard, just like I remembered it. I was too shy to make a move on him before, but I have learnt from my mistakes.

"Jules, I don't know if we should…" he manages, towering over me with his height, a single bead of pre-cum glistening on his head. "Someone might see us—"

But he hisses when I run the flat of my tongue along the thick vein of his cock, his hands closing into fists at his sides. I smirk, delighted with his reaction to my touch. I lick his balls and kiss his shaft next, before glancing up at him again.

"What were you saying?" I breathe innocently, my fingers wrapping around his length.

His eyes slowly peel off from where I am touching him to rest on me.

"I… uhm…" he starts but pauses again when I begin pumping him.

I hold his stare, my tongue swiping across my lips.

"What should I do next, King Féidhlim?"

His eyes darken, his fingers roughly wrapping around my curls.

"Open your mouth," he orders in a growl.

So I obey, ready to pretend I am a cock-sucking queen. I have never given head to anyone before, and Féidhlim must know that because, despite the impatience in his eyes, he slides his stick in my mouth slowly and carefully, making sure not to go too deep too quickly. While I appreciate the gesture, however, I have practised on bananas and balloons before, thank you very much!

I pick up the pace, moving my head back and forth, the pink gloss on my lips smearing his shaft. Féidhlim gasps, his grip over my hair tightening, his hand now applying light pressure against my skull to urge me to keep going. I brace myself and relax my throat—although it doesn't help much—before carefully swallowing his dick. When it reaches the back of my throat, my eyes grow glassy as my air supply cuts off, but the look on Féidhlim's face is worth it.

He watches me through hooded eyes, his mouth parted to allow his shallow breathing to leave his heaving chest. The simple act of witnessing the raw expression of pure bliss smoothing every line and crevasse of his features makes my pussy pulsate with want. Knowing that I am the one responsible for his surrender instils such power in me my walls have grown wet and demanding of their own accord. But soon, Féidhlim's long fingers break free from my hair to cup my face instead. He holds me still, his mesmerised eyes meeting mine.

"Jules… that's enough…" he breathes, battling for composure. "Good girl."

My lips slide away from his head, a trail of pre-cum linking my tongue to him as I catch my breath. He pulls me back up to my feet, his mouth meeting mine. My eyes flutter shut, my hands swiftly running over the bounds of his flat stomach and swollen chest below his shirt. I guide him to the white-clothed table and lean against it but he wraps an arm around my back, stopping me in my tracks.

"Not here," he tells me, his voice a low rumble in his chest.

He pulls me up to carry me to the centre of the room instead, where a white blanket rests over a cushioned surface.

"You thought of everything!" I can't help but exclaim when he places me down again, impressed with Féidhlim's keen sense of organisation.

He chuckles, allowing his muscular frame to roll on top of me.

"You're the one with a dirty mind, Princess Juliette," he announces against my lips. "I had this daybed brought in so we could watch the fish swim above our heads. Nothing else."

"I don't see why we can't do both, Your Majesty," I giggle, my fingers clasping around the nape of his neck.

"I'm afraid I'll need your full attention when I make you come," he rasps, slipping down toward my thighs.

I gasp when Féidhlim's mouth finds my pelvis over my dress and presses against it, his hands making their way up my legs to stop where the seam of my panties should be.

"You're not… wearing underwear," he hisses with a hard swallow, his blue eyes snapping back to me, brighter than usual.

"I had a feeling I wouldn't need it this evening," I reply boldly, playing it cool, despite my trepidatious heart on the verge of explosion.

I glimpse something dark shining in his gaze before Féidhlim inhales deeply and dives head-first between my legs. The motion is abrupt but precise, his mouth latching onto my clit; no time wasted. My head snaps back, my eyes sealing shut, a delicious cry escaping my throat at the pressure he applies to my swollen nub; the perfect blend of tongue-and-lip work with the occasional sucking of my bundle of nerves between his teeth. It doesn't take me long to shatter, my body pulsing against the daybed as the wave of ecstasy washes over me way too soon.

Féidhlim props himself up, locking eyes with me, the corners of his lips twitching into a smile. And I can't tell whether he is proud of himself for making me orgasm at the snap of a finger, or if he is mocking me for not being able to hold it in long enough. Either way, my already-flushed cheeks turn bright red with embarrassment, my arms folding over my face so I don't have to look at him.

Hashtag spot the virgin!

I felt more in control the last time he was between my legs, but I guess confidence comes and goes…

"Don't hide from me, Jules," Féidhlim tells me softly, his fingers wrapping around my wrists to pull my arms away from my mortified face.

His eyes find mine and all I see is... *love?*

He comes closer, kissing me tenderly at first, until the muscles in my body relax, ordering my arms to clasp around his back and my legs to wrap around his waist. Then, he leans in, his tongue entering my mouth for a slow dance. His pelvis presses against mine, and again I feel his rock, thick and hard.

Oh, how I want him.

All of him.

I toss his suit jacket away, my fingers swiftly pulling his shirt over his head next, my feet unwrapping from around his hips so I can pull his pants down completely.

"Juliette..." Féidhlim gasps my name, his gaze searching for mine, fidgety with lust. "Are you sure?"

I nod.

"Yes, I want *you.*"

And with that, his stare mischievously smiles at me as he finishes removing his clothes and shoes himself. So I slide my dress up, effortlessly freeing my breasts that bounce up and down before his eager eyes. He growls, his mouth latching onto one nipple, his hand cupping the other tit firmly. A squeal travels through the Ocean Zone area from my throat, my back leaning down against the white blanket under me until I am lying completely flat with Féidhlim hovering over my body.

He eventually leaves my breasts alone, propping himself higher to be at eye level with me. My heart somersaults against my ribs; the moment I have been so vividly waiting for is finally here. I thought I would be more nervous—scared even—but I am surprisingly calm. And ready. I nod at Féidhlim before kissing him softly on the lips, my hands gripping his firm biceps and my legs spreading wider under him.

"We can stop anytime, Jules," he reassures me, his gaze still on me as he adjusts his position, his cockhead now at my entrance. "You just say the word and I'll stop, okay?"

"Huh-huh," I hum with impatience, my head bobbing in yet another profuse nod.

He comes closer, almost hugging me in his strong arms, his pelvis jerking forward. And I know he isn't as rough as I would expect him to be with anyone else, but fuck me, it hurts! His mushroom head enters my walls, then his stiff shaft, my skin stretching to accommodate his length, my pussy moulding around him. I take a deep breath, hoping I am not grimacing too much from the tear and making a fool of myself.

"You okay?" he checks in with me in a low voice, depositing a kiss on my forehead, where beads of sweat have formed.

"Yep…" I lie, forcing a smile, and he kisses me again.

Féidhlim pushes himself deeper inside me, and I swear I feel the colour drain from my face.

How fat is his fucking cock?

He pulls out and jerks back in a slow motion, my walls screaming "fire" at me, despite my pussy still being wet; I know this because of the squishy sound it makes as he begins to thrust inside me. Soon he starts moaning in my ear, quietly, only audible to me, and the uncomfortable pain searing my insides turns into a kaleidoscope of butterflies fluttering in my stomach.

"Perfect," he whispers, his eyes squeezing shut as he slows down his pace, his pelvis now grinding against mine, applying just the right amount of pressure onto my clit. "Perfect isn't accurate enough to describe you, Jules," he quotes himself.

I gasp at his words, remembering our time on the beach when my world had cracked open into a sunny space of vast possibilities for the first time in my life.

I peek at the expression of sheer content that smears his face and I am struck; *am I the one making him feel like this? Me?* A sense of pride travels through me, calming down any anxious thoughts in the process. I relax, now fully able to enjoy the experience. To enjoy *him*.

Féidhlim's grinding grows more intense and soon I am overwhelmed by the satisfying weight against my clit, the excitement in his voice as he moans my name, the strong muscles of his body contracting over mine, the girth of his pleasing cock…

Oh my, he is big, and he fucks like a god!

Never have I ever felt so full.

Féidhlim suddenly hurls deeper through my walls, my eyes widening as he hits an unexpected sweet spot.

"Fé…" I cry, my voice squeakier than usual. "Do that again!"

"Yeah?" he manages, his teeth nibbling my ear. "There?"

His cock strikes my G spot one more time and I squeal, my eyebrows drawing in with the electrifying sensation seizing my lower abdomen. He grins, thrusting this exact same way until I break, my muscles spasming under him as I come undone. My ears ring and I see stars, enjoying every second of my orgasm. So I barely notice it when Féidhlim pulls out to pump his cum over my belly in a hiss, his white semen contrasting with the honey of my skin.

"Gods, you're perfect…" he breathes again, his chest heaving as he presses a kiss against my lips.

I watch him roll out of bed to grab a box of tissues from the round coffee table on his right. He cleans himself before swiftly coming back to attend to me next.

"How are you feeling?" he asks with genuine care and concern while helping me up.

A big fat grin spreads across my lips and he chuckles, handing me my clothes from the floor.

"We should've had sex a lot sooner," I purr, getting dressed.

"I know," he agrees, a naughty smirk darkening his eyes.

I giggle but it dies down the second my gaze lands on the white blanket that was under me, blood stains embedded in its fabric.

"Don't worry about that," Féidhlim tells me before I have time to process the damage our lovemaking has caused.

He grabs the blanket off the daybed and tosses it onto the floor as if indicating it is for the wash. I smile, grateful he didn't make a big deal out of my mess. Nevertheless, I effortlessly bend down, my sex aching between my legs, to reach for his clothes on the floor in thanks.

"Here," I say, handing him his suit trousers when a jewellery box escapes one of its pockets to fall at my feet. "Oh, sorry!" I blurt out, bending down again to grab the black leather container.

Féidhlim steps closer, panic clearly seizing his every muscle. I frown, my eyes jumping from the box to him, my heart doing cartwheels against my ribs.

"Fé… what's this?" I ask shyly, giving him the container back and gathering the last bits of strength I have left to keep my composure.

"One second," he mutters, throwing his clothes back on in a hurry. "This isn't exactly how I thought I'd do this but…" his voice trails off once he looks presentable again.

Our eyes lock and he clears his throat, graciously going down on one knee. His fingers pop the box open, a rose gold band with the most beautiful of opal stones—the light catching onto it to create rainbow-like waves—securely fastened between a crisscross of the same pinkish material. My eyes widen, my lips parting in genuine surprise.

"Princess Juliette of Reunion Island, *my* Jules, will you marry me?"

Chapter 30

Féidhlim

Twelve months later.

"*A Oisín, cuir ort do bhróga, le do thoil,*" (Oisín, please, put on your shoes) I sigh, grabbing the small pair of red runners off the floor for the third time.

"*Ní chuirfidh!*" (No!) my son, who has turned into a little devil this past year, argues, his blond curls bouncing around his round face as he avidly shakes his head. "*Tá Maim ag teastáil uaim!*" (I want Mama!)

"*Beidh Maim ar ais go luath,*" (Mama will be back soon) I tell him for the thousandth time in the space of a mere twenty minutes.

Aoife was only back ten minutes when she had to suddenly leave again to run some mysterious errand. Oisín wanted to follow her, like he always does, but she looked at me with an expression that screamed "I need some time alone," so I lured him into the royal kitchen with the promise of vanilla-and-caramel ice-cream; his favourite. It didn't take him long to gulp it all down, however—I swear Oisín has no tooth sensitivity, biting and chewing the treat like it were a chocolate bar—which then prompted him to resume with his questioning as to where his mama went.

I was nervous about sharing custody of Oisín with Aoife at first, fearing I wouldn't have enough time to bond with him, but our arrangement has been working pretty well for all of us so far. Oisín gets to come to the palace every day after school for his snack and play dates, while Aoife and I finish working. We have both been busy recently—me with my royal affairs, trying my best to lead our country better than my father did; and Aoife with her new business—so I am glad we always find a way to make it to our family gatherings at the weekends for Oisín's sake. He really does enjoy those.

And yes, to my utter joy and relief, Aoife and Oisín moved to Éire shortly after my father's funeral. Aoife settled back into her family home and opened her new restaurant only down the street. She is aiming for a Michelin star, which I know is coming. I offered her a position at the palace more than once as a chef, her cooking and baking being that good, but she declined each time, stating it was too early in her career to abandon yet another culinary project but that she would gladly cater for any event the palace hosts.

"*Go luath? Ach cén t-am?*" (Soon? But when?) Oisín's squeaky voice asks, grimacing when I get a hold of his little chubby foot to slip the shoe on it.

"*I gceann cúpla nóimeád, Baba,*" (In a few minutes, Baba) I say, keeping my tone calm to not let my impatience and frustration show.

"*Fuair Jules iad seo dom!*" (Jules got me these!) he exclaims, stomping his foot onto the warm tiles in the hall with pride once I am done securing the shoe.

His runners have laces but they are slip-ons, thank Gods.

"*Sea, fuair sí iad duit.*" (Yes, she did.) I nod. "*An chumhin leat cén tír ina bhfuair sí iad?*" (Do you remember which country she got them from?)

His face screws up, his nose wrinkling as he focuses on finding the answer.

"*An Spáinn?*" (Spain?)

I chuckle.

"*Beagnach ceart. Cen tír Eorpach eile gar don Spáinn atá ar eolas agat, Baba?*" (Close. What other European country do you know that's near Spain, Baba?)

He cocks his head, his index finger pressing into his cheek.

"*Mmm... Corcaigh?*" (Uhm... Cork?)

"*Corcaigh?*" (What?) I burst out laughing, my head tilting back. "*Ní hea, Baba, ní tír í Corcaigh.*" (No, Baba, Cork isn't a country.) I mechanically dry the tears of joy that have formed at the corners of my eyes. "*Cheannaigh Jules iad seo duit,*" (Jules bought you these) I tap the runners with the tip of my index finger, "*agus bábóg adhmaid le srón fada—*" (and a wooden doll with a long nose—)

"*An Ridire Pinocchio!*" (Sir Pinocchio!) he cries, a beaming smile spreading across his face.

"*Sea, Ridire Pinocchio.*" (Yeah, Sir Pinocchio.) My head shakes at the toy's title. "*Cad as dó?*" (Where is he from?)

"*An Iodáil!*" (Italy!) he screams with the perfect Italian intonation, his face screwing up and his little fingers coming together as his hand shakes the Italian way.

I nod proudly.

Juliette has been travelling the world these past couple of months, visiting country after country and living her dream before she has to get back to her royal duties. Her first trip after Éire was to France, then Spain, and Italy after that.

I was able to join her in the Netherlands before Éire's affairs got too busy. And then Aoife and Oisín met us in Denmark while he was on a school break, which was our very first family trip abroad.

Three months ago Jules went to Asia with Léo and K. And the time before that she was in Lithuania with El and Amrah before the five of them went to Russia together.

Was I happy to hear about Jules visiting El in Lithuania? Of course not; I was feckin' raging. Though I know they are friends, I will never be able to forget that they briefly courted. That, for a short moment, she considered having him as her marital companion. That he tried his best to get rid of me and succeeded. That he told me very openly he had feelings for her. How could I ever trust El after everything that went down? He tried to make up for it by helping me find Aoife and Oisín and assisting us against my father, but I will never be able to trust him around Jules.

Jules, who always comes back to Éire between her trips to shower Oisín with presents, which he loves. Jules, who always stays at the palace for a couple of weeks just to be with me, which I am grateful for. Jules, who never holds it against me when I can't accompany her on her travels, which I admire. But this is all coming to an end. Africa was her final adventure, her twelve-month grace period from her parents reaching its expiry date.

The front doors suddenly open and footsteps echo behind us.

"*Sì, molto bene, Oisín,*" (Yes, very good, Oisín) the familiar melodic voice sings in Italian.

I turn around, my heart stuttering in my chest.

"Jules!" Oisín exclaims, racing to the female I have been courting for twelve months like a little lion, his curls flying around his face.

She giggles, dropping to the floor to welcome him in her arms. She holds him tight against her, pressing big fat smooches over his mane and rosy cheeks.

"It tickles!" he chuckles, his body twisting sideways in her embrace, his t-shirt now showing his little ballooned belly.

Juliette releases her grip, warmth lighting up her eyes when her gaze finds me over Oisín's head. The corners of my lips stretch into a loving smile as I take her in. Her skin glows darker than it did three weeks ago before she left the rainy Éireann weather to go explore the Giza pyramid complex in Cairo. *Gods, every time I lay my eyes on this female I find her even more beautiful than previously!*

"You're home," I murmur in her ear, relief washing over me as I clasp my arms around her frame, the sweet scent of coconut and vanilla enveloping us.

I cup her face between the palms of my hands, my thumbs stroking the soft golden skin of her cheeks as I kiss her softly, my lips craving hers.

"Ew…" Oisín complains, turning his back to us to join his mother by the door instead, where Jules' green hardshell suitcase stands.

We chuckle, our heads shaking because no matter how often he sees us kiss, my son's reaction remains the same.

"You should've told me you were coming back early, I would've come to pick you up," I tell Jules, tucking a curl behind her ear.

"I wanted to surprise you," she replies softly, linking her hands around my waist. "Plus, I got to spend time with Aoife."

She turns around to wink at her.

"Yep, we hadn't had time to catch up properly in ages!" Aoife joins in while stopping our three-year-old from tripping over as he attempts to pull the heavy suitcase behind him.

"What are you talking about? You spend more time with Jules than I do," I argue, grimacing at Aoife while getting the suitcase away from our little monster.

"Well, Fé, you're always in your business chamber…" Jules rolls her eyes.

"You're more than welcome to visit me there," I purr in her ear, the whisper only loud enough for her to hear, which prompts her cheeks to grow red. "In fact, I insist that you do it more often in that white dress of yours I like so much."

Jules gives me a look, her lips twisting into a grin as she playfully slaps me on the arm. She nervously glances at Aoife and Oisín but I shrug; Oisín is too busy wondering what presents Jules brought him back from Egypt, and his mother is too preoccupied with keeping him away from the suitcase to care about us.

"Before I go," Aoife starts eventually, hugging our son goodbye for the rest of the day. "I just want to confirm your reservation for this evening at seven p.m."

My eyebrows draw in but Jules nods swiftly.

"We'll be there," she tells Aoife, pulling Oisín up into her arms.

I chuckle, listening to Juliette's adventures in Cairo while we wait for dessert; how she fell off her camel's back while riding in the desert, scratched her knees, and lost one of her sandals in the hot sand. How I wish I was able to travel with her...

"It was so much fun, though!" she exclaims, her eyes beaming with happiness at the memory. "But I missed you..." she admits quietly, getting up from her teal velvet chair to settle on my lap instead. "So much so that I needed to come back home early. To *you*."

She leans in for a kiss, which I eagerly accept because I too have missed her dearly. I counted the days until she would be back in my arms—where she belongs—safely tucked away from the rest of the world and its dangers.

"I can't believe you're here, Jules," I breathe against her lips as she kisses me again, her arms wrapping around my neck.

My cock bobs under her in my chinos. She is wearing her white dress, the one I mentioned earlier, and the same one she had on that evening at the aquarium. I swallow, my hand travelling from her knee to her thigh, curious to see if she is wearing any underwear. She gasps and so do I when my fingertips reach her bare sex, her skin warm and smooth.

"Fé... Aoife's in the kitchen," she manages through hooded eyes, her cheeks blushing under my touch, her fingers twisting over the collar of my grey suit jacket.

"The kitchen is on the other side of the restaurant," I remark in a low voice, my mouth brushing her ear. "We're completely alone here."

My index and middle fingers push through her folds, burying deep inside her, while my thumb rubs small circles over her clit. A quiet cry escapes her lips and I smile, pressing a light kiss against her hot cheek.

"*Shh*, princess. Someone will hear you."

She swallows hard, her eyebrows drawing in as her teeth sink into her bottom lip in an attempt to remain silent.

My fingers thrust in and out of her perfect cunt in a subtle squishy sound, the pad of my thumb eager against that sweet spot of hers, swollen and sensitive.

"Don't fight me, Jules," I mutter, pushing my digits deeper into her while adding pressure to her clit. "Come for me, *now*." I curve my fingers, reaching her G-spot to pound against it the way I know she likes.

"Yes, my king," she squeals, struggling to keep quiet.

Her face buries in my neck as her body shatters around my fingers at my command. The grip of my right arm tightens around her back, securing the love of my life against my chest as she rides her orgasm like a queen on my lap. She eventually takes a deep breath, her body perfectly moulding to mine, the palm of her right hand resting over my racing heart.

What can I say? Making her come always gets me on a high, too.

"Féidhlim… I love you," she whispers, her eyes meeting mine, a satisfied grin smearing her relaxed features.

"I love you, too, princess," I murmur, bringing my lips to her beautiful curly hair.

Footsteps clack on the oak flooring, a young waiter strolling our way with two white plates in his hands. He glances up at us, his face turning red before bowing politely; I don't know if it is because of who we are, or because it is obvious I was up to no good with Jules on my lap. Either way, he places the desserts on the table and bows again.

"Two chocolate bread and butter puddings, Your Majesties," he announces. "And your flutes of bubbly are coming."

He points at his colleague with the flat of his hand before heading back to the kitchen. I frown.

"I'm afraid there's been a mix-up. We didn't order champagne," I tell him, but he is now too far away to hear me.

"I did!" Jules says, adjusting herself on my lap while remaining seated.

Her head cocks as she gets lost in her thoughts. When she looks me in the eye again, her fingers mechanically play with the collar of my shirt.

"I talked to Léo," she announces.

"How is he?"

"Good," she replies dismissively. "He and K are getting married."

"What? That's amazing!" I chirp as the second waiter places our glasses on the table and leaves. "When's the wedding?"

"Soon. In six months."

"That *is* soon," I chuckle, my brow hiking.

"Yes, and they agreed to take over for my parents when they pass," she shares, her expression more serious than ever.

My face screws up.

"But that'll make Léo king of Reunion Island," I state the obvious.

She nods.

"Yes, which is only fair if I am queen of Éire," she says in a small voice, her fingers nervously twisting over my jacket. "If… you still want me to be your queen, that is."

Her eyes search mine and I blink, my heart booming in my ears.

Is she—

"King Féidhlim," she goes on, grabbing the flute that is meant for me from the table. "Will you marry me?"

She hands me the glass in which an engagement ring awaits. My mouth drops as I am astonished by the question and frankly surprised by her timing. She wriggles uncomfortably on my lap, her eyes fidgety, and I feel her confidence slipping away. So I grab the flute from her delicate fingers, grinning like a fool in love.

"Of course, I'll marry you, Jules! I've been waiting an entire year for this, remember?"

I eagerly down the champagne to reach for the ring; a thin white-gold band with a *claddagh* engraved through it. I pass it around my ring finger, and Jules smiles, delighted she got the size right.

"Here's yours," I say next, my fingers closing around the jewellery box hidden in the inside pocket of my suit jacket.

Her eyes widen.

"Do you… always have it on you?" she asks.

"Always when you're around."

I kiss her softly on the lips before opening the black leather container. Her eyes sparkle as they rest on the engagement ring for the second time, only now she nods profusely, an excited giggle escaping her throat as she hands me her finger.

And it is a perfect fit.

Epilogue

Elmas

I swing my left arm above my head, stretching like a cat over my sunbed on the thin white-sand granules of my private beach in Calella, Barcelona. The blue-and-white-stripe umbrella protects my face from the harsh midday sun, while I enjoy the heat radiating over my legs.

A vamp sunbathing—What a peculiar picture!

The waves crash onto the shore, white foam bubbling a couple of feet away from me on the grainy ground. I wave my hand in the air, the family heirloom on my finger catching the shiny rays of the sun.

Gods bless the Hakimi witches!

If it weren't for them, I would be hiding inside my hotel suite right now.

I take a deep breath, the fresh smell of sea salt caressing my nostrils. My eyes flutter closed behind my black shades, seagulls chirping in the distance as my body relaxes against the cushion of my seat.

Life is beautiful when you are a prince.

I stay there, simply being until my throat gets dry and urges me to roll over to the concrete coffee table on my left to grab my Blood Mary cocktail when my eyes lock on the screen of my phone. I bring the paper straw to my lips, casually sipping my drink while scrolling through the notifications with the pad of my thumb. My eyebrows arch with shock when I read the headline of *Lrytas*, a Lithuanian online media—"*King Féidhlim of Éire Is No Longer a Bachelor!*"

What the…

I check *Delfi* next: "*Princess Juliette of Reunion Island to Be Éire's Next Queen!*"

No fucking way!

As if my heart isn't battered enough, I click on the *15mn* website to triple check—"*She Is The One!*" with a photo of Julie and Fé kissing as they leave his baby mama's restaurant in Éire.

Fuck me…

It is one thing to admit defeat when the female I like is into someone else—truthfully, I think I lost like a winner—but it is another for their union to be rubbed in my face and for the whole world to know she didn't choose *me*. My heart stings, my chest a constricted mess, the backs of my eyes prickling with hot tears I thought were long gone by now.

Buzz.

Buzz.

My phone vibrates in the palm of my hand, Julie sending me an attachment image, followed by a smiley face emoji. I sigh, pinching the skin between my eyes with my free digits.

Why on Earth did I agree to remain friends with a female who doesn't reciprocate my feelings? Well, because I still thought I had a shot with her after she found out about Fé's son… and after she met his Aoife… and after she said no to his first proposal… and after she travelled the world mostly alone… and after she came to visit me, but still wasn't into me…

Idiotas. (Idiot.)

Buzz.

Buzz.

Another text from Julie. I brace myself, clicking on the notification to read her messages. I am instantly welcome with the photo of her ring finger, a big, fat opal stone decorating it. I can't help but smile despite the hurting of my heart, because that ring is simply perfect for her.

Well done, Fé… you nailed it. Again.

Julie: I went back home yesterday afternoon and this happened!! (heart emoji) (grinning face with smiling eyes emoji)

She already sees Éire as her home…

Julie: I was so afraid he'd say no... (smiling face with tear emoji)

I mechanically chew the skin of my cheek, gathering the little bit of strength I have left to respond.

El: Amazing! So happy for you Julie.

Another lie.

Julie: (heart emoji)

I lock the screen of my phone before placing it back on the coffee table. I stare right ahead at the perfect blue sky and calming ocean, my lips closing around the paper straw that started disintegrating inside my glass. I sip my Blood Mary, hoping to wash down my sorrow, my heart heavy against my ribs.

Next in the
While You Can
series...

Enshadowed

While You Can

About the Author

Emilie Ocean—a fiction writer and a polyglot hailing from Reunion Island—has carved a niche for herself in the literary world. Armed with a BA degree in LLCE from Blaise Pascal University, France, and an MA degree in Literary Translation from Trinity College Dublin, Ireland, Ocean has established herself as a prolific writer and ghostwriter who specialises in science-fiction, fantasy, romance, and erotica. Her passion for languages is evident in her ability to fluently speak Reunionese, French, English, and Spanish, which she seamlessly incorporates into her writing. Ocean's work is a testament to her dedication to the craft of writing and her ability to transport readers to fantastical worlds through her vivid imagination. Her credentials and talent make her a force to be reckoned with in the literary world. Ocean currently resides in Galway, Ireland, where she lives with her partner and furry companion.

Stay Tuned!

Follow Emilie on Instagram (@author_emilie_ocean).

Follow Emilie on TikTok (@authoremilieocean).

Visit Emilie's website here:

Made in United States
North Haven, CT
10 May 2024